The Contract

D E McCluskey

&

C William Giles

You are now contractually obligated to enjoy this book...

D E McCluskey & C William Giles

The Contract
Copyright © 2019 by D E McCluskey & C William Giles

The moral right of the author has been asserted
All characters and events in this publication,
other than those clearly in the public domain,
are fictitious, and any resemblance to real persons,
living or dead, is purely coincidental

All rights are reserved

No part of this publication may be reproduced,
stored in a retrieval system, or transmitted in any form
by any means, without the prior permission, in writing, of
the publisher, nor be otherwise circulated in any form of binding or
cover other than that of which it was
published and without a similar condition including this
condition being imposed on the subsequent purchaser.

ISBN 978-0-9934490-8-6

Dammaged Productions
www.dammaged.com

The Contract

For Craig, Foetus, Gilesey.
This book would never have seen
The light of day without your input and enthusiasm.
You will always be Carl to me for some reason!

1.

THE DAY WAS beautiful. The sun was shimmering in the deep blue sky. Heat flies were rising from the hot sidewalk, causing the air around them to distort and warp in fanciful ways. The wisteria trees in the gardens were in full bloom. Their pods were hanging low from their branches, offering much needed shade to the three children who were playing a game of tag on the well-manicured lawn.

The peaceful, idyllic scene was broken only when a car pulled onto the driveway of the detached house. The vehicle was long, black, and expensive. The honk of the horn alerted the playing children to its presence, and instantly, they forgot what they were doing and they stopped to wave at the driver.

'Daddy's home,' the man in the driver's seat shouted from his open window.

'Daddy!' the smallest of the children, a girl, no older than five, shouted as she ran towards the car. 'Daddy, did you bring us anything? Did you?'

'When have I ever not gotten you anything from one of my trips? Eh?' the man replied.

The children, all three of them, stepped back to allow the heavy car door to swing open. The driver climbed out and stretched his short but powerfully built frame. As the children gathered around him they were all staring up at him with expectant eyes and hero worship.

'So, who's been good for their momma?' he asked, reaching back into the car to retrieve a plastic bag from the back seat.

There was a chorus of 'me, me, me' as they all jumped up and down, grabbing at the bag that he was holding just out of reach of the tallest child; a boy of no more than ten.

The Contract

'Stop teasing them, Kurt,' a female voice called across the well-tended garden, from the direction of the large, front door. Just inside the house stood a woman; she was in her late thirties but still with all the assets and vigour of youth. Her long, mousy blond hair was tied back into a ponytail, and the white t-shirt she was wearing clung to her every curve.

Kurt looked away from the jumping children towards this woman—his wife. A smile spread across his face as his eyes roamed over her figure. 'Why should I stop?' he laughed. 'You tease me all the time.'

He was still laughing as his attention returned to the children. He lowered the bag, allowing them to grab at it. Like a mischievous monkey, the older boy snatched it from his hands and ran off, back into the shade of the drooping wisteria, lording the spoils over his younger siblings. Kurt watched them go, smiling.

'Well, that's me done for a few weeks. Can you handle me sticking around?' he asked, making his way across the garden. The beautiful woman in the doorway opened her arms out towards him.

'Hmm, I don't know about that,' she replied. 'That depends on if you've got a gift for me, too?'

'You know that I'd never leave you out, don't you?' He swooped her up in his arms, lifting her with ease from the floor, and kissed her tenderly on her lips. 'My gift for you is in my pocket,' he whispered into her ear, briefly raising his eyebrows.

'I think I can feel it,' she giggled in reply.

At that moment, his leg began to vibrate, and a ringtone came between them. He put her down onto the floor and reached into his pocket.

'Have you changed your ringtone?' she asked absently.

Kurt pouted and shook his head. 'Nope! I honestly have never heard that tone before!'

'Well, change it back, it's horrible!' she replied as she turned into the house.

She was right. The ringtone was loud and abrasive to his ears. It sounded like a tuneless wail of trumpets and drums. Like some stupid battle call from a third-rate, biblical epic. He fumbled at the button on the side of his phone, but he couldn't lower the volume. 'I'm sorry baby, I'll have to get this,' he said with an apologetic smile.

He looked at the screen and grimaced at the name it was displaying. He winked at his wife before turning away and walking back towards the car with the cell phone to his ear. 'Marcus, it's good to hear from you,' he spoke, putting one hand to his ear to block the noise of the squealing children playing with their expensive toys on the grass. 'No, no, it's all taken care of. He's not going to be a problem anymore, to anyone.'

As he laughed, a loud crack cut through the lazy noises of the day.

Everything changed at once.

The children stopped laughing, the birds stopped singing, even the incessant chirping of the insects stopped, instantly! The only sound that could be heard was the echo of the blow reverberating from the staccato walls of the large house.

In a shower of reds, whites, and some grey, Kurt's head exploded. The power of the bullet that had been fired from the high calibre sniper rifle travelled, unimpeded, through his forehead, before exiting from the back of his head, taking with it a fair amount of hair, skin, skull, and brain. The ugly mixture of these things splattered onto the shining, immaculate paintwork of his expensive car as Kurt's body flew backwards, recoiling from the impact of the lethal projectile.

His ruined body crumpled onto the hood of the car, causing the thin metal to buckle and crease beneath his weight. The phone fell from his hand, still connected to whoever Marcus was, before cutting the connection as it smashed on the concrete of the driveway.

His twitching torso slid from the car, flopping unceremoniously onto the drive. His body slumped next to the broken remains of his phone.

Almost immediately, another sound filled the air. It was the sound of screaming. It was an eerie sound. A concoction of adults and children crying out in anguish, in unison.

The screams, coupled with the loud report from the rifle, brought neighbours out of their homes. Once they had assessed the situation, most of them hurried back into their homes, fearful of whatever had happened, too fearful for their lives to offer any help to the stricken woman and her children. All they could do was usher their loved ones back into the relative safety of their own homes.

The neighbours knew what this woman's husband did for a living, and they wanted no part of whatever drama was unfolding on their street.

The Contract

They watched from their windows as the woman rushed over to the car and cradled the body of her husband in her arms. Her formerly pristine, white t-shirt was now slick with dark red blood and grey matter.

The children were, motionless, watching the scene as if it was happening on a huge TV set, their new toys and gifts forgotten, discarded in the grass. Their eyes were wide, and their lips were trembling, as their mother screamed and wailed for help. Help that was not, for now, forthcoming.

~~~~

From a small copse of trees in the park on the other side of the road, a small plume of smoke rose. A few moments later, a young man emerged from the same bushes. He was of indeterminate age, and his black clothing clung tightly to his thin, but athletic frame. His unkempt, almost bleached-blond hair and tight beard were in sharp contrast to the darkness of his attire.

As he exited his hiding space, he closed the long attaché case that he was carrying and, in no hurry, set off in the direction of the carnage he had just caused. He walked purposefully, pushing his way through the small crowd that had braved the threat of more shooting and gathered to see what all the screaming was about. No one gave him a second look as he strode up the driveway towards the stricken woman, who had recently stopped screaming, but was now sobbing as she held what was left of her husband in her arms. The man took a moment to ruffle the hair of the middle child, a girl, who was motionless, her face transfixed on her sobbing mother and dead father. She didn't even notice him pass.

The woman, however, did. She looked up at him. Her eyes were pleading, her mouth was quivering. She pushed her dead husband's body towards him, as if he were an offering, in the vain hope that the man was a doctor, a surgeon, or a miracle worker.

He was none of the above.

He simply leaned into the dead husband, placed an object onto his chest, and then walked away.

2.

THE NEW YORK Yankees were playing the Boston Red Sox at New Yankee Stadium. A little over fifty thousand people were crammed in to watch the home team host their biggest rivals. For over one hundred years, the Yankees and the Red Sox had held the oldest and fiercest rivalry in American sports. A rivalry that has been the cause of too many barroom brawls over the North-Eastern United States.

Today would be no different. The sun was shining, the sky was clear, and the air was filled with the smell of fresh bread, fried foods, hotdogs, and beer. A perfect Sunday afternoon for sports.

Five minutes before play was to commence, a small, fat man was led into the Jim Beam Suite. His seat was right behind home plate. This suite was one of the more exclusive seating areas in the stadium, perfect for a baseball fan, with enough money, to lavish themselves with nothing but the best. Six large men accompanied him, each of them wearing uncomfortable-looking double-breasted suits, with the jackets suspiciously fastened.

Their emotionless faces scanned the area, absorbing every detail they could, looking for threats, real or potential; anything that looked out of place. The seats around the fat man were all occupied, and as he was shown to his, most of the patrons about him made a point of reaching out to shake his hand. With a jovial smile, accompanied by a thick sheen of sweat, he heartily shook every one that was offered to him with a tight, friendly squeeze.

'Sir, it's so good to see you.' 'Sir, we need to talk. I have a little something for you.' 'Sir, would you do me the honour of …' were the typical greetings offered to him. He took them all gracefully, before finally arriving at his seat.

The Contract

Satisfied that everything was in order, the six big men relaxed as the fat man wiped his hands on a white handkerchief from his top pocket.

As one of the men sat down in the seat next to him, the fat man nudged him with his elbow. He leaned in, offering his boss an ear. He pointed to one of the men who he had just shaken hands with. The big man took note of who it was with a curt nod.

The business was done. Now it was time for fun.

An organ signalled the countdown to the start of the game, and the whole stadium stood to greet the teams as they were announced, running on to the field.

It was show time.

~~~

Heading into the seventh inning, the game was as tight as it could be. As the day was hot, sweat was covering the fat man's body, staining his armpits, even through his jacket. He continuously mopped at his brow as he enjoyed the game.

'Ladies and gentlemen, please show your appreciation for your next batter this evening. Roger Lamont ...'

The fans were on their feet. Roger Lamont was the New York Yankee's highest scorer this season, and a sure-fire game-changer.

The crowd fell silent as the pitcher eyed the catcher behind Lamont. A small nod and a wink told him everything he needed to know about how to pitch the ball. After a quick rub on the crotch of his trousers and an adjustment of his fingers, he was ready to give the curveball of his life. Fifty thousand people held their breaths as the pitcher began his run. The crack from the connection between the ball and the bat rang out around the stadium, and forty thousand of the fifty thousand present went wild.

It was a home run.

The roar of the crowd caused a flock of birds that had been nesting within the rafters to take flight, escaping whatever monster, or predator could cause a noise like that.

The fat man was suddenly transported away from the game, away from the life he had lived for the last thirty years and was suddenly a baseball hungry kid again. He was alive with dreams of playing out his fantasy of batting for the Yankees in front of the adoring masses. A fantasy that had been cut short by his next love. Money, business, power, and ultimately, greed.

He danced as if he had made the hit on the field himself. Unadulterated joy and passion for the sport he loved coursed through him as his body jigged on the spot. He beamed with the love that can only be felt when your team is winning, live, and you think of all the fresh money you've made on the illegal betting ring that was run from the kitchens of your restaurants. Still in rapture, he turned around and saw thousands of people jumping up and down, just like him.

A young man who was stood directly behind him caught his eye. Everyone else in the stadium was caught in the moment, a blur of motion and emotion, whether waving their arms, jumping on the spot, clapping, or cheering. But this man was not. He was motionless. There was no emotion or elation, or … anything else in his face. To the fat man, he resembled a blank canvas, a chunk of marble ready for an artist to fashion something from. He was striking to behold rather than being impressive. Dressed in black, with short blond hair, short beard, and unusual, striking eyes. The youth unnerved him, but he couldn't understand why. With a shiver sprinting down his moist spine, he turned away, back towards the celebrations in progress.

He would have sworn an oath on his dear mother's life that the boy hadn't been there when he'd arrived at his seat, otherwise he would have had his men check him out and move him along at his insistence. They were as wary as he was of anyone other than the usual sycophants and the easily intimated in the area.

As Lamont continued his slow jog around the diamond and the crowd continued to dance him along, the fat man spared another quick glance back. The boy hadn't moved. He was staring forwards, towards the game, both hands in his pockets. All around him, Yankee's fans were singing and cheering their man who was running past them, waving lazily to the crowd.

Biting his lower lip, the fat man turned to speak to Vinny, the bodyguard, who was currently as engrossed in the game as everyone else was, and he struggled to get his attention.

There was a blur from the corner of his eye as something flashed past. Before he could react, let alone raise an alarm to his men who were stationed all around him, whatever it was drew tight around his throat. Instinctively, he raised his hand to his fleshy neck, and his stubby fingers

The Contract

attempted to claw whatever it was away. His fight was in vain, as the wire already had a grip on his thick neck, and the tightening continued.

The celebrations continued. His security detail, jumping up and down, hugging each other, were unaware of what was happening to their employer. Backs were patted and high fives given and received. All of this ensured that no one noticed as his arms flailed, attempting to contact one of them, any of them, to help him.

He knew it was a garrotte, he'd used them several times before, but, in the arrogance of his position, had never thought that he would be on the receiving end of one. As it pulled tighter, he felt the cold wire dig into his doughy, fleshy folds, cheese-wiring through his soft flesh, cutting him, allowing blood to flow. His blood, mixing with his sweat, stained the top of his collar pink. His eyes bulged as the crowd continued to shriek and roar.

His eyes welled up, and through his blurred vision, he caught sight of the huge video screen across the field. As the thin wire twisted again, and his breath was cut from his body, his attention wandered over to it. It was playing a video in high speed. He'd never seen it do anything like this before. Normally it was of the field of play, or of people kissing in the crowd, but today it was playing images that he recognised from another life. Images of the streets where he grew up. All the loves of his youth: the games, the fun, and the baseball of course. It then fast-forwarded to his teenage years and the young lusts, loves, and fumblings with various crushes. His older teens followed then, filled with violence, knives, guns, money, gambling, prostitution, drugs, and more. These were the years that had defined him, but he knew that there was so much more which had been lost.

Sadly, now, it was all too late. The video on the screen was now playing a soundtrack, one that he guessed only he could hear. It was the sound of tolling bells and beckoning trumpets. Sounds of screams and pain. He saw white, then dark wings flap across the screen before his vision blurred, and reality came crashing down around him. At that point everything began to darken.

He felt wings, *maybe the ones from the screen,* he thought, flapping around him. The breeze they created hit him, and him alone, in the face. No scream was forthcoming— he didn't have enough breath in his body to build one— as the last of his life ebbed away. Eventually, screams did come, but they were not from him. They were the screams of the home crowd as Roger Lamont finally made it back to home base.

Blood gushed from the wound in his neck, ruining his expensive, pinstriped shirt with its crimson essence. His tongue lolled from his mouth, bloated, swollen, and purple.

His attacker released the pressure on the garrotte, allowing his lifeless body to slump down in his seat. Only when the fat man was back rested in his expensive chair did the youth reach inside his jacket and produce a large, white feather. He leaned over the dead fat man and placed it into the top pocket of the sweaty and bloody jacket.

~~~~

As the fat man fell back into his seat, and his very last breath gurgled from his mouth in pink bubbles of saliva and blood, Vinny, his bodyguard, stopped celebrating. He turned to see his boss, his uncle, his godfather, slumped in the seat. At first, he didn't notice the blood on his shirt and jacket. His initial reaction was that the fat man had had a heart attack. *I told him he needed to look after himself,* he thought, before his eye wandered. He then saw the blood seeping from his mouth and from the wound in his neck.

He knew that his career was over. How could the Don be killed in a public place, surrounded by his men, and a few thousand sycophants?

Another of the Don's men noticed Vinny kneeling to check the fat man's body. Immediately, he stopped celebrating too and ran to assist. This alerted the other four men, who all rushed to his side, knocking into, and over, many of the fans who had paid good money to watch this game.

'Did you see anything? DID YOU SEE ANYTHING?' Vinny shouted at the men. His jacket was open, and his gun was drawn.

At the site of the gun, the crowd began to panic. Screams, this time of a different nature, erupted as the body of the Don was discovered. Chaos ensued, and the crowd began to run every-which-way to distance themselves from the dead body and from the six men with the guns.

No one noticed the slim, blond, man as he turned and began to ascend the stairs towards the exit. The sole bastion of peace and order in the chaotic madness that the Jim Beam Suite had become.

Seamlessly, he mingled in with the crowd and disappeared.

The Contract

3.

THE TWENTY-FOUR-HOUR gym was on the fifteenth floor of the office block in downtown Wichita, Kansas. At this time, all the offices were closed, most of the lights were off, and the only people around were the security guards who patrolled the corridors and offices, shining their torches into darkened rooms, stifling yawns. They tended to stay away from the fifteenth floor as there were usually people in and out of the gym at all hours of the day. Tuesdays were normally the quietest night of the week. People had already burnt out all their weekend aggression and were storing their energies to battle the next one.

Julie Horrocks was alone in the plush suite. That was exactly how she liked it. Dressed in her tight-fitting, spandex gym clothes, she loved nothing better than getting up at four in the morning, running to the gym, and having a nice long workout, before the hustle of her daily life began. Her long, dark brown hair had been tied back in a ponytail, a bottle of water had been tucked into the cupholder before her, and her headphones were in, blasting out some electronic techno as she tackled the cross-trainer. This was her cool-down machine after her rigorous routine was over. She was looking forward to a ten minute relax in the hot tub and then a nice cool shower to liven herself back up.

This was her routine, and she loved the release of endorphins to set her up for another gruelling day in the bear-pit that was her office. A bear-pit where *she* was the 'mamma-bear!'

Stepping off the machine, she took a long drink from the water bottle, and wiped the sweat from her brow with a small towel. She headed for the showers. She was already looking forward to the heat of the hot tub as she entered the changing rooms. The caveat on the wall stated that users used the hot tub at their own risk.

She knew how to press buttons and turn dials.

On entering the small room, she activated the heater and then the bubbles in the large, round pool in the centre. The steam began to rise, and she turned the lights down to a low, ambient glow. She stripped off her sweaty gym clothes and stopped to admire her athletic, but still curvy, figure in the mirror that ran from the ceiling to the floor. A wicked smile crept over her face as she made her way to her locker to retrieve her mobile phone.

The dirty bastard will love these, she thought as she snapped a few photos before sending them to her boyfriend. She knew he'd be asleep, but it would be something nice for him to wake up to.

Still smiling, she rummaged inside her sports bag and retrieved her two-piece swimsuit. After a quick change, she went back to the hot tub and dipped her toe into the water. 'Perfect,' she whispered, before leaving the and turning on the water in one of the many shower cubicles. She wanted to rinse herself off before dipping into the hot, bubbling water, and having her well-earned relax.

She stepped into the cubicle, putting her hand under the falling water to test the temperature. She liked it hot. The heat opened up her pores, allowing her skin to breathe and discharge all the toxins from her dermal layers. Once detoxified, she could fully embrace the dulling effect of the warm hot tub.

She caught the water in her cupped hand and brought the refreshing liquid up to her face testing the temperature. Satisfied, she stepped in, closed her eyes, and raised her face into the stream. She let the water bless her with its magical refreshment as it poured down onto her face, shoulders, then between her breasts. The warmth of the water mixed with the coolness of the air caused her nipples to tighten. This made her think of Raj again, her current beau. A smile broke on her face as she turned, allowing the liquid to continue its flow down her long, dark hair and back. The tingle that washed over her aching body in the wake of the clear liquid felt magnificent.

Her enjoyment of this luxury was halted, however, when there was a sudden change in the room. A cold blast hit her. It wasn't a hard blast. Just the kind that hits you when someone enters into the locker room. *Someone else can't sleep,* she thought as she put her head back under the fast spray.

After a few moments submerged under the faucet, she realised that whoever it was who had come into the locker room hadn't arrived at

The Contract

the shower cubicles to wash yet. She poked her head out of the thin glass door and peered about. The black tiles on the walls gave the room a timeless class, but they absorbed all illumination. She couldn't see anyone in the shower room, so, assuming that she was still alone, she shook her head and immersed herself back under the flow of the warm water.

A few moments later, she reached out to turn the water off, anticipating the deep relaxation of the hot tub. She rubbed her face to red the excess water from it and attempted to exit the cubicle.

A strong, gripping pressure on the back of her head shocked her. Her eyes snapped open. It took a moment for the outline that she could see through the steamed glass of her cubicle to take form.

It was a man! She wasn't one-hundred-percent sure, but the presence *felt* like a man. She knew how paranoid that sounded in her head, but it was true. She whipped her thick, wet hair from her face and looked through the cubicle. He was standing directly in front of her, right outside the glass.

She felt the scream rising in her stomach as she tried to squirm away from him, but the cubicle was too small. There was simply nowhere to go. Another strong hand clamped over her mouth, stemming her impending scream.

All she could do was scream with her eyes.

A deep panic set in as she felt herself being pushed back against the cold, dark tiles.

Rape!

This was her only sickening thought.

He's going to rape me.

There was a brief reprieve from her terror as once he pushed her, he didn't advance any further inside the cubicle. Even through her fear, she knew that there was something unusual about him, something strange that she couldn't put her finger on. Then it dawned on her. His strong, piercing, blue eyes had never left her face.

She was young, extremely attractive (even if she did say so herself), and very naked, but not once had his eyes strayed from her face.

His short blond hair and beard were now dripping with her shower water, but never once did his eyes blink.

Then something happened, something that scared her more than she had ever been scared in her whole life. She couldn't tell due to the stream of warm water all over her body, but she thought she might have wet herself. It was horrible.

His deep, unmoving, blue eyes turned black. An unfathomable, impenetrable black. They looked like thick, sickly pools of molasses. The dread that had begun to rise in her moments earlier heightened. She had never witnessed anything like this before. If asked, she would have said that it was impossible for someone to change their eye colour at will; but that was what she witnessed.

The pressure in the hand over her mouth, preventing her from screaming, was tremendous as it pushed her head towards the black tiled wall. His young face was emotionless; there was a complete lack of enjoyment, excitement, or even fear in it. His new black eyes bored into her as he reached around with his left hand and grabbed a fistful of her hair. Slowly, he began to tighten his grip, pulling her head further back.

Her disbelief that this could happen in her gym was the only thing that had stopped her from wriggling and thrashing, trying to escape. That initial shock proved to be her downfall; and a fatal error. He removed his right hand from her mouth, and she took in a long, deep breath, choking on the water as it poured between her lips. He then inserted two of his fingers into her mouth. She gagged. He responded to her involuntary reflex by pulling her head back further while keeping her jaws apart with his fingers. This allowed the shower stream to flow into her mouth.

She thought about biting his fingers, but her jaw was open too wide and she had no control over it. The water filled the cavity of her mouth quickly, all too quickly, and it began to overflow out of the sides and down her cheeks. It bubbled as it poured! There was no air getting into her lungs as there was no-way she could swallow and breathe fast enough; such was the relentless pressure on her mouth and throat.

A bizarre sensation overcame her, as her legs weakened. Her body began to flow, just like the water that was filling her. She felt herself lift, up and out of her body, like she was twisting and turning in the air. She wanted to scream; but no sound would issue as she continued her ascent. She stopped twisting and found herself in the strange position of being able to look down on herself from above. Her brain couldn't conceive of what she was seeing. To her, she was no longer being assaulted and drowned by a stranger in the shower. It looked like someone else, someone who looked like her. She was aghast that the girl

The Contract

below, the one being assaulted in the cubicle, was now covered in blood rather than water. The now sanguinary shower flowed down, coating and staining her naked body. Naturally, the blood was thicker than the water and its thickness clung to every inch of her exposed flesh.

What should have been water flowing down the plughole in the centre of the floor, was now thick, dark, semi-coagulated blood. As it splashed to the floor, it did not drain straight away. Instead, it blazed. It was liquid fire, flowing and smoking. It raged and burned. Her feet and ankles reddened as her skin blistered. The blisters popped and oozed as her legs began to scorch and melt. Newly exposed bone was visible between the rips and slits of her skin. It was white against the black, charred flesh and blood from the already cauterizing wounds.

It *was* only water, but sadly for Julie's floating essence, the reality was how she perceived it.

Under the shower of fire and blood, the man held her. Her arms flailed uselessly against the blood-stained glass and against him. Her strength was fading in accordance with her life force.

From above, Julie watched herself fade. A bizarre kind of music— trumpets, harps, and chanting—filtered into the shower room, seemingly coming from everywhere. The sounds merged and blared as they got louder. The shriek of the trumpets morphed into a sickening, high-pitched wail. It was a horrible sound, like unseen voices screaming from deep within an abyss before it transformed again, becoming the screams of medieval childbirth. Floating high above the scene of horror, she clamped her hands to her ears, attempting to block the abomination of noise. It was a useless gesture. The sound was coming from *inside* her head.

The screams signalled an end to her plight as she felt herself being drawn down, back towards her dying body. She knew that her end was nigh as she was sucked into her flagging body. She stared up at the ceiling. The water continued to pummel into her face and mouth, but now her stomach was full. She could swallow no more. The effort of trying had damaged her gullet and watery blood was vomiting up from her throat and out of her nose. It was dark, unoxygenated blood, straight from her lungs. Water had rushed into them, flushing them, filling them full to ruination.

Damaged and haemorrhaging, unable to breathe, her body allowed her a few more, feeble attempts at escape. Her hands tapped shakily on the walls of the cubicle as her legs twitched in the red water that was struggling to flow down the drain.

Julie Horrocks drowned.

The liquid fire was gone; the blood shower was no more than simple cooling water flowing over her lifeless corpse before draining away around her perfectly pedicured feet. The blond man held her for another moment, ensuring that his task was complete. Gently, he eased her dead weight onto the shower floor; he already knew that she was gone.

Julie's murderer reached inside his wet top and produced a single white feather. With reverence, he placed it between her blue and swollen lips. He turned off the shower before stepping back out of the cubicle and strolling, almost casually, out of the changing rooms.

He didn't bother to dry himself, he simply left Julie Horrocks dead in the cool, clear water.

The Contract

4.

IT WAS EARLY morning in Washington, DC. The sun was only just rising over Pennsylvania Avenue. Agent Cox and Agent Symes had been called into an emergency meeting on the fourth floor of the J Edgar Hoover Building, the headquarters of the FBI.

Agent Symes was struggling with his chair. He was a big man, at least six-foot three, and his wide frame complimented his height. The chair was not meant for such a profile. Agent Cox, however, did not share his partner's discomfort, and even offered a stifled giggle as he watched Symes squirm.

Cox was the older of the two. Symes, in his early thirties, had been promoted from the military, while Cox, in his mid-forties, was a career agent with over twenty years with a badge.

'So, we think it could be a serial killer, but one that's working his victims at a faster rate than most of the others we've encountered. There's been three victims in as many days.' The rotund man standing at the large whiteboard at the head of the room was looking at pictures of three victims. One young man, one old, fat man, and a rather attractive young woman.

'What makes you think these murders are related?' Cox asked as he studied the before and after pictures on the board: the young man with his head blown off, the fat man garrotted on the seat in a sports arena, and the young woman, naked in the shower. 'They're all in different geographical locations, and all of them look like they were killed with different methods.' Cox shrugged. 'So, what's the link?'

'The link, Agent Cox, is this.' The robust man, who happened to be a director of the bureau, clicked the small device he had in his hand and the whiteboard changed. The three faces disappeared and were replaced by three pictures of white feathers. Two of them were pristine white, while the other one looked damp and a little greyer than the others. 'These were found at all three of the scenes.'

'So,' Symes chirped in. 'Bird feathers. Two of the victims were outside, and the third could have carried the feather in with her, inadvertently.'

'Maybe, but these feathers were *on* the bodies of the victims,' the man at the front replied.

Cox sat forward, studying the three feathers on the large screen. 'Are they real?'

'No!' Symes quipped. 'We've got some nut-job leaving virtual feathers about the place!'

Cox shot him a look, telling him to shut up. 'I mean, are they organic? Are they from a real bird?'

'Well, they are organic, yes, but we have no idea from what bird. Or, even if they're from a bird. The guys in the labs are sourcing some ornithologists right now, to see if they are from a rare species.'

Cox walked to the front of the room and leaned into the whiteboard. 'If they are a rare species, then they must be huge. Are these feathers to scale, Frank?'

Frank investigated his files. 'They appear to be larger than Ostrich feathers, but that's no indication of how big the bird might be.'

'Even so, it must be pretty fucking huge,' Symes butted in as he joined his partner at the front of the room.

'Could it be a synthetic feather, created from organic matter?' Cox asked, ignoring his partner.

'That's a distinct possibility, yes. But still, we have no record of where the original material could have come from,' Frank replied, looking up at the board.

'So, what do we know about the victims?' Symes asked, looking away from the board towards Frank.

'Well, here's where it gets interesting,' he replied, sitting down at the table at the front of the room. Both Symes and Cox followed suit, sitting back in their original locations. 'All this information will be in your case folders, by the way. The first victim, if you really want to call him that, Kurt Mills. He was shot and killed outside his own house, in a nice suburb of Baltimore. He was killed by a single, high calibre gunshot to the head. We've retrieved the bullet that killed him, but ballistics are baffled as to the make and calibre. It maybe some sort of custom.' A

The Contract

picture of the recovered slug appeared on the screen. All three men looked at it. 'The rifle that it was fired from was not recovered from the scene. At present, we've got no one who can even hazard a guess as to what it was. All we know is that it's very high-calibre.'

Symes's face changed, his eyes widened, and he shook his head.

'What's up, Agent? Does this shock you?' Frank asked.

'No, sir, I'm more shocked to hear that there's a nice suburb in Baltimore!'

Frank smiled and shook his head. He clicked the small device in his hand again, and the picture on the screen changed to the 'before' picture of the young man.

'Kurt Mills! A successful businessman and a loving family man,' Frank continued. 'Or, at least that's what his obituary will say. In reality, he was a successful drug dealer and also a hit man for hire. The FBI have been watching him for a while now, trying to build a case against him and get evidence on who he was working for. We haven't found anything, as of yet, to stick. He normally never did any of the 'wet work' himself, and for the benefit of the rest of the world, he was legit. He had a wife and three children, plus several *goombahs* dotted around the state. But we do know that he's directly responsible for at least fifteen murders in the Baltimore and Washington, DC area, alone. God only knows how many more, further afield.'

'This is impressive reading,' Symes said as he flicked through the dossier that had been handed to him on entering the room. 'You guys have done your homework.'

'That's what we do, Agent Symes,' Frank retorted, flicking the screen to the next slide in the presentation. 'This next one is pretty impressive. This man was garrotted in one of the most expensive suites in Yankee Stadium. If you can believe this, he was murdered right in the middle of a game against the Boston Red Sox. What we can't believe, gentlemen, is that not one witness has come forward to say they saw anything. He had six, count them, *six*, bodyguards with him at the time of the incident. We haven't yet been able to locate a single one of them. It's my guess that they're all either sleeping with the fishes right about now or they are out on the lam.'

Frank took a moment to pour himself a glass of water from the large jug on his desk. He offered the jug to the agents; they both declined.

'The victim's name was Salvador DeGrassie.' He paused for a moment after mentioning the name. He smiled as both agents looked at each other. 'Yes, gentlemen, you're right. The same Sal DeGrassie that we at the FBI have been trying to get to for years. His name has been linked to everything from racketeering, prostitution, and drugs, to gun running, money laundering, murder … you name it, Sal DeGrassie's liked for it. Married with at least six children, possibly more as God only knows how long he's been putting it about the city and state of New York.'

'Jesus! How did anyone get to him in Yankee Stadium?' Cox asked as he looked at the pictures of the dead, fat man slumped in his expensive seat.

'That's the Jim Beam Suite,' Symes added. 'It's not just *one* of the expensive suites, they're *the* most expensive seats in the house. That stand would have been filled to the rafters for a home game like that. Surely there must have been someone who saw what happened.'

Frank shook his head. 'Not a one … allegedly! This third victim is a real piece of work, and when I say that, I mean it. She was gorgeous. Julie Horrocks, thirty-two years old, single, loaded. Wichita, Kansas. One of the top criminal defence lawyers in the country. She made millions defending and getting releases for every little piece of scum of the country. She was damned good at it too. Some people say she was *too* good. It was hinted at that she had top judges in her pocket and most of them in her pants as well. Legend has it, she would do anything for an acquittal, and I mean anything. Then once the 'anything' was done, the doer would be blackmailed. She was found drowned in her local gym three days ago.'

'Drowned? Could it have been an accident?' Cox asked looking confused.

'Yeah, I suppose it could have been if she hadn't been standing in the shower cubicle at the time.'

Symes's face creased as he squinted towards Frank. 'She drowned in the shower?'

'Someone held her head up to the shower nozzle and kept her mouth open until she drowned. The crazy bastard then left his calling card. This single white feather.' Frank clicked the handheld remote again, and a picture of a wet, but magnificent, bright white feather appeared on the screen.

The Contract

'So, what do we know about this guy? Always assuming it is a guy. Have we got anything to go on?' Symes was flicking through the third file; he was admiring one of the photographs of Julie. It was a black and white shot of her in a courtroom wearing a tight skirt with a long split in it, a white blouse, and glasses. 'That is one waste of a serious hard body!'

Cox shook his head and hit his partner with his file.

Symes took the hint and put the photograph back in the folder.

'I won't lie to you guys. We've got nothing. Zip! No prints anywhere on the three sites, no DNA, no fibres, nothing except these fucking feathers. It's our thinking that this guy is a professional assassin. He may even be foreign, brought in specifically.'

'Is there any relation between any of these murders, other than the feather, I mean?' Cox asked.

'Nothing! Nothing at all. As far as we can see they're all unrelated cases. Bound together by the single white feather. Gentlemen, I've got other business to attend to this morning. You will, of course, have the full resources of the Bureau at your disposal. Please consider yourselves briefed. Now do me a favour, bring this bastard in, preferably alive. So, if you would excuse me ...' Frank ushered the two men out of his office and closed the door behind them.

5.

A LONG, FOUR-by-four limousine with blacked out windows, was idling at a traffic light in the middle of nowhere, Ohio. The lights were temporary, having been set up to allow tractors and farm equipment access to the long roads that dissected the cornfields on either side. The darkened windows of the vehicle proposed absolutely no access to the rear of the stretched car. Only the front windows offered any view inside the vehicle. The driver was alone in the front. The large, African American male was wearing dark sunglasses. He looked vigilant but bored waiting for the lights to change.

He was tapping his hands on his steering wheel as he looked out of the windshield and up at the lights swinging on the wire above the dirt road. He considered jumping them and continuing the journey to the location of the next gig, but, knowing that he was a man of colour, driving an expensive car in the middle of Hicksville, USA, it was best to adhere to the law and wait out their course. He also knew what his current employer would be up to in the back of the car, and he thought it best that no law enforcement got a peek at that level of debauchery.

The partition was up, and that could only mean bad things were happening.

He checked the mirrors, looking for any sign of local police cars hiding within the swaying rivers of corn on either side of the road. Just because he couldn't see them didn't mean that they weren't there. His long years on active service in Afghanistan had taught him that.

He could hear the faint thump, thump, thump of his boss's music pumping through the partition, and he shook his head. *How the fuck can anyone call that music?* he thought as the joyless drivel filtered through. He reached over to the radio in the dash and attached his mobile phone to it. He selected a collection of blues that he had stored in the music app

The Contract

and selected a playlist. The beautiful and melodic guitar introduction to BB King's *Three O'clock Blues* filtered through the cabin, and he sat back, relaxing into his seat, enjoying the song.

This was a good job, and it paid well. Driving Lovin' L Duke around the country, from gig to gig, making sure that he got to where he needed to be in one piece. It didn't mean that he had to like the guy, or his music for that matter, but he did have to look out for him.

~~~

In the back of the limousine, it was a far cry from the serene atmosphere in the front. Lovin' L Duke, a muscular black man covered in dark tattoos with strange symbols shaved into his tightly cropped hair, was sat on one of the long, leather seats. He was naked, except for a pair of white boxer shorts and black sunglasses.

Loud rap music was pumping from the speakers, and he was smiling while jigging about, attempting to dance. In front of him were two women. One was white, and the other was Asian. They were both naked and making out with each other, obviously for the Duke's approval. There was another woman, again white and naked, who was snorting a long line of white powder from a mirrored surface.

The Duke leaned forward and opened a small compartment set into the car's suite. Inside was a decanter with six glasses. Inside the decanter was a dark brown liquid. It was brandy, very expensive brandy.

'Don't mind me, ladies,' he laughed, pouring himself a large glass. As he leaned back, he couldn't resist giving the Asian girl's backside a lick. The distasteful look on the girl's face indicated that they were there for the money and not for the Duke himself.

Inside the compartment, next to the glasses, was a semi-automatic pistol. His eyes focused on the gun, and a grin broke out across his dazed and confused face. He picked it up and pointed it at the woman who was snorting the powder from the mirror. 'Stick 'em up, bitch,' he slurred as he pulled the safety off the weapon.

The woman's red eyes stared down the barrel of the gun. 'Whatever, Duke,' she replied, wiping her nose, not even a little bit impressed with the gun.

'BANG,' he shouted, squeezing the trigger. The dry clicks of the pistol repeated three times; none of them registered in the woman's face.

Laughing, he dropped the pistol onto the floor and took a long swig from his glass.

~~~~

The driver was still waiting for the lights to change. They had been on red for at least five minutes, and it was beginning grate on his nerves. He toyed with the idea of blowing his horn. *What good will that do me?* he thought as the song on the stereo changed to John Lee Hooker and the funky blues sound of *Dimples*. This was one of his personal favourites. He turned the volume up just a little bit more to drown out the rubbish that was booming from the rear.

As he looked down at the dials, something caught his eye in the mirror. He knew that there was nothing behind them for miles and miles. They had taken this route on purpose, the *scenic route,* as The Duke had called it, driving through endless fields of corn. But now, behind them, was a man. He was dressed in black from head to toe, with a hood up and his hands in the front pockets of the top he was wearing.

Something about this youth didn't seem right. Not one for being under-cautious, the driver reached over to open the glove compartment, allowing it to drop, revealing the gun stowed within easy reach inside. He never once took his eyes from the approaching figure.

As he got closer, the youth removed his hood, allowing his bleached blond hair to blow in the wind. The driver could see that he was really nothing more than a boy. He couldn't place his age, but he was a lot younger than his own forty-two years. His throat dried as the boy approached, and his hands became twitchy on the wheel, longing for his weapon.

He was now rueing the decision by The Duke, as he liked to be called, to take this scenic route. He'd wanted it so that he could have some *special time* with the ladies back there. *There's nothing ladylike about those tramps,* he thought absently as the boy continued to get closer. *If I had my way with them, they'd be as dead as those other whores back in Afghanistan.*

The arrival of the youth had brought back bittersweet memories of his tours away with the Corp. Reminiscences of the atrocities he had enacted, encouraged, and enjoyed, on those *fucking ragheads*. A smile crept over his face.

The Contract

In the short time it took for him to recollect, the traffic lights changed from red to green, and back to red again. The whole sequence had passed him by, unnoticed.

In his dream-like state, he also didn't notice that the music from the expensive cabin speakers had changed too. Gone were the dulcet tones of John Lee Hooker, only to be replaced by an eerie cacophony of trumpets and drums.

A knock on the window snapped him out of his daydreams of the rape and murder of helpless women, while their husbands and fathers, bound and gagged, were forced to watch, helpless to the atrocities that were happening to their loved ones before them. He blinked twice as the youth appeared at his window.

'What the fuck?' he mumbled.

With fast, well trained reflexes, he reached down to the glove compartment to grab the gun. As he did, a bang heralded the smashing of the driver's side window. It crashed in on him, covering him in thousands of small, glass squares. An iron-like grip on the back of his well-muscled arm stopped him an inch or two from the handle of his weapon.

'What the fuck do you think …'

The driver didn't finish his sentence. He turned to see the impassive face of the young man looking at him through the broken window. He saw the fist coming, but there was very little he could do about it, such was the grip that the boy had on his arm.

He felt the impact in his neck, and everything blurred as a tidal wave of pain engulfed him. His gullet was crushed. Like a deep-sea diver who had run out of oxygen, he grasped at his throat, battling for breath. Panic set in, but no air was forthcoming. He thrashed and raved, gasping, scratching, trying to tear through the fabric of his skin to allow the sweet gasses that his body craved, in. Within a few moments, his fight began to slow, and he slumped back into the expensive leather seat.

He was only peripherally aware of the strange music coming from the speakers, beginning to blur.

As his eyes continued to bulge and his hands clawed in desperation at his ruined neck, he saw the strange young man reach into his pocket and produce something. The driver's last coherent thought before the darkness came to carry him away, never to bring him back again, was, *what the fuck is he going to do with that feather?*

As he died, collapsed against the driver's seat in the limousine with a large, white feather tucked into the top pocket of his shirt, the young man opened his door. He shifted the driver's body over onto the passenger seat as if he were moving a hollow toy doll, he then climbed in and began to drive, ignoring the red traffic light swinging above the road on the thin wire.

~~~~

In the back of the limousine, the party for four was still in full swing. The girls who were making out had now started to go one step further. The Asian girl was sitting back in the seat, while the white girl with the red hair had buried her head in between her legs. The Duke was loving what he was watching.

The third girl looked half asleep with a rolled up fifty-dollar bill stuck up one nostril and white powder in her dark hair like the most expensive dandruff on the planet. The Duke was loving this also. He began to rub at the front of his white boxer shorts, fully intending to join the two girls who were enjoying each other, when a muffled bang rocked the car.

It was only a small tremor, but enough to put him off his stride. He fumbled for the remote control that had fallen down between the seats and turned the music down. All three girls stopped what they were doing, the girl with the red hair wiping her mouth as she turned to look at him.

'Shhh,' he commanded, putting a finger to his mouth.

All three girls were silent.

He listened. 'I thought I heard something. Are we moving?' he asked, not really expecting a reply.

The girls didn't offer an opinion either way. After a moment or two, he heard the door slam. 'Damned driver must have taken a leak or something,' he laughed, pointing the gun at the girls who were performing for him. He smiled. 'Carry on ladies, you're being well paid for this shit.' As he turned the music back up, the two girls continued with their business. The Duke smiled as he continued to rub his crotch, watching what they were doing. He nodded to himself as the momentum of the car continued. *That's better, we're moving again…*

~~~~

The Contract

The scent of alcohol and drugs populated the backseat of the car. There was an air of unease within the girls. As much as they were there to perform for their client, aided by the drugs and money in a healthy supply, none of them were comfortable with the situation. They'd heard bad things about this employer. Apparently, his 'bad boy' reputation was well earned, and there had been rumours of him going too far with the girls, ending up with some of them in hospital. Those girls had been paid silence money afterwards, a lot of it, but that didn't stop these from being wary, and more than a little intimidated by him. Of course, in their line of business, they were expected to get crazy, and they were experienced enough to be able to deal with whatever was asked of them. The customer was always right after all. However, there was something unspoken that made this particular transaction feel different from the outset. They all felt it, but none of them had communicated their doubts to the others. Everything about it felt wrong somehow, as if the assignment was doomed from the moment each of them wiggled their bikini-clad asses into the limousine and flashed their playful, business-like smiles at the client. Their discomfort had heightened as the journey progressed. The drugs they were being forced to use and the gun that was being waved in their faces only increased their desire to get the job done and get the hell out of this car in one piece.

The bad atmosphere was shattered, literally, when the partition between them and the driver exploded. A shower of blackened glass and plastic rained down on the four people in the cabin.

The Duke sat back, watching the explosion through wide eyes. The two girls performing oral sex screamed and jumped out of the way of the flying debris. As the third girl opened her sleepy eyes to see what the disruption was, the fifty-dollar bill fell out of her nose.

A slender, blond man erupted through the hole that had just opened from the driver's cabin. In one unbelievable show of athleticism, he rolled through the small opening from the front into the back. His eyes roamed around the car, taking in the three naked women, the drugs, the alcohol, and the gun. He turned to look at The Duke, who was still staring wide-eyed at the newcomer. He spoke one word. It was directed at the women, and not the scared, semi-naked man holding the gun in his shaking hands.

'OUT.'

It wasn't a request; it was a command.

To the women, it sounded like a thousand people had all spoken at once. It was as if the voice hadn't come from him but had come from everywhere else. They began to panic, not believing what they were seeing. The blond man simply reached out and laid his hand on the door handle. An audible 'click' resounded through the cabin, and both rear doors sprung open as if detonated by small explosive charges. Undeterred, the three ladies took their chance to escape this madness. Grabbing clothes and money, they literally fell over each other as they made their escape from the limousine.

The cool air from outside filled their lungs, and the daylight hurt their eyes. They milled around outside of the car for a few moments, not really knowing what to do. Then, realising that they had been released, in a fashion, from this contract, they dressed and made their way towards the freeway that they could see, maybe two miles off in the distance. None of them spoke, but the Asian girl and the red head supported the dark-haired girl along the way; she'd had a little too much of the white powder.

~~~

'Man, this coke is HOT,' The Duke mumbled as he watched the youth tumble, athletically, into the back of the limo. Everything seemed to be happening in slow motion, and he sat back watching it unfold with a semi-vacant grin spreading across his face.

In a slow daze, he reached for the gun that was in the side arm of the seat, this one was loaded, meant for business, not for pleasure like the last one. He held it up towards the party-crasher. He was amused to see that his hands were shaking, rather badly.

'OUT!' he heard the voice, *or was it voices?* he thought, while the doors blew open. As the fresh air entered the cabin and hit him like a wall, he came to his senses and realised that this wasn't a drug induced hallucination. The boy really had crashed through the partition, and the bitches, all three of them, were leaving. He sat and watched as they fell over each other trying to escape this situation. *Let the fuckers go,* he thought. *I'll be speaking to Julio about them tomorrow!*

Once the women were gone, the doors remained open and he eyed the escape route they had taken jealously. He mentally calculated if

The Contract

he could make it out there with them, away from the weird white dude who was now sitting opposite him. For what seemed like an eternity, the blond man stared at him. The Duke still felt like he was in shock, facing the intruder, pointing his trembling gun loosely in his direction. He could still see through the open doors. The realisation that they were in the middle of nowhere was not lost on him. They were surrounded by cornfields for as far as he could see. He cursed his decision to take the *scenic route* so he could entertain them bitches, and he wished that he was now in the city, on his turf. He knew that he could hold his own in the city; out here, he was at the mercy of whatever this redneck piece of shit wanted from him.

It was only a few seconds that passed, yet it seemed like a lifetime before he decided that his best bet was to go for the door, to head for the freedom beyond, into the cornfields. Sadly, for him, that option was taken away, very quickly, as the doors slammed shut of their own accord.

Something dawned on him then. It was the realisation that he was trapped! Trapped inside this car with some throwback from the film Deliverance, wanting God-only-knew what. For the first time in a very long time, since being a runner for the local street gangs when he was a kid, The Duke was scared.

He noticed blood on the white guy's hands, and he knew immediately that it could only have come from one place, given the stranger's entry point. The blood must have been from his driver.

'S'up with Charles?' he asked, trying his very best to cut the waiver from his voice. His body was still shaking, and his teeth had joined the party. They were chattering away in the heat of the day.

He wondered where the imagery that the guy's booming whisper had evoked came from. It told of visions, legions of men— or were they demons—charging and shouting in unison. He pondered if he had snorted too much coke and smoked too much of his weed, and all of this was some kind of weird, fucked up hallucination. *It might even be an overdose!*

His mind, always one for running away with him, began to reminisce about being that young hustler in his neighbourhood gang, on the first rung of his particular ladder. The first rung in a ladder that had led him up to a life of stardom and luxury, drugs, and whores. He'd made it on his own and no one, especially a freaky, pale, white redneck, was going to take it away from him … was he?

He realised that the man hadn't answered him yet, so he gripped the pistol tighter and asked the question again. 'I asked what's up with Charles?'

The man still didn't answer, he just cocked his head to one side as if he didn't understand the question.

'Look, man!' He was trying his best to sound authoritative, and not like a little child who had just dirtied his diapers. 'I'm going to give you one chance to get the fuck out of here before I start blowing holes into you. Y'hear me, redneck?'

There was conviction in his voice, and he sounded confident, only it was all a charade; inside he was petrified.

Without even registering that he had asked a question, the white man picked up the decanter of expensive brandy and, in the wink of an eye, he was on top of him, pushing him onto the leather seat of the car and pouring the contents of the decanter over his bare chest.

A ghost of a smile caressed The Duke's lips as he watched the liquid soak into his dark skin. He enjoyed the sensation. *Yeah, this is all a hallucination,* he thought as he looked up to the strong white man holding him down. *He's kind of cute too.*

Now he knew he was hallucinating. He had never, not once in his whole life, found another man cute, *at least not a white dude,* he added in his head. *This is really happening! Am I just sitting here letting this fucker do this to me?*

The white man produced a lighter from his pocket and sat staring at him.

The Duke stared back. He was in a state of reverie; he was awed by this man's presence. He thought he could hear music coming from somewhere distant. It wasn't the kind of music that he'd have appreciated normally, there was no beat or bass to it, no thump, but it was growing on him, drawing him in. It sounded like something he had heard once or twice as a child, maybe in the few times that the sorry excuse of a mother he'd been 'blessed' with had dragged him to church. It was the sound of trumpets, of horns, of a battle and a triumph. The sound built and built, quickly becoming deafening, to the point that he had to put his hands over his ears to block it. His initial pleasure at the music had now become

The Contract

a contortion of agony as the discordance was now threatening to deafen him.

The youth holding the lighter didn't seem affected by it at all.

The sound could not be blocked by covering his ears. It seemed to him that the wails of the triumphal horns, the raging angelic wrath, and the distant thumping of drums of war were all inside his head. It was firing up to a crescendo, a cacophony of noise that was making his ears bleed, literally. Blood began to pour between his fingers and down his cheeks. There was a distinct and agonising popping sound as his eardrums burst. The pain ripped through the sides of his head. He dropped the gun and watched as it bounced silently and uselessly from the car seat. He witnessed it silently discharge, and he saw the bullet hit the youth in the shoulder. There was no blood. The man didn't even flinch. The bullet bounced off him, harmlessly, and lodged in the padded roof of the luxury car.

The Duke returned his eyes to the stranger who was now straddling him. *What the fuck has happened to his eyes?* he marvelled, as the man's once piercing blue eyes turned a dark, endless black. His own eyes moved to the lighter in the youth's hands, and realisation dawned on him of what he was about to do.

Everything began to move in slow motion again.

The stranger flicked open the lighter and gazed lovingly at the flame as it danced, reflecting gently in the obsidian abyss of his pupils. He then lowered it. All too quickly the dancing yellow flame was joined by its blue cousins as the brandy caught fire, spreading across The Duke's chest and stomach. He stared in disbelief, helpless against what was happening to him. In his head, he screamed in pain. Confusion rained down on him as he wasn't sure if the sounds had even made it from his mouth as the horns continued to deafen him. His torso was now bucking in response to the fire, as his flesh began to bubble and cook. The layers of fat beneath his skin melted and dripped at an alarming rate.

The pale man quietly got up and stepped out of the back of the car, closing the door firmly behind him. The Duke, screaming in agony now, watched him leave through wide, pained eyes.

~~~

The boy walked to the front of the limousine and opened the door. Thick, black smoke was pouring through the smashed partition, and it billowed out through the open driver's door. The smoke and the screams filled the air in equal measures. He reached in and pulled the body of the driver out, laying him on the ground by the side of the limo.

He stepped off towards the corn field, where he stopped and turned back towards the heavily smoking vehicle. He held out his arms, as if in worship, before bringing his hands together in a clap.

~~~~

Inside the vehicle, The Duke writhed in agony. He was still conscious and could see the boy standing at the side of the road, his arms raised. The music of the trumpets and horns was growing, and the agony of the raw fire on his skin was unrelenting. Just when he thought he could take no more pain and was ready to succumb to the inevitable, the sounds became louder and the heat even more intense. This coincided, exactly, with the pale man's hands coming together.

As they clapped, the sound of trumpets, although in his head, blew the windows out of the car. The influx of air inside the car accelerated the inferno within, allowing it to blaze out of control.

There then followed an explosion, which did not drown out the scream of the ex-rapper inside.

~~~~

Once the explosion and resulting carnage was spent, the youth strode towards the conflagration that used to be a luxury vehicle. Without even a flinch, he leaned into the pyre that was the interior of the car and pulled out the still burning remains of the man inside. Lovin' L Duke's flesh dripped from his bones like cheese from a pizza. He was dead, but the boy's work wasn't finished yet.

He lined the melted corpse up next to the body of the dead driver on the bare asphalt, he plucked another feather from the inside of his hooded top and placed it onto what was the forehead of the singing star.

His task now completed, the pale, blond stranger turned and walked away into the fields of corn.

The Contract

6.

THE OFFICE SPACE that had been assigned to them was large. It was probably too big for just them, but the Bureau had wanted them to have the best resources available for this case.

'Maybe we're going to get a few secretaries in here with us, eh?' Symes quipped as he sat back in his seat, looking up at the large whiteboard before him.

Cox laughed. 'Yeah, right. With your reputation, you know who we'd end up getting.'

'Brenda Reid?' Symes replied with a sly-dog wink and a raise of his eyebrows.

Cox shook his head. 'Think again, man. We're talking Carrie McKenna.'

Symes whistled as he took in a sharp intake of breath. 'That battle-axe?'

'She's probably the only one you haven't been sent to human resources about.'

Symes laughed aloud. 'And for good reason too. Anyway, what do we have here?'

'This, Agent Symes, is the reason we're here.' Cox stood back from the board, taking it all in. There were several photographs of crime scenes, some showing the dead bodies, others showing the locations of the murders from different angles. Three victims, two male and one female. Each of them sectioned off from the others, showing the broad spectrum of the investigation. He was shaking his head as he covered his mouth.

'Cox, you would be a terrible poker player, you know that?'

'Hmm?' he asked turning around to look at his partner.

'You, your body language.'

'I just can't get a handle on this case. Nothing about these murders add up. There's no correlation between them.'

Symes picked up one of the thick, brown folders off the table and leafed through it. Pictures and documents adorned the inside. It was depressing reading.

'So far, all we have is that Mills here,' he pointed to the photograph of the young man, 'he hired a boat from one of DeGrassie's holding companies. Apparently, it was for a corporate fishing trip. It only happened once!'

Symes put the folder down and stood next to his partner, looking up at the board. 'But other than that, they had nothing to do with each other,' he added, mimicking his partner's stance. 'For all intents and purposes, they've never met.'

'Horrocks,' Cox pointed at the picture of the attractive young woman. 'She once had a meeting with DeGrassie regarding representation. The case never made it to court due to the witnesses being unwilling to testify.'

'Too scared to testify, you mean?' Symes added.

Cox nodded. 'Three victims, one calling card, tenuous links at best.'

'Four, possibly five victims!'

Both men turned as a large black man strolled into the office and tossed another folder, similar to the other three, onto the table that was behind the two agents. 'Sorry guys,' he said throwing his hands in the air in a gesture of surrender. 'The director asked me to personally ensure that you got this. Don't shoot the messenger! If the body has a feather on it, it's yours, apparently!' he laughed as he walked out.

Symes picked up the file and leafed through it as Cox turned back towards the board.

'I know this guy!'

Cox turned back to look at him, eyebrows raised.

'Well, I know *of* him. He's in the charts right now.'

Cox took the file from him and looked through it. His brow ruffled at the graphic nature of the photographs. They displayed the badly charred remains of a human, and the body of a well-dressed black man with a swollen neck. His eyes shifted to the corresponding photograph of a large, muscular black man. 'Nathan Croft! Doesn't sound much like a rock-star to me.'

The Contract

'Rap star,' Symes corrected him. 'Lovin' L Duke. His song out now is called, erm...' Symes took out his phone and began tapping at the screen. 'Here we are. It's a nice little ditty called, *Smacking Them Bitches*. Smacking is spelled with a double K, them is spelled as D E M. Fucking morons with this shit.'

'So, what do we know about our Mr Croft?' Cox asked flicking through the files.

'The internet is our friend, Agent Cox,' Symes said logging onto the computer terminal. 'OK, let's search our database and see who this Lovin' L Duke really is.'

Cox leaned in over his shoulder as Symes typed the real name of the rapper into the search engine. 'OK, Mr Croft was born in Compton, Los Angeles in 1980. Father: Unknown. Mother: Elizabeth, or Lizzy Croft. She has multiple arrests for prostitution, drug possession, and get this, jaywalking. I'd have thrown the book at the bitch!'

Cox laughed.

'Our Mr Croft started his career early. Juvenile warnings for drug running, robbery, and assault, at the age of nine. Good job, mom! His first real bust is at sixteen for possession with intent and a firearm offence. It all goes downhill after that. Theft, burglary, assault, drugs, drugs, drugs, wearing a hat in church!'

Another laugh from Cox...

'Then, in '97 he's involved in a drive by shooting. He's on the receiving end. He takes four bullets, two in the chest, one in the neck, and one in the leg. He's on a life support machine for three months, all at the taxpayer's dollar, I might add. He recovers and is in traction for another six months where he develops a skill in writing rap songs. A real poet. He's signed up to Crak Ho Records. Mom shed a tear; she was so proud. Or she would have been if she hadn't been dead by then of an overdose. His first song was called *Long Legged Lovelies*. Sounds nice doesn't it? Then it's all back uphill from there. Multimillion-dollar deals, limos, mansions, swimming pools, movie stars! The Compton Hillbillies...'

'And then found burnt to death in the back of a limo in Shitsville, Ohio!' Cox added.

'Looks like we're going to need another board.' Symes left the room, leaving Cox staring at the file in his hands, shaking his head.

7.

THE TWO AGENTS were travelling on a small jet belonging to the Bureau. Before them were four files, the contents spread across a small table. Cox sat staring at them; his greying hair unkempt and his eyes tinged with red.

Symes returned from the bathroom and sat back in his seat while continuing to look at his phone. 'Christ! Cox, you need to have a listen to these lyrics. This is what our man Nathan got famous for.' He leaned in, putting his elbows on the table, and holding the earpieces from his phone out before him.

'Man, you know that using the internet up here is costing you a fortune, don't you?' Cox replied, ignoring the invitation of rap music.

Symes winked without looking up from his phone. 'Not me, man! This is the Bureau's dollar.'

Cox sat back and closed his eyes. 'Go ahead. Enlighten me with this mastery of the English language.'

'You ready for this? This is *Long Legged Lovelies*. I'm not even going to try to do it in the rap style, so you'll just have to put that bit together in your own head.' He cleared his throat and carried on. 'I'm a sexual beast, and I like you the least, on your pussy I'll feast … you long legged lovelies.'

'That's bringing a tear to my eye, man. You could put that in a Valentine's Day card,' Cox laughed, still with his eyes closed.

'It gets better. Listen! I'm a fucking tyrant, and you know what I want. That's a bit of a stretch in the rhyming stakes if you ask me. We're going to do it 'til you're silent, you long legged lovelies.' Symes looked up from his phone and smiled at his partner who looked almost asleep. 'Hey, this isn't a lullaby, you know! You want me to keep going?'

The Contract

'Please, no!' Cox replied, opening his eyes, and leaning forward. He began looking through the files again. 'So, what do we know about the women?' He sorted the three photographs of the prostitutes who had been in the back of the limousine at the time of the attack.

'Well, all three of them were strung out on coke at the time. Apparently, it's a perk of the job!' Symes sucked in a breath as he turned the photographs of the two white women and the one Asian woman, around. 'Jesus, I think I'm going to have to interview these three myself.'

Cox shook his head and took the photographs away from him. 'You're not getting anywhere near them. You're a fucking goat!'

Symes smiled and sat back. 'Well, all three of them, interviewed independently of each other, have all said the same thing. Basically, they all described some sort of superhero attack. They said it happened fast, the guy smashed the partition before jumping through and ordering them to leave the car. By all accounts, they were glad to get away. The Duke had a bit of a reputation.'

'Is their testimony reliable?'

'Who knows? They have to do whatever the client wants. If that includes snorting coke, then so be it.'

Cox closed his eyes again and sat back in his seat. It wasn't long before light snores were coming from him. Symes smiled and reached over and turned the photos of the girls around to look at them better. 'Shit, man, I need to find out where you hire girls like that.' He then sat back in his seat and closed his eyes too.

~~~~

It was eleven thirty pm by the time they reached the murder scene; a small farm service road, roughly two miles away from the freeway.

'Welcome to nowhere,' Symes quipped as they got out of the car.

The scene was well illuminated, and there was still quite a presence of law enforcement around the tent that had been erected over the burned-out limousine. Khaki clad officials were milling around the area, some of them were holding large clipboards and making notes, but most of them didn't look like they had a clue what they were doing, or even why they were there.

A large, black woman with her hair tied back in a bright pink hair tie made her way over to them. The material of her uniform was stretched tight over the bulk of her body, clinging in the heat to every curve. She flashed a very pretty smile at the two men. Cox recognised the relief in her face. It was the same relief that most police chiefs showed when they realised they could finally hand a case over to someone who knew what they were doing.

Symes's eyes roamed over her curves. 'Why hello, sugar,' he whispered to Cox, who nudged him in the ribs to shut him up.

She was wearing a golden shield on one breast; the word SHERIFF was emblazoned across it. Cox reached inside the overcoat he was wearing and removed his FBI credentials. Symes did the same.

'Well, haven't the FBI sent us over the two handsomest agents to get us through this mess,' she smiled.

Cox was instantly annoyed with this woman. It was eleven thirty pm, the temperature was somewhere in the mid-seventies, he was tired, and here she was being all nice and smiley. He returned her smile anyway, begrudgingly.

'That's right, ma'am, we're from the FBI. I'm Agent Cox and this delightful man next to me is Agent Symes.'

Symes leaned in and took her hand. Cox noted how he held it just a little too long. He rolled his eyes as he watched the sheriff gush a little at the attention. *This guy could charm the birds out of the trees,* he thought.

She fluttered her eye lashes at the larger man and flashed a smile, filled with perfectly white and straight teeth. 'Well, it's my pleasure to make your acquaintance, gentlemen,' she replied, not taking her eyes off Symes. She cleared her throat a little and got back to business. 'We've tried our utmost to keep the scene as free from contaminates as we can, but you know, when you're conducting an investigation…'

Cox watched as khaki clad law-enforcement personnel traipsed all over the scene. He exhaled slowly through his nose. *That scene isn't going to be worth shit,* he thought, and he could see in Symes's eyes that he was thinking the same thing.

'The coroner has concluded that between the driver being killed and the burning of the car, there was at least fifteen minutes, maybe a little longer,' she informed, while leading them towards the crime scene. 'The fire was started using brandy as an accelerant. Good brandy too, the

The Contract

bottles in there were worth over a couple of hundred bucks a pop, damn waste of good liquor if you ask me!'

Cox couldn't resist a smile. Despite his initial reaction to her, she'd grown on him. He and Symes had always made the effort not to rush into these scenarios with the 'Big Bad FBI and You All Will Bow to My Lead' kind of attitude the way some agents liked to run things. He thought that you got more done if you were cordial and inclusive.

'Them girls were damn lucky to survive,' she added.

'Why do you say that, Sheriff? By all accounts the girls were ordered to leave the car prior to the burning,' Symes asked.

Cox could hear the confusion in his voice.

'Well, every year we pull at least three bodies out of this corn. Damned stupid people, they just don't realise that you can get very lost in there. There's at least fifteen square miles of corn in this area, and we are standing right slap-bang in the middle of it.'

'So, do you think the murderer wanted some privacy to do what he did?' Cox asked, more thinking aloud than asking an outright question.

'Hmm, I don't know. If the driver was killed half a mile further down the road, then why drive all the way to within two miles of the freeway before doing what he did? It also doesn't seem to go with any of the other M.O.s. I mean, he killed a guy in Yankee Stadium during the Red Sox game. This guy doesn't do privacy,' Symes disagreed.

'Well, whatever he was doing, it seemed that he wanted to cover his tracks. We found the trails that relate to all three of the girls. The driver and the rapper are here …' Cox noticed that she said the word 'rapper' as if it was a swear word. 'But we haven't found anything that would relate to the killer. Add that to the fact that we haven't found a shred of evidence that there even *was* anyone else in there with them, all except that damned white feather. God damned freakiest thing I ever did see,' she added with a shiver. She then crossed herself before kissing the hand that she used and offering it up to the sky.

'What makes you say that, ma'am?' Cox asks.

'Well it just doesn't look right. Everything in the area burnt to a crisp, and those damned feathers just sitting there, one in the driver's top pocket and the other on the rapper's head, as white as the KKK! Not a fleck of dirt or ash on them. It just 'aint right, damn it.'

8.

THE INTERVIEW ROOM was a far cry from the incident room back in Washington, DC. It was small, stuffy, and impersonal. A tiny, rectangular window filled with frosted glass was the only source of natural light. Cox was sat at the table, his head bent over touching the wooden surface. He banged his forehead against the wood. Exhaustion, frustration, and hunger were all eating at him.

Symes was at the door, seeing the young girl out; she was one of the witnesses from the limousine. Cox could hear him talking to her, but not what he was saying. His voice was too low. The girl giggled, before handing him something and then leaving.

'What a waste of time and energy,' Cox breathed as he sat back and looked at his partner.

Symes was busy looking at the object that the girl at the door had given him. 'Business card,' he said with a grin, before throwing it onto the table. With a groan, he sat down on the chair opposite Cox and looked at him. 'So, what do you think of all that?'

Cox sighed again. *I'm doing a lot of that these days,* he thought. 'He said - she said stuff!' He pushed the yellow legal pad that was before him away and towards his partner. 'All three of them were pretty much out of it for the whole experience. All we've got is that the attacker was a man, he was young and blond, or maybe mousy brown, he was clean shaven, with a beard. He had superhuman strength and agility. All three of them commented on that. One of them commented that he moved 'cat-like.' The other two said that he leaped through the partition like a gymnast, or words to that effect. The red-head likened him to Plastic-Man.'

Symes smiled. 'She was my favourite,' he said.
'Why doesn't that surprise me?'

The Contract

'Well, we've got nothing from the scene of the crime, and nothing from the witnesses. I don't know, man; this just doesn't add up for me. There's got to be something we're missing.'

'There's nothing from the driver, not even any spittle on his face from the aggressor, no skin underneath his fingernails. He didn't put up any kind of a fight. The gun in the glove compartment hasn't been discharged. This guy is a fucking ghost.'

Cox was shaking his head as he listened to his partner's depressing diatribe. 'There has to be some significance with the feather.'

'The only connection between the victims is the fact that they all seem to be pretty despicable people. It's like someone is judging them on the way they lived their lives,' Symes said as he flicked through the legal pad in his hand.

'All three of them said that his voice had a booming quality to it. Two of them said that it was like there were a hundred or more people shouting. Have you ever heard of people experiencing enhanced hearing while under the influence of drugs?'

'I've heard of it, but nothing like what the Asian girl described,' he looked through the pad. 'Umm ... Sue! She said that as the man ordered them to get out, it sounded like, and I quote, "God's own voice!"'

'Well, we've got a big fat nothing here. We know it's a man, and that he's white, and he could be an Olympic-like gymnast with the power to throw his voice.' Cox stretched and yawned. 'All these dead ends are tiring me out. I'm going back to the hotel to have myself a whiskey and a big long sleep. You coming?' He looked up at his partner who had picked up the business card that he had received from the witness. He already knew the answer to his question.

'Umm, no. You go ahead. I'm going to go over a little something with Sheriff Mourier. You never know, it might become a lead.'

'Symes, don't go fucking around with the local law enforcement. I never saw her as your type anyway, man.'

Symes's brow ruffled as he looked at Cox with a big smile across his face. 'You hurt me, man. Like I've even got a type!'

Cox shook his head and got up from the table. 'Just don't go fucking this up. We might need her and her leads later. I don't want an atmosphere between you two.'

'Like I've ever left a lady in a weird atmosphere.'

'We're going to need to get back to it in the morning. So, don't be staying up all night. You got that?'

'Can I at least take the car, dad?' Symes replied, laughing. 'We're going to talk about the case, that's all.'

Cox nodded. 'Well, you won't be needing that business card then, will you?'

Symes held the card to his chest and smiled at his partner.

As Cox walked out of the door, the sheriff was stood by her desk. She had obviously been home and gotten herself ready as her hair was hanging loose and had been curled. She had makeup on and nice clothes.

Cox turned back to look at his partner, his eyebrows were raised. 'Just talking about the case?'

'Over dinner. obviously,' Symes replied with a smirk.

'I don't know where you get your energy from, I really don't. Just don't fuck this up. OK?'

Symes held both his hands up as if to ward Cox off. 'I won't. Just a bit of dinner and some backchat about the case. I'll be back in the hotel by ten thirty.'

'Alone?'

Symes laughed.

'Well, if you're going out there to woo the lady, then you had better put that away.' Cox pointed at the business card from the escort that was still in Symes' hand.

Symes looked at it and grimaced, comically. 'Good thinking, partner. I knew I could rely on you.'

He left the room, and the sheriff fixed her top as he passed her. 'Ma'am,' he said tipping his head in a nod.

'Agent Cox,' she replied looking more than a little sheepish.

The Contract

9.

THAD CARR WAS in a bad mood. He had walked through the office that morning and passed the open-plan desks without so much as a 'hello' or 'good morning' to any of the other workers. He had reached his destination and entered it, closing the door to his own plush office behind him. People in the open-plan area looked at each other, raised their eyebrows and smiled.

Normally, Mr Carr, or Thad as he liked to be known, was a pleasant, even jovial, man. He was in his early forties, although due to his extensive fitness regime and (mostly) good living, he could easily pass for early thirties. The consensus between the women of the office was that he was the most eligible bachelor in the company and that he was very pleasing on the eye.

As he closed the door, he rested his back against the cool, frosted glass and sighed a deep, resounding sigh. He loved this job, and normally he loved his workforce, but he hated the first day back in the office after his annual vacation. He always came back with the knowledge that his in-box would be stacked with trivial matters, *matters that any one of those lazy bastards in there could have handled while I was away!* The last thought depressed him. He needed time to ease himself slowly back into the work ethic. He sat in his luxurious leather chair and closed his eyes. He was a deep believer in zen, and right now he needed to find his, just to get him through this first day.

After a moment or two of collecting his thoughts, he leaned forward and pressed a button on his desk phone.

'Mr Carr, what can I do for you?' the electronic version of his administrative assistant's voice asked over the speaker. Jean was new, and she was shaping up to be an excellent addition to the team, but she hadn't gotten the hang of calling him Thad yet.

'Jean, I think I need half an hour or so, just to prepare myself for the day. Can you screen my calls and bring me in a coffee?'

'No problem, Mr Carr,' the officious voice on the other end of the line replied.

'Excellent!' He sat back in his chair again, put his hands behind his head, and leaned back, closing his eyes.

His thoughts rolled back to his days out of the state, fishing and partying in the Everglades.

~~~~

With his feet up on the desk and a zen smile on his face, Thad Carr was slowly coming back from a salacious daydream. He opened one eye and glanced at the pile of papers before him. With the smile on his face fading to the resigned look of a man with impending work to do, work that was not going to go away on its own, he leaned over and pressed the intercom button.

'Jean?'

The electronic voice of his secretary replied. 'Yes, Mr Carr?'

'Could you bring me that coffee now rather than later? I'd love a latte with a double caffeine shot and a cinnamon cookie if you could.'

'Yes sir, not a problem. I'll run down and get it for you now. Do you want anything else?'

He smiled. He loved subservient women. 'No, thank you, just the latte and cookie will be fine.'

'Ten minutes, sir.' He could hear the delight in her voice as he released the button. This pleased him. He fired up his computer and began his day by picking up the first sheet of paper from the large stack in his inbox.

As he immersed himself in the work at hand, the reminiscences regarding his time in the Everglades were still emerging. A nice little tingle within his trousers entertained him as the debauchery and revelry they had partaken in gave him a small sexual thrill. *I'll take care of myself a little later on, then I might call Kate.*

Kate was his current squeeze, hand-picked from the office. Ambitious, hungry, and very liberated. He liked her because he knew that he could manipulate her into doing anything that he wanted. *It's good to*

The Contract

be the king, he thought with a smile. Mel Brooks's *History of the World, Part One* had always been one of his favourite films.

The secret lives that he and Mike lived while on their vacations always caused his mouth to water. They made him smile, no matter how bad life was treating him. Sometimes, he knew his smile could be more akin to a hideous sneer, but he couldn't help that. *It is what it is.*

As he waited for his coffee to come, he scoffed and reached for another sheet of paper from the inbox. A small noise disturbed him. It sounded like a rumble of thunder from outside his office window. He turned his head and glanced out at the rapidly darkening Georgia sky. A sickly green-grey shade was spreading through the morning. The clouds looked pregnant, ready to drop their downpour over the expectant city. If anything, this put him *more* in mind of his time in Florida. There had been many a thunderstorm down there, and he always revelled in the darkness and warm humidity of a storm.

The sly look of his secret knowledge returned to his face. It was there for just the briefest of moments, replaced by a mild startled look when the bright flash of lightning caught him out. He chuckled to himself, thinking about one particular girl they had chased during another thunderstorm. She had very nearly gotten away from them in the difficult conditions. *Almost, but not quite*, he thought.

He stared out at the main office through the frosted glass of his door, at the coloured blobs of the other employees passing by. *Look at them,* he laughed to himself. *Scurrying along in their day to day lives, trying to make ends meet. None of them know what it's really about. Not when you have the power of life and death in your very own hands. Knowing what it feels like to brandish it at your will, to dish it out at your own discretion.* He put his feet back up on his desk and started to read another memo.

His earlier bad mood was now entirely forgotten.

A ceiling tile began to move silently above him. As it slid aside almost five inches, a long, thin loop of wire inched down, almost but not quite hitting Thad's scalp. He felt something brush the short hairs on the top of his head and absent-mindedly flicked his hand, thinking it was a fly buzzing around him. That was another reminder of the Glades, the endless stream of fucking insects. It was particularly noticeable when there was a lot of dead meat lying around, as well as the scent of fresh blood in the air.

He returned to his mundane report with thoughts of thunder and lightning, naked girls, fan boats and gators! Warm rain falling in downpours was running through his mind. A glow took over him, filling his senses. An erection was threatening to appear as he mused on everything they had done. He could almost smell the blood in the water.

That final distraction proved to be his downfall.

Another rumble of thunder followed by a rapid flash of lightning told him that the storm was getting nearer. The flash coincided with the continued journey of the metal wire.

It crossed his eye-line.

At first, he didn't react, thinking it was just the lighting.

The thin, almost invisible, wire grazed his cheek, and he swatted at it. It hit his chin, and then it was too late.

He looked up quickly, allowing the wire to drop past his chin and slip beneath and around his neck. Almost as quick as the flash of lighting, the loop that the wire was tied in tightened as he craned his neck. Instantly, it closed, cutting into his soft flesh. His hands rose up instinctively in a vain bid to grasp the noose, which now had him at its mercy. The more he struggled, the tighter the wire became, cutting off the air supply to his throat, disabling his ability to speak, or even scream.

Terror took hold of him, and his fingertips began to bleed as he frantically clawed at the garrotte around his neck. The thin wire cut further into his flesh, slicing through the dermal layers of his straining neck. Blood began to flow freely as the wound opened further, caused by the thrashing of his legs behind the desk. If there had been any witnesses to this event, it would have looked like Mr Carr was dancing, or attempting to get away from a troublesome wasp or insect that was bothering him.

In his peripheral vision, he caught sight of the window. The rain was now raging against the glass. To his tearing eyes, however, it wasn't rain that was coming down so heavily. It was fire! Liquid fire! It was pouring from the heavens and steaming as it hit the buildings and pavements below. Smoke rose from the streets as the molten flames dropped past his window, hissing on their descent.

The force behind the wire became more insistent, and in his struggle, he could feel himself being lifted from his seat. The strength of the pull was impressive, lifting him further and further until he was out of the seat completely and onto his feet. He looked up. It was difficult to see

The Contract

anything as his eyes clouded from the strain put upon them, but he was desperate for some understanding. He needed to know what was happening to him in the relative safety of his own office.

What he saw above only melted his mind even further.

His eyes followed what he could see of the wire. It consisted of a single, slender but strong, metal strand. As he followed it up towards the ceiling, the strand began to grow wider. Its width expanded, and instead of metal, it was a soft, pink, almost flesh-like tendril. Becoming wider and thicker, it was a twisting and turning muscle. As it tightened, pulling him further up towards the ceiling, he saw that the white tiles had gone. He was lifting towards an enormous, gaping darkness.

The obsidian swirled, it morphed before his petrified eyes. It became a maw, an abyss. The edges of the hole sprouted teeth. Long, sharp, dangerous teeth. A sulphuric smell emanated from it. His confused mind likened the smell to spoilt eggs, but a hundred, no, a million times worse. He was dangling now with his legs kicking uselessly in the air. His fingers were struggling with the muscular vine that was now wrapped, tightly around his neck.

The hole, above him, began to elongate, as if it was ready to greet him, to embrace him. The dark, filthy mouth descending towards him, sprouted more teeth from what had clearly become jaws. Flesh formed around them, wet, dripping, green flesh. The teeth were stained dark with what he only could think of as blood. Viscous liquid was dripping down the pale pink flesh of the grotesque tongue that he was hanging from. Hot, putrid breath issued from the orifice, as the tongue stole his head into the dark chasm. Screams echoed inside the darkness, screams that he recognised. These, coupled with the unmistakable smell of the Florida Everglades beneath the rank sulphur, brought to mind alligators.

His legs spasmed, kicked out, knocking papers and files from his desk. His desperation to survive made his heart thump in his chest with a slow, dreaded beat. His ears were ringing. Or where they? Were these the sounds of trumpets blaring triumphantly, and drums beating to the march of soldiers? Were they in the distance, or were they in his office with him, right now? He no longer cared about the pain of the tongue wrapped around his neck. He no longer thought about the fact that he couldn't breathe. All that consumed him right now was the horrible, screeching, musical disharmony exploding in his ears.

The music, if anyone could call it that, was getting louder, closer. His only hope was that someone from the main office would hear it and come in to investigate. Maybe they could cut him down from the vile, dripping alligator in his ceiling.

The fire had ceased to fall from the sky outside his window and had started to fall from the ceiling inside. The jaws, of the alligator from Hell, began to close around his head. This was when his bladder gave way. His suit trousers stained dark, before dripping with his own steaming piss. His tongue lolled from his mouth, bloated and purple. Blood and thick, pink spittle dripped from his mouth, onto his desk.

A single white feather fell from the hole in the ceiling where the tile had been pushed away and landed gently on the desk, next to the pool of blood and saliva. There was no longer an alligator languishing in the ceiling, just a small hole where a tile had been moved. There was no longer fire falling from the tiles, or from the sky outside. All there was, was the limp, dangling body of Thad Carr, area manager and murderer of twelve innocent women.

A few moments after Thad expired in the jaws of his imaginary alligator, Jean came into the office with his coffee. She carried it in on a tray which also contained a small plate with a few cookies on it 'to keep him sweet.' She knocked at the door and entered without his beckoning, which was the norm. Her head was down, mindful of not spilling his coffee. Mr Carr hated spilled coffee. 'Oh, Mr Carr, the angels must be crying in Heaven today, sir. That rain is coming down something fierce ...'

At that point she looked up.

The sight that she beheld, she would carry with her for the rest of her days on Earth. Mr Carr, the nice Mr Carr, was hanging by his neck from the ceiling. Blood stained his shirt and fingers. Urine stained his pants and pooled below him, mixing with the blood and saliva. His tongue protruded from his mouth, swollen and purple. Papers and files had been strewn across the floor around his upturned chair. For the briefest of moments, Jean absorbed the whole scene before her grasp on the tray faltered and she spilled the coffee over herself and the floor. As the porcelain cup and the metal tray crashed onto the expensive carpet, she began to scream.

It was a long while before she stopped.

The Contract

10.

COX WAS ALONE at the breakfast table. His plate had previously been filled with French Toast, eggs, streaky bacon, and maple syrup, but was mostly empty now as he sipped on his second cup of coffee. The one thing he loved about living in hotels for his work was the breakfasts.

'Everything OK for you, sir?' the pretty waitress asked as she began to clear away his dishes.

He looked up at her and smiled, snapping out of his own thoughts. 'Oh, yeah. The breakfast was excellent.'

'Can I get you anything else?'

'No, I'm just waiting for my ... Oh, no worries, here he is now,' Cox said pointing to the large figure of Symes who was making his way through the dining room. He was on the phone, and his face looked serious.

'Are you with him?' the waitress asked, her cheerful face becoming vexed. Cox thought that there may have even been more than a bit of anger.

'Yeah, we're on a job, he's my partn—'

'Yeah, well, tell him from me that he's a fucking asshole.' With that she snatched up his dishes and disappeared off towards the kitchen.

'Right ... yeah, I'll let him know. Yes, we'll get it sorted out for this afternoon. There're only a few loose ends to tie up here anyway. Not much else we can do. Right, five-thirty, no problems, we'll be there.' Symes hung up the phone and sat at the table opposite Cox. 'Looks like there's been another one. Savannah, Georgia, yesterday at roughly ten fifteen am, Eastern Time. We've got wheels up at the airport, at seventeen thirty.'

'Did you find anything else out about the case last night?'

Symes was looking around for the waitress. 'Huh?' he asked, distracted.

'Last night, when you were out with the sheriff. Did you get any further information?'

His partner pulled an annoying, goofy smirk, before exhaling. 'I think the sheriff is going to want to handle the details of this one on her own. Her department is more than capable of sorting the crime scene. We did get into some pretty tight details though,' he said raising his eyebrows and smiling.

Cox shook his head. Then, a thought occurred to him. 'What time did you get back last night?'

'Well, we went back to her apartment at about eleven. I was back here for a nightcap about one-thirty. Why?'

'Was the night porter a pretty little blond?'

Another grin spread across Symes's face. He squinted his eyes. 'Yeah, why?'

Cox shook his head as he stood up from the table. 'Maybe you should order your breakfast on the road.'

Symes saw the young, pretty waitress come out of the kitchen. She spared a glance over towards their table. There was a lot of venom in that one look. Symes stood up, throwing the napkin he had been unfolding on the table. 'Maybe you're right,' he said. 'I'll grab a breakfast burger on the run.'

'How the hell do you do it?' Cox asked, genuinely interested.

'Believe me, sometimes I don't know.'

'Did you? You know?' Cox made a gesture; it was obvious exactly what the gesture meant.

Symes nodded. 'Come on man, we need to check out.'

As they left the dining room, Cox heard the waitress slamming something on a table behind them.

~~~~

After a rather awkward couple of hours with the sheriff, transferring the official investigation into the murder of Nathan Croft, aka Lovin' L Duke, over to the regional FBI agents, cox and Symes were sat in the FBI jet. Cox was at a small table, the normal jumble of files and photographs spread out before him. Symes was sat at the table on the

The Contract

other side of the fuselage; he had a large map of the United States spread out before him. There were several red dots on the map indicating the locations of the murders. He was shaking his head.

'There's no pattern. Nothing. None of the locations have any relevance, none of the victims have any relevance.'

'Except for the fact that they all have dubious backgrounds,' Cox added.

'Well, all of them except for this latest one.' Cox scrambled around in the pile of papers at his desk, eventually locating the one he was looking for. 'Here we go. Thaddius Carr! He was an area manager for Fulton's Finance. A national subprime finance company. They specialise in giving loans to people with bad credit in exchange for almost extortionate interest rates.'

'Do you think this could have been a customer venting his anger? But doing so by jumping onto the 'White Feather Fever' that the press is fuelling?'

'No, whoever killed Carr is the same person who killed DeGrassie. I'd bet my house on it.'

'I've seen your house; I'm not going to take that bet. I don't want to be stuck with that run-down shithole.'

Cox smiled. 'No, this hit was too good. He hung a man, in his own office, at ten am, Tuesday morning. Literally ten feet away from a crowded, open-plan office. This has all the hallmarks of our man.' He picked up a sketched drawing that had been compiled from the descriptions given by the three prostitutes in the Duke's limousine.

'I still think that looks too much like Brad Pitt to be widely distributed,' Symes said. There was humour in his voice, but not too much in his mannerisms. 'So, right now we have murder one: an assassination of a known gangster on a quiet residential street. Murder two: A 'made' Mafioso, garrotted to death in Yankee Stadium—during a freaking Yankee's Red Sox' game, by the way. Murder three: A high profile prosecutor known for her shady dealings, drowned to death in the shower of her own gym. Murders four and five: A famous rapper with a decidedly bad reputation and his driver, who we found out was dishonourably discharged from the US Marines, for excessive use of force, causing the deaths of three families in Afghanistan. Now, murder number six: A seemingly innocent financial manager, hung by a wire in his own office. This is fucking great reading. I think it would make a great book.'

'Well, I wouldn't read it,' Cox replied rubbing his eyes and sitting back in his chair. He picked up his drink, rum and Coke, and sipped it.

'Why? Are you more into romances?'

'Fuck you,' Cox laughed, leaning his head back on his seat. His eyes were closed, and he already looked half asleep. 'You know that this isn't looking good for us, don't you? The press has already got a hold of it. The White Feather Fever, they're calling it.'

'I think they love the fact that we're six murders in and haven't even got a line on who it could be.'

'Well, let's just see how things pan out in Georgia.' Cox relaxed into his seat and crossed his arms over his chest. Within a few moments, he was asleep.

The Contract

11.

SAVANNAH, GEORGIA, FOR a large city, was relatively tame. There was a criminal element, as there was everywhere else in the country, but here it was rather small and sporadic. A murder in strange circumstances, like the one of Thad Carr, had set tongues wagging for miles around. So, the arrival of the two FBI agents to investigate another White Feather Fever killing was big news.

After their three-and-a-half-hour flight, they checked into their hotel in downtown and set out to find the offices of Fulton's Finance.

They didn't need to look too hard for it. There was still a large police presence at the scene. 'Listen, Symes, no banging the help this time eh?' Cox whispered as they parked their rented Oldsmobile.

A large man wearing a dark blue uniform with bright ginger hair and hands as large as shovels made his way over towards them. He was smiling, holding out one of his huge appendages. 'Sergeant Malley, at your service, agents,' he greeted them with a genuine smile.

'I don't think you're going to have much to worry about this time Cox!' Symes whispered with a conspiratorial wink.

'Pleased to meet you. I'm Agent Cox and this is Agent Symes.'

Sergeant Malley shook hands with the two men, both of them noting how strong his grip was. *Jesus, I'm glad this guys on our side, I'd hate to have to fight him.*

'I suppose you're going to want to go straight inside?' the big man asked, putting his hat back on his head.

'Yeah, if we could. It's been a bit of a whirlwind these last few days. I don't think I've ever done as much travelling, and I'm ex-military,' Symes chirped in following the man.

'You been to all the sites then?' the sergeant asked as he led the two agents through the taped off area leading into the tall office block.

'Yup. Every one of them,' Symes replied, smiling.

And broke the hearts of the women at every one of them too, Cox thought before instantly regretting it. He genuinely liked Symes. He was reliable, he was loyal, and he was an excellent agent. Everything you wanted in a partner. Cox just wished that he'd learn to keep it in his pants once in a while.

He rolled his eyes as he watched Symes wink at a young female police officer standing guard at the doorway to the building. She blushed, laughed, and dropped her head.

'Carr's office is on the sixth, you want the elevator?' Malley asked as he strode off through the small lobby.

'Yeah, that'll be fine,' Symes answered, pushing the button.

When they got inside, the three men took up most of the room. As the door closed, sealing them inside, Malley turned towards them. 'I'm glad you guys are here. We heard that this was part of a bigger case, a federal case! When the press came along, they wanted to interview me. I told them that I don't really have any jurisdiction in this case, as another White Feather Fever case is surely a job for the feds.'

Cox nodded and smiled at him, then shared a quick look with his partner. *Brilliant,* he thought. *This guy has single-handedly given the press exactly what they need to blow open this case.*

They stepped out of the elevator into a nice, if not overly exuberant, lobby area. Thick carpets and warm wooden features adorned the room. There was a large sign on the wall informing visitors that they had reached the offices of Fulton's Financial Services.

Symes sighed as they passed several police officers who were milling about the lobby, all of them trying their very best to look busy. 'How many officers have you got hanging around here?' he asked the big police sergeant.

'About twenty. Every one of them are at your disposal, gentlemen. Actually, most of them aren't even on duty, I think. It's just that when a big old case like this one comes about; everyone wants a slice of that pie. I'll tell you, there's a lot of people who are plenty excited about all this.'

The three men pushed through the big glass doors into the reception area where they were greeted with reams and reams of yellow and black crime scene tape.

The Contract

'Jesus, it looks someone's had a party with this stuff,' Symes laughed as he ripped a long swathe off the reception desk.

'We put that all over the reception, just in case we got any prints,' Malley said, tucking his thumbs into his police utility belt. The smile on his face made him look like he was very pleased with himself and proud of his boys for being so forward thinking.

'Is there any evidence that suggests that the perpetrator came out this way? Any witnesses?'

'Nope,' he replied, his grin not even faltering.

Symes shot his partner a look. Cox got the meaning of it within the first nanosecond. 'Okay, good work, sergeant. Now, can we see the office where the murder took place?'

'You sure can. It's just this way.'

Malley took off in the direction of the office. Neither of the agents needed much, or even any, help to figure out where he was heading. The abundance of crime scene tape indicated where they needed to go.

'Do you think they ordered too much tape or something?' Symes asked.

'Either that or Sergeant Malley has shares in the company who supply it,' Cox answered with a grin.

They turned a corner only to be greeted by another mass of tape, which covered the fire doors that were between the reception and the main office. Three policemen pushed past them, out from the main office. They were laughing and joking until they saw the two agents. Then they bowed their heads and hurried out of the hallway.

The room they entered was deceptively large. There were fifty, or so, desks all centred, with several smaller offices around the walls. One of the offices was decorated in even more of the yellow and black tape.

'Thad Carr's office is the one with the—'

'I think we can tell which office it is, thanks,' Cox cut in, holding his hand up to the sergeant.

He took the hint and stopped talking.

'How many people have been through this scene?' Symes asked as he watched the other officers passing in and out of the crime scene, seemingly without a care in the world.

The sheriff pulled a face that Cox didn't really want to see. It confirmed for him everything that he was already thinking, that the crime scene had been compromised.

'Well, when the secretary screamed, it opened the floodgates to all the looky-loos.'

'The what?' Symes asked making his way over to the partially open door.

'The looky-loos, that's what we call them. The rubberneckers, the ones who want to see the grossness for themselves.'

Symes exhaled slowly, putting his hand to his head as if he had a headache. 'How many?'

The sheriff closed one eye and squinted with the other towards Symes. 'Maybe thirty.'

'Thirty? Jesus Christ, you could have sold tickets. What happened then?'

'Well, then we turned up. The first responders.'

'How many of them were there?' Cox asked, trying to be a bit more diplomatic than his partner.

'Four, initially,' the sergeant answered. His voice had become almost a whisper as his head was beginning to bow.

'What do you mean, initially?' Symes asked.

'Well, I told you before, this is a big deal for us. You federal guys will have a better handle on this, but …'

'Look,' Cox asked holding his hand out to the big man, 'How many have been in and out of the scene?'

'Including CSIs? All of them, maybe twenty.'

Symes threw his hands in the air. 'That's at least sixty people. Jesus, we can wave goodbye to any evidence, then.

'OK. There's no use crying over something we can't do anything about. Sergeant Malley, what do we know about the victim?' Cox interjected, calming the atmosphere.

'I know him real well. In fact, I went to school with him. We're both from Bloomingdale; it's about a forty-five-minute commute from here. It's not the kind of place where you'd expect to find the victim of a serial killer. Savannah, for its size, is relatively safe.'

'The victim?' Symes asked rolling his hands.

The Contract

'Oh, yeah. Well, he is, or was, forty-two years old. Single, actually a dedicated bachelor. He went to school the year below me. Bloomingdale's a small town, everyone knows everyone else.'

'Any recent movements? Any history with the police? Criminal records?' Cox asked. The profile of this victim just didn't sit right with him. He didn't fit in with any of the others. They all had criminal records, bad, nasty people. People who would throw their own grandmothers underneath a bus for a few bucks. This guy seemed nice and quiet. 'Can you give me any information on his recent movements? Any dealings that he might have had out of town?'

The big sheriff thought for a few moments. Cox fancied that he could see real cogs turning just underneath his red hair.

'Well, he's not long back from vacation. Same two weeks every year. I think it's Florida he goes to. He goes with one of his friends he's still tight with. He used to play football. I mean he wasn't a star or anything, but he made the—'

'Sergeant Malley,' Symes interrupted, his loud voice cutting through the sheriff's ramblings. 'Do you know where about in Florida he went to? Also, we're going to need to talk to this close friend. Does he have a girlfriend, or anyone else in town he hung with?'

'Yeah, I'm sure we can do that for y'all. You know, we might not even have to ask around. We're a tight community around here, and in Bloomingdale. If there's something to find, the Bloomingdale boys will find it.'

Symes began to turn away, ready to assess what was left of the crime scene.

'Well, when I say Bloomingdale boys, I mean girls too. We have a number of the fairer sex working for us these days.' Malley's thumbs were still tucked into his gun belt, and his grin was even larger than before. His face looked like it was beaming with pride that he relayed the information that their police force had had the foresight to employ women.

Symes nodded to him. 'I'm really going to need that information sergeant,' he snapped.

Malley took the hint and turned away. 'Right away, Agent Symes. I'll have that for you within the hour.' He walked off snapping and barking orders at his officers.

'Malley,' Cox shouted, and the tall sergeant turned back. 'While you're doing that, me and Symes are going to take a little look around. I'm going to need all photographic evidence of the scene, the inventory, and anything that was bagged and taken away. Can you do that for me?'

'Yes, sir, right away.'

As they watched the big man amble off, Symes turned to his partner and smiled. 'How the hell do they ever solve anything in this place?'

'Right. I'm going to take a look at the scene. Symes, can you have a look at the crawl space between the ceiling and the ceiling tiles?' Cox asked.

'Yes, sir, right away, sir!' Symes answered mocking the sergeant.

Cox laughed and walked deeper into the office.

~~~~

Symes retrieved a high stepladder and removed a couple of ceiling tiles. A deluge of white powder tumbled down, causing him to cough. He spat it out and brushed the residue from his hair before blowing the rest away. He peered up into the hole and looked at the crawlspace above. He was astonished to find that it was rather large. Even a man of his size wouldn't have any trouble crawling through it. *A thin guy could easily get through here*, he thought. *If I could just ...* Reaching inside, he found a couple of sturdy pipes and pulled himself up.

The ceiling consisted of a line of tiles and then a line of boarding, presumably there for maintenance purposes. He boosted himself up into the space, resting himself on a beam that ran the full length of the office. He manoeuvred himself into a crouched, sitting position before pulling himself along.

'Cox! Cox, can you hear me?' he shouted from his elevated position.

'Yeah! Where are you?' Cox replied.

'I'm in the crawlspace above the ceiling. There're beams up here that run the entire length of the room. I'm over Thad's office right now. Can you get over there and meet me?'

As Cox made his way into the crime scene, he noticed the little things. The items on the desk that had been knocked over and put back in the wrong places, the pot plant that had been knocked over and set right, leaving soil and footprints on the carpet. He'd seen it all before, he knew that it was due to the over-enthusiastic first responders, and the office workers wanting to get a look at the dead body, not caring about due process or evidence. He sighed, releasing the air slowly out of his body. He felt like a balloon, slowly deflating. He looked on the desk and was dismayed even further to see a plastic evidence bag discarded on the top, as if it were an afterthought and not the whole topic of this investigation.

Inside the bag was a long, perfectly formed, and perfectly white, feather. 'Brilliant,' was all he could bring himself to say. He jumped a little as a voice from the ceiling broke his train of thought.

'What did you say?' the voice asked. Cox had forgotten that Symes was in the crawlspace.

'Err, nothing. I was thinking to myself. What am I doing in here?'

'I'm right above you. I'm about to move a ceiling tile.'

Cox looked up as he heard the small scratching sound of the mineral fibre rubbing against another tile and then the metal seating of the structure. A small flurry of white powder descended over the Agent below. Cox blinked to avoid getting any in his eyes, and he spat as some fell into his mouth.

'Did you notice the white powder?'

'Yeah,' Cox replied wiping it out of his hair.

'Don't you think that Carr would have too? OK, I'm lowering a wire down the crack in the tile. It's the same kind of wire that Thad's body was strung up with. Can you sit in the chair?'

'Not really. I don't want to disrupt the evidence.'

'Are you serious? Like it hasn't been fucked up beyond any repair already?'

Cox snorted a small laugh of derision, a laugh with very little humour in it. 'I get you. OK, I'm sitting in the chair,' he replied.

'OK, I'm going to try to loop this around your head. Can you pretend that you're actually doing some work for once?'

Cox nodded. As he sat in the chair, he felt the wire hitting him on the top of his head. It bounced off his hair three times before he felt it on the back of his neck. He then felt it lifting up again and having another attempt at his head. Again, it missed. It was beginning to annoy him. He grabbed at the wire. 'There's no way that you're getting that over my head and around my neck.'

'That's pretty much my point here. It must have been one hell of a lucky shot to nab his head without him knowing. And then there's another thing. Grab the wire and pull on it with all your strength,' Symes requested.

Cox complied.

'Ow... fuck!' he heard his partner shout from above.

'What?'

'The wire would have cut right into my hands there. That's not even half of your weight. There's no way on God's green Earth that a normal man could hike a fully-grown adult male up out of his seat and suspend him from up here using this wire, or any other wire for that matter. There's not enough leverage for one. It would take an enormous amount of upper-body strength to even get the wire tight, much less lift him up.'

Cox took a note pad from the inside pocket of his jacket and began to make notes.

'OK, so, now I've lifted you, and you're all dangling and shit. So, I tie the wire off on the gangway up here and begin to make my way out of the office, the same way I got in, by the way, there's no other way in or out. Time me from right ... now!'

Cox pressed a button on his watch as he heard Symes shuffling about above him. He got up from the chair and followed the noises.

A short while later Symes shouted, 'Stop timing.'

'Two minutes and thirty-seven seconds.'

'I'm making a timeline here. So, Jean Fetcher comes in with coffee, she said that she was gone no longer than five minutes, that's the narrow window that this guy has for sneaking in through the roof, unheard, looping the victim, using his unholy strength to lift the victim ... how long would it take for him to die, do you think?'

'Statistics say anywhere between four to six minutes,' Cox replied. The figure was off the top of his head, and he didn't much care for the fact that he knew the answer.

'Correct. So, then another two and a half minutes to get out of the office, again unheard, and out through the small entrance that's in the men's restrooms, unseen and unmolested. Any of this make any kind of sense to you?'

'The timeline's far too narrow!' Cox mused.

The Contract

'Not only the timeline, but the whole hanging too. It's like this guy just appeared up here, used his super-strength to kill Thad, dropped a white feather, and disappeared again. Maybe we *are* dealing with a super-hero here?'

Cox felt like he should have laughed at Symes's suggestion, but the whole thing had gotten him unhinged. The last thing he felt like doing was laughing.

~~~

Later that evening, the detectives were relaxing in the bar of their hotel in Savannah. Sat at a table with empty plates in front of them, both men were leaning back in their booth holding brown beer bottles. A small, but impressive collection of other brown bottles had begun to gather on their table.

A group of young women entered the bar, making a loud announcement to all the single men at all the tables around.

Most of the men were staying in the hotel on business, all of them alone, and maybe hoping for a little company for the evening, or perhaps a little longer. Cox thought he saw several wedding rings being pulled off and shoved into pockets.

The group hadn't gone unnoticed to Symes's trained eye, and Cox shook his head as he took another swig of his cold beer.

'Adam,' he spoke, breaking Symes's attention away from the women, who were checking him out too, looking over and giggling before looking coyly away again.

'Yeah?' he asked.

'What are we doing on this case?' Cox asked, looking deeply into the brown glass as if trying to see how much liquid was left inside.

Symes shook his head at his partner. 'What do you mean, man? We're working it, just like any other we've done.'

'Do you think we're chasing our tails? We've got next to no leads, despite loads of witnesses.'

'A whole stadium full of witnesses …' Symes laughed.

Cox nodded, his eyes were now focused on the red and white label on the bottle that he was trying his best to peel off without ripping. 'Exactly, man. A whole fucking stadium. We've got three strung out prostitutes who actually saw the perp up close and personal but have nothing to offer. We have a street full of sober neighbours, and now an office filled with bright-eyed and bushy-tailed employees, who all saw ... zip! All of this, even though some of these murders were nigh on impossible to pull off. Do I need to go on?'

'We're making a difference. We always do. You just watch this space, man. We're going to do a job on this guy. We'll catch the son-of-a-bitch! It's what we do.'

Cox could see that Symes was trying to reassure him, but he could also see that he was getting distracted by the obvious flirting of the women at the bar. He looked around him, all the other single men at the tables were watching them too, but quickly looked away when they saw that they only had eyes for one guy.

'Do you really think that this time? Or, are you just saying that? What if this thing is even bigger than the FBI?'

Symes laughed aloud. He slammed his bottle on the table before him, attracting some looks from around the room, especially from the older woman behind the bar and the three young women on the other side of it. 'How can you even think that?' he laughed. 'Man, there's *nothing* bigger than the FBI. Remember that!'

Cox was laughing now too. He took another swig of his beer before pulling the label all the way off the bottle. 'I don't know. Do you think that maybe, just maybe, we're looking at a group of organized killers, and not just the one superhero villain? Maybe even a group of vigilantes. I mean, all the victims have been loathsome individuals. The locations are so far apart too. It would be difficult for one man to be acting alone. He'd have to have considerable resources to even get close to the victims. DeGrassie for instance. Those tickets for that suite are not cheap, they're also notoriously difficult to get if you don't have a season ticket.'

'I hear you man, but the time scales don't make it impossible for it to be one man. I'll get a cross reference of all the available flights between the different locations. When we get the passenger manifests for the times of the flights, that should link them up with the times of the murders. Then, we should be able to see if there are any names that keep popping up. If not, then we get the surveillance cameras. We can get a team of facial recognition experts to sift through them, see if any faces pop up. Bingo, we have our man.'

The Contract

Cox looked over at his enthusiastic partner. He couldn't help but smile. Symes could always be relied upon to come up with a good idea when the investigations were looking bleak.

'OK! Let's jump on that first thing in the morning. Right now, though, I'm going to bed. We're staring down the business end of a thirteen-hour shift here. Don't stay up too late,' he warned, eyeing the woman at the bar. 'We got a lot to do tomorrow.'

Symes was already looking past him, towards the bar. 'I'm just going to have one or two more. You know, to help me relax.'

Cox took his coat off the back of the chair and slung it over his shoulder. 'Yeah, you relax, buddy?' he laughed. 'You go right ahead and do that.'

As he walked towards the exit, he turned around, just in time to see the three women from the bar sit themselves down at the table that he had just vacated. *Unbelievable,* he thought as he pushed the door open, stepping into the warm Georgia night.

~~~~

Back in his room, Cox was looking through the transcripts of all the interviews they had undertaken that day. The stack of paper used was extensive, it was the last thing he wanted to do, *especially after a few beers,* he thought. He took his trousers off, unbuttoned his shirt and sat down heavily at the small table in the room.

He picked up the first sheet of yellow paper and began to read.

He read for over an hour, until his eyes grew tired and the words on the paper no longer made any sense. He put his pencil down on the pad that he had been making notes on and stretched. His mind wandered to what, exactly, Symes was getting up to right now, but he cast that thought away. He had given up any thoughts of a wife and family for his career. *But that doesn't mean I don't want a bit of fun from time to time,* he thought.

With a long, breathy yawn, he looked at his notes again. They weren't extensive for what he had been reading, but then most of the witnesses, or the employees, had all been pretty much telling the same story.

From what he had; all he could glean was that Thaddius Car was an only child. His parents had died within two years of each other when he was in his twenties. He had worked at Fulton's Finance since leaving high school and had earned himself a managerial position. He was a keen fisherman and had won awards locally, and even a few nationally. He didn't hold a passport, but he did have a driver's licence. He rented a house in Bloomingdale, in a nice area, where he lived alone, not even a dog. He talked sometimes about girls he had been out with, but he never had a steady girlfriend, or boyfriend for that matter. He did have a few close friends. One fact that kept coming up in conversation was that he took the same vacation every year. To Marathon in the Florida Keys.

Cox underlined Marathon. This had piqued his interest and he thought it warranted further investigation.

He sat back in the uncomfortable hotel seat and looked at the pad. Basically, Thaddius Carr was Mr Nice Guy. The typical boy-next-door. Probably the boy that most of the mothers in Bloomingdale were hoping their daughters brought home for dinner.

'None of this fits the MO of our man,' he mumbled. 'All the others have been gangsters and murderers, people who didn't care about who they trod over, on their own personal path to wealth. So, why Thad?'

Cox knew that the answer to this question was not going to come to him via divine inspiration, so he resigned himself to sleep. As he pulled the covers up over his head and snapped the light off from the switch above him, he had one, last, envious thought about what Symes was doing. He shook his head and closed his eyes, hoping that sleep would come quickly.

It did.

The Contract

12.

COX WAS ALONE, again at the breakfast table, he was getting used to eating his morning meal this way. He was enjoying the eggs and bacon and the delicious, freshly squeezed orange juice that was in an abundance. Around him on the table were the notes that he had taken from the interviews and from the rushed internet search he had undertaken last night regarding Marathon.

'Do you want more coffee, hun?' The woman's voice took him by surprise, and he looked up, startled to see the barmaid from last night holding a half full jug of coffee, ready to pour at a moment's notice.

'Oh, yes please. But do you have any decaf?'

She looked at him as if he had two heads and one of them was sprouting snakes. He shook his head and pushed his cup towards her. 'Regular is fine,' he said with a smile.

'You alone this morning?' she asked, looking around the room, obviously for any glimpse of Symes.

'Yeah, my partner hasn't shown up yet. He will though.'

She offered him a cheeky wink and a secret smile. 'I don't know about that. I think I might have tired him out a little, last night. If you know what I mean!'

Cox squinted at her, shaking his head.

'Your friend certainly knows how to treat a lady. Just don't go telling my old man now, you hear me?' She walked away, laughing. Cox noticed as she moved that she was doing so with slight discomfort. *He's a fucking machine,* he thought with dismay.

Just then, Symes made his way into the restaurant, looking more than a little dishevelled. His normally tidy hair was messed, and he clearly hadn't shaved. A light brown fuzz was building on his chin. His eyes looked red.

'Jesus, Adam. You look like shit!'

Symes closed his eyes and grimaced, his whole face looked like it was ready to fold in on itself. He held out his hand as if to quieten his colleague. 'Easy now, partner. I think I need some coffee. A lot of coffee!'

'How much were you drinking?'

Symes shook his head. 'I wasn't drinking. I just don't think I've gotten any sleep.'

As he sat down, Cox pushed his untouched coffee cup over towards him. 'I'm not so sure you're going to want to order any. Your waitress is a big fan. She's certainly got a spring in her step this morning.'

Symes opened his eyes, the red rim around them glared at Cox. 'Which one?' he asked, there was no humour in the question, neither was there a brag or a swagger, it was just a question.

'The barmaid from last night. She told me that you'd be looking rough this morning, she said that she rode you pretty hard.'

'Yeah, she did. But that's not why I didn't get any sleep.'

Cox was at a loss. 'Was it something to do with the case by any chance?'

'No, man. It was something to do with the three girls from the bar,' Symes replied grabbing the still steaming coffee cup from the table before him.

Cox's jaw almost hit the table. 'The *three* girls?'

Symes took a sip from the cup and put his hand over his eyes. 'Yes, the three of them.'

'Together?'

Symes nodded as he put the cup back onto the table. He grimaced as he rubbed his neck.

'Christ, man. You need to see someone. I think you have an addiction.'

Symes looked at him. There was a small smile on his face, but his eyes looked like they were pleading. 'Is that really a thing? Sex addiction?'

'Yeah, it is, and I think you have it.'

'Do you know anyone who deals with it?'

The Contract

Cox's face fell a little, and his eyes became serious. 'Yeah, man, we'll get you some help, but first we're going to have to get onto this case. You feeling up to it?'

'Yeah. I'm up for it. I just need to sort my head out first.'

'Well, here's your chance. Your girlfriend's coming back over with the coffee.' Cox pointed over towards the back of the room where the waitress was heading their way with a beaming smile on her face and a full, steaming jug of coffee.

'Oh, fuck!' Symes swigged the last of the coffee and stood up. He smiled and waved at the waitress who stopped in her tracks, her smile wavering. He then turned on his heels and made his way out of the restaurant, double quick.

Cox was left alone. He picked his coat up off the back of his chair while looking over towards the waitress. Her shoulders had begun to slump, and a splash of coffee spilled out of the jug, leaving a small steaming puddle. 'I'm sorry, we have to go. Government business and all that,' he said, shrugging his shoulders. 'I'm – um, sure he'll call.'

With that, he got out of the restaurant almost as fast as Symes had.

~~~~

Within the hour, they had checked out of their rooms and were sat in the hired car on their way to the airport. Cox had booked them on a flight from Georgia to Florida Keys Marathon International. Their flight wasn't until later that night, but Symes didn't seem to want to linger in the hotel for any longer than he needed to.

They had been in the car for forty-five minutes, and Symes had been asleep for at least forty of them.

'Hey, man! Welcome to the land of the living,' Cox announced as the big man's eyes fluttered open.

He looked out the windows, scratching at his chin as he did. 'Where are we?' he asked. His voice was thick, like he needed a large swig of water.

'We're on I95. Beautiful isn't it? The airport is about ten minutes away. I hope you're feeling nice and fresh after your nap.'

Symes nodded. 'Look, I don't want to fall out over any of this. I just don't …'

Cox looked at him for a moment before turning his head back towards the road. 'Look, man, I get it. You're a young, single guy who, for some reason unbeknown to me, has a magnetism with the ladies. Shit, I wish I got even a quarter of the action you get. Just don't let it get in the way of the business, OK?'

Symes shook his head and rummaged around in the back seat. He opened a bottle of water and took a long swig, screwed the top back on and nodded. 'I won't, man. But that thing you said, about going to see someone, when we get back to DC? I'm going to check myself in. Anyway, tell me why we're off to Marathon in the Keys. Not that I'm complaining mind you.' He offered his partner a small smile.

'Well, when I went through the notes last night about who Thad Carr is, all I got back was that he was this monumental nice guy. There wasn't one bad report about him. The worst I got was that he could be a little moody sometimes.'

'In my experience, no one is that nice,; Symes offered. 'He' got to have some sort of glitch; we just need to find out what it is.'

'Well, apparently he spends two weeks of every year in Marathon. Supposedly, he's a keen fisherman. The day he was killed was the day he got back. So, I thought it wouldn't do any harm to check the place out, ask a few questions and see who he spent his time with.'

'Yeah, be nice to catch a few rays too,' Symes said with a Cheshire cat grin.

The Contract

13.

TWO DAYS LATER, Cox and Symes were sat in the restaurant of a nice hotel in Marathon. They had arrived the day before and spent the day introducing themselves to the local police force and familiarising themselves with the Marathon scenery.

To Cox's chagrin, the town of Marathon was gearing down from the notorious spring break. However, there were still gangs of young students staying in the hotel, lounging around the pool, wearing next to nothing. None of this was doing his partner any favours. He was like a child caught overnight in a candy store.

Cox had booked them adjoining rooms with a large breakout room where they could run their investigation. It was a tactic to keep him away from the tantalising flesh on show at the pool.

It was eight am, and both men were casually dressed.

'Man, this place is wild,' Symes said as he looked out of the window towards the pool view below them.

'You do realise that you're here to work and not to socialise, don't you?'

Symes turned away from the window and shot him a look. There was humour in that look, but there was also a bit of concern. 'That's not what I meant,' he laughed. 'I meant it's wild out there now, and spring break, at its wildest, was last week. Why would a single guy, who was allegedly down here for the fishing, book into a hotel that was synonymous with wild parties and hedonism?'

'I was thinking the same thing. Everyone in the office was saying that he normally met a friend down here and they spent the full two weeks fishing in the Everglades,' Cox said looking through the folder before him.

'Do you think he was gay and maybe he was embarrassed about it? They might have come down here to mingle with the crowds to hide their tryst.'

'That's a good take. My instinct is telling me that there's something there, something hidden. We're just going to have to drag that info out of people.'

Symes smirked. There was a glint in his eye that Cox recognised, and once again he shook his head, knowing what was coming next.

'If I can mingle in with the crowds, you know, get to know them a little, so it won't be such a bone up their ass when we start asking questions and probing a little deeper.'

Cox laughed. 'Bone up their ass?'

Symes laughed too as he poured himself a cup of coffee from the machine on the table by the window. 'Well, um, you know what I mean. Anyway, back onto planet murder …' he shrugged.

'Well, either way, I've lined up a few interviews already. Mostly with staff. Carr sounds like a man of routine, it's my bet that he's stayed at this same hotel for at least the last six years, so I'll meet with the manager. He's been here for fifteen years, so I'm hoping that he'll know something about the man.'

Symes nodded.

'You're going to speak to the service maids and the guys behind the bar. You're going to be professional, and you're going to keep your grubby hands to yourself. Capiche?'

'Yes, sir,' Symes saluted as he made his way back to the table, with a steaming cup of coffee in his other hand.

~~~

Wearing only a pair of swimming shorts, Agent Adam Symes was stood on the dry side of the wet bar. He was sipping on a non-alcoholic cocktail that he had asked to be made up specifically, so it looked like an alcoholic one. A group of college girls sat around a large plastic table, all of them wearing next to nothing, and all of them eyeing up his muscular physique. He looked over a few times, liking what he saw, and delivering a few winks and smiles where he deemed necessary.

An invitation for him to join them was sent, completely non-verbally, but he knew from their body language that he would be

The Contract

welcomed. He also knew that if, *no scratch that... when*, he made his way over, he would be having wild sex with at least three of them within the hour.

This wasn't a conceited thought on his behalf, it was just the truth.

With a smile, he took another sip of his 'mocktail' and began to saunter over. That was when something in his peripheral vision caught his attention.

There was a man practically hiding in the well-manicured bushes that surrounded the pool area. He was dressed in the full, ridiculous, uniform of a valet and was doing his very best to catch his attention. With a sinking heart, Symes looked over towards the group of beautiful, expectant young women, and the man vying for his attention. *Adam, you're here for work. You can spend leisure time when your chores are done,* a sensible voice spoke in his head, he had no idea where it had come from. He returned to the bar, depositing his drink and, to the obvious disappointment of the group of women, he addressed the concerns of the young valet.

'Are you looking for me?' he asked the younger man.

'You're with the guy who's been asking around after that Carr guy, aren't you?'

'I'm Agent Symes, with the FBI. My partner and I are trying to ascertain the movements of Thaddius Carr. Do you have information?'

The young man's eyes shifted, and he rubbed his hands absently on the legs of his trousers, Symes noted that they left a little damp stain in their wake.

'I might have.'

Symes had forgotten all about the group of girls now, this young man had his full attention. 'Just let me tell you that anything you tell me may become part of the investigation, and you may be required to stand testimony in a court of law, if and when the investigation comes to a conclusion. You understand that?'

The young man grimaced, wiped the stubble on his chin and looked away, toward the pool area. 'Look, I heard you and your buddy asking about him. He comes here for two weeks every year. They do a bit of partying, and then they go. Easy as that. Straight in and then straight out again.'

This was the bit they already knew, but Symes had a feeling that this man was trying to tell him more. 'You said they. Who's the other guy?'

'I'm getting there, man. You know, if I'm seen talking to you here, I could lose my job, my contacts too, if you know what I mean.'

Symes knew what he meant. It was common knowledge that if there was anything anyone needed, legal or illegal, for a small fee it could be obtained from the valet guys. This guy had all the looks of a small-time hustler. The shifty eyes and the sweaty hands were a dead giveaway.

'Every year they come here. They book the same rooms. They're close for the full vacation. Sometimes I get them girls, other times I get them ... you know, other stuff. They usually hire one of those fan boats and go fishing out on the Everglades. Sometimes they're out there all night.'

'You're not really giving me anything here. Just sounds like two dudes enjoying their vacation. I'm going to need a little more,' *or I'm going to go back to that group of girls and do a little partying myself,* he concluded in his head.

'Well, I got a little something that the hotel manager won't tell you. It's bad for business, see. But, every year, while these two guys are here, spending and partying, at least three or four girls go missing. I'm talking, never to be seen again, man. Sure, people go missing from around here all the time. Gangsters, prostitutes, or maybe drunk people who go out into the 'glades and are never seen again. But sometimes the girls who go missing when they're here are local girls, or girls just out here to party, you know what I'm saying?'

Symes was nodding. Both the girls and the drink had been completely forgotten. This was exactly what they were out here looking for. 'And you know this ... how?'

The man's head bowed low, and Symes heard him exhale, a slow, laboured breath. After a moment, when he looked back up, his eyes were pink. Symes could see tears welling up. 'My sister's missing! She was last seen in a bar in town with those two dudes.'

'Do you know the name of the other man?'

'Fitchett. Matt Fitchett. I know this because I looked into them when Nicky never came home.'

'Have you corroborated any of this with the local police department?' Symes asked.

The Contract

The young man looked at him as if he was stupid. 'I don't *corroborate* man. I'm the fucking valet! How do you think I get through the month earning minimum wage and tips? I'm only telling you this because she's my *sister*, and she's missing. I don't want to give any of this to the joke of a PD around here. If you talk to them about missing persons, then I'm sure they'll *corroborate* with you regarding the extensive files they have. Just don't mention that you've talked to me. I can't afford the hassle.'

'You didn't tell me your name! Have you got something to hide?'

'Yeah? Maybe I have. Everyone has something to hide, don't they? Speak to Juanita at reception. She'll give you all the info you need. Cross her palm though, man. I don't want anything. All I want is to find the fucker who made my sister disappear.'

'Juanita?'

'Yeah, I'll tell her you're coming to see her.' With his speech over, the young man slunk back into the bushes and disappeared.

Symes hardly noticed the group of girls as he rushed out of the pool area, heading back towards the restaurant, where he knew his partner would be working. When he got there, he found Cox at a large table, once again surrounded by several files and papers. His head was in his hands.

'Jesus, man, you look like you've gone twelve rounds with a prize fighter.'

Cox looked up at his partner, wearing just his loud swimming shorts and flip-flop sandals. 'Thanks, Symes, so nice of you to notice.'

'How are the interviews going?'

Cox pushed the papers away from him and stretched his arms in the air. He took in a big yawn. 'Not good. That officious little prick of a hotel manager isn't the least bit concerned about helping the investigation; he's more interested in how many people are at the bar. As this isn't an actual, official part of the case, I can't force him to open up.'

Symes sat at the table and leaned in. A huge smile wrapped itself around his face. 'Well, it's a good thing that I'm doing a good job, isn't it?'

Cox looked at him. His face wasn't giving away anything of what he was feeling or thinking.

'I made contact with, or rather I was contacted by, a guy who was happy to impart some information regarding our very own Thaddius Carr. Apparently, it seems, that Mr Carr *was* down here on vacation every year with a male friend. I don't think they're a couple in the way we were thinking about it, but … him and Mr Matthew Fitchett were partners.'

'Go on,' Cox encouraged him.

'It seems that whenever these two come to party, a number of young women go missing! Never to be seen again.' Symes sat back, the smug grin still on his face.

'This is exactly the kind of thing we're looking for. If Thad Carr is involved in something, something nefarious, then that could get him the attention of our white feather guy.'

'Exactly what I was thinking.'

'So now we've got something to take to the manager. Maybe get him to open up a little,' Cox said, getting up.

Symes held his hand out, stopping his partner from leaving. 'No, I've got a contact. She's not going anywhere. Let's eat before we get onto it.' He smiled as he saw that the mention of food seemed to agree with his partner, and he sat back down, shifting his files out of the way to pick up the menu.

~~~~

An hour later, fed, watered, and refreshed, both Cox and Symes were walking through the foyer of the hotel.

'Hi Adam,' came a voice from behind them. Both agents turned around to be confronted by a gorgeous vision with long brown hair, big, Disney eyes, and a toned, curvaceous body, hidden only by the merest of hot-pink fabric that stretched the definition of bikini to its limits. 'You never called,' she accused while twirling her hair around her fingers.

I thought that they only did that in comedies, Cox thought as his eyes couldn't help themselves but roam over her body. She showed no sign of being creeped out by the older man ogling her. She looked as if she was used to it.

'I've got work to do, honey, I told you that,' Symes spoke to her as if she were a student and he was the history teacher.

'What time will you be finished? I can wait.'

Symes shot his partner a guilty look before walking over to the delight in pink. 'Listen,' he whispered. 'I can't talk right now, but I promise I'll speak to you later. It might be late though.'

The Contract

The young woman's face transformed from forlorn to happy in the wink of an eye. 'Tonight?'

'Yeah, tonight. Now, go on, run along, I've got work to do.'

She leaned in and planted a kiss on his lips before running off.

Symes turned back to his partner and offered a sheepish grin. Cox was still staring at the young woman's behind as she made her way towards the pool area. 'Holy shit,' he uttered, unable to tear his eyes away. 'I don't know whether to congratulate you on thinking about your job or slap you for not going off with … that!'

Symes began to laugh. 'Believe me, man, it's not everything it's cracked up to be. I hate it when the women are more into themselves than you, you know what I'm saying?'

Cox lowered his head, a little embarrassed with himself for staring. 'Who's this girl we're meeting?'

'Juanita. She works on the reception desk.'

'Does she know we're coming to see her?'

Symes nodded. 'The valet told me that he'd have a word with her.'

Cox rolled his eyes as he eyed the young Hispanic woman sat at the desk in the reception. She was busying herself with something on the computer and didn't notice them approach. He was acutely aware of the tight outfit she was wearing and the potential effect it was having on his partner.

'Hi,' Symes offered her his hand to shake; she gave a little jump as if he had scared her.

She smiled. Her white teeth were in stark contrast to her dark skin, dark hair, and brown eyes. Cox could see that this girl was stunning.

'You must be Juanita,' he continued. 'My name is …'

The young woman turned her head and shouted out into the back room. 'Juanita, the FBI agents are here.'

'Send them through. Carmichael is out this afternoon. Nobody will care if there has been anyone back here or not,' an older voice filtered out from the room.

The young woman flashed her bright smile back at Cox and Symes. 'Agent George Cox and Agent Adam Symes, you can go right on in. Juanita will see you now.'

Cox and Symes looked at each other before entering behind the desk and following the direction the young woman was ushering them towards.

As they entered, an older Hispanic woman stood up. She was of indeterminate age, but the dark hair, pulled back on her head, was turning grey at the roots. Her once beautiful face was showing the signs of aging that people get from too much exposure to the sun. She smiled as they entered, flashing them her white teeth. 'What can old Juanita do for the big bad FBI?' she asked, indicating towards the two seats opposite her at the small desk. 'Please, sit.'

'We're going to need some information regarding two of your guests. Well, two of your past guests. They were here last week,' Cox began.

Juanita looked at the two men, there was a warm, pleasant smile on her lips. 'Why, gentlemen,' she was speaking in a light Mexican accent. 'There were so many guests here last week. It's hard for us to keep track of all the comings and goings during spring break. You can see how busy we are this week, and this is the end.'

'I think you'll remember these two. They were—'

'I think, maybe you need something to jog your memory. Eh?' Symes interrupted, putting his hand in his shorts pocket and pulling out his wallet. He took out a twenty-dollar-bill and placed it on the table before the woman.

Without looking at it, she took the note and slipped it into the gap in her opened shirt, tucking it into her bra. 'Do these two guests have names?' she asked with the same gentle lilt to her voice and the same smile on her lips.

Cox knew this game only too well. 'Actually, they do. Thaddius Carr and Matthew Fitchett. They've been coming here for the last…'

'I know them. Not very nice boys. We all thought that they were gay when they began coming here. That was before they were caught with a young student in the towel hut, just down by the pool.' She indicated the door with her head, shaking it at the same time. 'Nasty business, that, but, as they say: boys will be boys.' The woman shrugged. 'The girl didn't want to press charges against them. She already had a reputation and didn't want it to spread any further. The boys apologised and the whole matter was swept away.'

The Contract

Cox noted that Symes's face had brightened. The first time since finding out that the beauty on the desk wasn't Juanita. 'Can you tell us exactly what happened?' Symes asked, leaning forward on the small desk.

The older woman smiled. This close to her smile, Cox noticed that her teeth were not as white as he had originally thought. There was a hint of decay to her smile, and the twinkle in her eyes told him that she was enjoying the telling of this poor tale. 'Well, let's just say, a girl who will go into a towel hut with two boys is eventually going to find the kind of boys who would do that to her. If you understand me?'

'What happened?' Symes asked again.

'Well, when someone eventually responded to the screams, her lip was thick, like she had been hit. Her eye was swollen, and she was naked. One boy was tops and one boy was bottoms, if you catch my drift,' Juanita replied, looking Symes right in the eye.

'OK,' Cox interjected, easing a little bit of the tension in the office. 'So, what happened after that? Were they arrested? I checked Mr Carr's file and it was clean of arrests.'

'As I said, the boys apologised. I think they gave her a little "compensation" for her troubles and maybe a little bit to the management too. All parties wanted to avoid troubling the local authorities. Nothing more was said or done. The management kept it to themselves, and there this nasty little tale ends.'

'How long ago was this?' Symes asked.

The woman looked at him and shrugged her shoulders. 'My memory isn't what it used to be.'

Symes sighed and took out a ten-dollar bill this time and slipped it to her across the desk.

She clucked her teeth, took the bill, and hid it in the same place she hid the last one. She breathed out a loud, exaggerated breath. 'That must have been about six years ago. We all thought that that would be the last that we saw of them two, and it would have been a good riddance to bad trash; but no, they were back the next year, and the next and the next. They spend big when they're here, but there is another price we pay.'

'And none of this has been reported to the police?' Cox asked.

Juanita looked at him, her eyes were hard. 'You think reporting the likes of this to the police makes any difference down here? As long as they get what's theirs, there are *always* other ways to look, Agent. Are we done now?'

Juanita began to get up from her chair. Cox reached out his hand and stopped her.

'Not quite.' He looked over at his partner, then back to the woman. 'There's a little more to be gained if you can get us what we need. The hotel will make us jump through hoops to get a guest manifest that will have all the details we need.' Cox reached into his pocket and removed his wallet. He removed two fifty-dollar bills and placed them on the table. 'We need the address, and other info you can get us on Matthew Fitchett. Can you do that for me?'

Juniata eyed the money on the table hungrily. 'Yeah, I can do that. When do you want it?' she asked, reaching out for the money.

Cox's hand fell onto hers, stopping her from retrieving it. 'Well, seeing as Carmichael is out, how about right now?' he said.

Juanita smiled. 'I had a feeling that this information was going to be important to you.' She opened a drawer underneath the table and pulled out two orange card files. Inside the files were slips of paper. 'So, I prepared the information early for you.' She slid the files across the table with one hand, while taking the cash with the other. Again, she stuffed the dollar bills into her bra. 'I think that concludes our business here, gentlemen. I'll wish you good afternoon. I have a lot of work to do.'

Juanita stood up and motioned towards the door, welcoming the men to leave. They both took the hint and left, Cox carrying the orange folders.

'Well, I think that was a good bit of business,' Symes said smiling at his partner as they left the stuffiness of the small office, back into the humid Florida air. He opened the folder and read the very first page. It gave them all the information they needed. The name and address of Mr Matthew Fitchett.

'Well, look at that. It seems our boy is a Floridian after all,' Symes said, pointing at the address at the top of the copied invoice.

'Jacksonville. This invoice is from two years ago. Are there any other addresses for him?'

Symes leafed through the thin folder. 'Well, it looks like our boys took turns in paying for the hotel bills. Last year was Thad. This year it was M Fitchett, same address as the last.

The Contract

'Excellent. I'll go and book us a flight to Jacksonville. We need to have a little conversation with our man here.' Cox closed the file and went to walk off, back towards the reception.

'Hang on, Cox,' Symes said, grabbing his arm. There was a wide smile on his face. 'There's no rush, is there? I mean, there's not been a murder, so were not expected to be there.'

Cox knew what Symes was angling for but played along anyway.

'Get the flight for tomorrow. I've got a little bit of ...' he pulled up his shorts, rather theatrically and winked towards his partner, 'unfinished business.'

Cox sighed. *He does have a point though, we've worked our asses off on this one,* he thought. He gave a small, slow nod. 'I'm sure there's no flights out of here tonight anyway. But I suspect that there will be early tomorrow morning.'

'Sure, but not *too* early,' Symes smiled.

The cat who got the cream, Cox thought.

'I'll see you tonight for dinner and drinks then,' Symes grinned before making his way towards the pool area and a group of semi-naked young ladies.

14.

THE FOLLOWING DAY, the two agents were driving along I95 towards Springfield, Jacksonville. Cox drove while Symes relaxed and recovered in the passenger seat with his hair blowing in the wind created by the open window. He was wearing a dark pair of sunglasses, which clashed with the paleness of his skin underneath his two-day-old stubble.

Cox shook his head. 'I've got no sympathy for you whatsoever. I said relax, not go out and get yourself absolutely shit-faced.'

'That's the thing, man. I hardly drank anything. I think one of those little bitches must have spiked my drink,' Symes replied, directing the air-conditioning vent towards his sweating face.

'But you still managed to sleep with two women in the same night?' Cox gripped the steering wheel, his knuckles turning white as he looked at his partner.

'I don't even remember. Well, not until this morning anyway.'

'I can't believe you. I really can't. You have absolutely no control. I can't believe you slept with Juanita *and* the girl in the pink bikini. Talk about poles apart, man.' Cox turned away from the road to look at Symes, suffering next to him. He frowned. 'Come on! Juanita? Jesus, she must be old enough to be your mother.'

'She's not as old as she looks,' Symes replied with a small shudder. 'We're turning right here! Onto Concord Boulevard East. Our man's street is …' he looked at the address again on the top of the paper he was holding. 'Here we go, onto Meade Street.'

They turned onto a small, suburban street. There were only a few houses dotted around, and all of them had their lights off. They found the house they were looking for, which was dark too. There was a rather expensive looking vehicle parked in the driveway.

The Contract

'Would you look at that car?' Symes said, sucking in a breath in order to make him whistle. 'When I retire, I'm going to get me a car just like that one.'

'I think you'll have to retire when you're one hundred and thirty-two to afford one of those,' Cox replied.

'Our man here moved from Georgia to Jacksonville to work for the bank twelve years ago. It looks like he settled down rather nicely. He's single and a respected member of the community.' He closed the file he was reading from and looked at his partner as they pulled up in the driveway. 'If you ask me, it's all the hallmarks of a serial killer.'

Cox expected his partner to be laughing at this quip, but he wasn't. 'Well, let's go and meet John Wayne Gacy then.'

As they alighted the car, they were greeted with the small, silvery tinkling sound of breaking glass. It came from inside the house. Instantly, the two men were alert to the situation. Both agents removed their guns from their holsters and were ready for action within the wink of an eye.

Symes eyed his partner, who indicated towards the house, directing him to go around the back of the property. Symes understood and took off, silently, through the small trees that lined the grounds.

Cox took the front porch. With his back to the wall, he peered through the window into the darkened room within. He couldn't see anything out of the ordinary. The room looked tidy, like any other nice front room.

Another tinkling of glass caught his attention, and he felt his blood pumping in his ears as adrenaline began to course through his body. He'd been in situations like this before, but he would never lose the fear of the unknown. That fear kept him sharp and alert. He had always been grateful for it as it had saved his life on more than one occasion. He knew from his training that once you became used to the fear, you became a danger, not only to yourself, but to your team.

A moan escaped from inside the house. To Cox, it sounded male, and it sounded like whoever uttered it was in pain.

Readjusting the grip on his gun, he turned away from the window and focused on the porch door. Slowly, he grasped the screen handle, knowing that it wouldn't be locked, he pulled it open. The scream from the hinges was amplified in his ears ten-fold. Once again, he knew from his training, and from the fact that this wasn't the first time he had ridden this carousel, that noises always exaggerated themselves in a person's conscience when they were trying to be stealthy.

Unperturbed by the racket the door had made, he grabbed the handle on the front door. The coldness of the metal burned him for a moment, and he fought the urge to remove his hand, to warm it, but he knew that he might lose a crucial few seconds of advantage if he did. He turned the handle and wasn't surprised to find that the door was also unlocked. As he pushed it open, ever so slowly, the hackles on the back of his neck began to tingle. His senses told him that there was someone inside. There was a feeling of unease, of struggle.

He heard a thump followed by another moan.

This time he traced the sound to an upstairs room.

There was also a smell. It was metallic with a coppery undertone to it. His experience told him that it was blood.

With his own blood racing through his head, pounding with the rhythm of his heartbeat, Cox began to make his way towards the staircase before him.

Movement to his left caught his eye and, silently, he swung his gun around towards whoever, or whatever, was causing it. He was relieved to see Symes coming out of the kitchen, gun raised and silent. The bigger man winked at him, and nodded his head towards the staircase, indicating to his partner that he would cover him as he made his way up.

Another light thump and a muffled groan got Cox moving again, albeit slowly and cautiously. Advancing on his tiptoes, he stepped onto the first stair of the fifteen before him. He winced a little at the creak, but once again, he knew that the sound had been amplified in his head. Whoever was upstairs wouldn't have heard that sound. He knew it, but it didn't stop him from swallowing heavily and tightening his grip, once again, on the handle of his gun.

He took another step up, followed by another, then another. The soft bumping and scraping that had come from above had stopped, as had the moaning. He turned, checking where Symes was, and was thankful that he was right behind him, covering the room below, making sure that they didn't get outflanked from down there by the partners of whoever was upstairs.

Eventually, he made it up the whole set of stairs and was confronted with a long landing with four closed doors around him.

The Contract

On closer inspection, not all of them were closed.

Cox squinted, trying to focus on the sliver of light that was stemming from the only door that was slightly ajar. He wanted as much intel as he could muster from inside before he went crashing in, guns blazing.

There was a flicker of movement, and he took it as his cue to go. He rushed towards the door, stopping with his back to the wall just short of it. He motioned to Symes to get into position on the opposite side of the frame. His partner understood and complied.

Cox thought for a moment about announcing himself, informing whoever was in there that there were two, well-trained, and armed federal agents outside, ready to come in. Giving the perpetrator a chance to give themselves up. Then he thought about the murders that had been committed. He thought about the brutality of them, the merciless way they had been carried out.

He wanted to take this bastard down.

Without warning, he kicked the door in, raising his gun, covering the room as per his training.

What he saw inside filled him with revulsion.

In an instant, Cox knew where the coppery smell in the house was originating.

It was from in here!

Even though he was a seasoned professional and had seen his share of death and mutilation in his years as an FBI agent, nothing he had witnessed, ever, could have prepared him for this scene.

'Jesus Christ,' Symes muttered from behind him, before he heard the tell-tale noise of a person baulking, attempting to keep down the rise of bile coming from his stomach. This affected Cox, as he knew that Symes had spent years in the military, including tours in Afghanistan. He had seen more than his share of atrocities too.

This was bad!

The body, it was of indeterminate gender, was hanging by its arms, naked, from the ceiling. Its hands had been bound together by a thick leather belt and fixed to a sturdy looking light fitting. A pillowcase had been placed over its head.

That was where the normal, if you could call it normal, stopped.

From below the neck and arms, all skin had been flayed from the body. Peeled off in thick, deep strips of flesh.

If this person wasn't dead before this, then they certainly died during this procedure, Cox thought, forcing his gaze to go against every instinct it had to look away; he needed to make an accurate assessment of the victim.

Laid out on the bed were strips of skin. They had been laid, neatly in rows. With a gorge rising from his stomach, Cox noticed two of the strips had blue, discoloured nipples still attached to them. One of the strips had a hole in the centre of it. *The bellybutton,* he thought. Next to that was a small withered penis and two other lumps, which cox assumed were testicles. He then made his determination over the corpse's gender.

Directly beneath the body, on the damp duvet, were clumps of a yellow, jellylike substance, which Cox identified as body fat. There were also copious amounts of blood and faecal matter.

'Jesus Christ,' Symes muttered from behind him. 'Whatever happed to this guy, it didn't happen fast.' He did a sweep of the room. 'Holy fuck! Look at that …'

Cox snapped his attention away from the horror before him and looked towards where his partner was pointing.

Among the faecal matter that had amassed underneath the body, something that didn't quite belong there had been placed at the top. Like a flag depicting a climber's accent to the top of a mountain, was something that Cox really should have seen before, but hadn't. A single white feather had been planted in the shit. Its stem piercing the crust, while the whiteness of the strands remained impeccable.

'A feather,' was all he was able to say.

Both agents, ignoring the smell and the gore of the room, leaned in closer to take another look.

A small shuffling noise came from beneath the bed. Cox, instantly alert, flicked the safety catch on his gun and aimed it. He eyed Symes, who was already doing the same thing.

Fighting to keep his breathing in order, so as not to hyperventilate, Cox lowered himself to his knees to peer into the darkness, where the noise come from. A sheen of sweat covered him from head to toe, and he felt the grip of his weapon begin to slip in his hand.

A small dog, which must have been hiding, waiting for these two meddlesome humans to leave before continuing its strange, but tasty lunch, darted out.

The Contract

'What the...' was all Symes could say as the pooch ran between his feet, bolting towards the door. A long, pink strand of flesh was trailing from its mouth as it bolted out of the room and down the stairs.

Symes turned to watch it go.

Cox, who had fallen back onto his rump as the dog jumped out, relaxed. He eased himself back up into a standing position; there was a smile on his face despite the scene that they had found themselves in.

That was when he saw *him*.

For the first time, he came face to face with the man they had been hunting all over the USA.

The boy, wearing a black hooded top and jogging bottoms, was stood, as still as a statue, staring at him. His face was emotionless, but his deep, blue eyes were piercing. Cox fancied that he could feel them burning into him, ripping him open, exploring everything, every fibre inside of him. He felt naked before him. He knew that there was nothing that he could hide, nothing that he could deceive him with.

The young man moved, as quick as a flash, and hit Symes on the back of the neck. Cox watched as his partner crumpled into a heap on the floor in slow motion. The youth then turned back to look at him. His blank expression hadn't changed.

All of Agent Cox's training deserted him. Even though he had been in the presence of clear and present danger many times in his career, at that moment, he had no idea what he was supposed to do. As he raised his gun towards the young man, he felt like he needed to scream. He wanted to shout at the whatever it was he was looking at; he wanted to scream at him, or it, and tell it to never come back, ever again.

All that he managed was to stutter a feeble, 'Hands up!'

The youth still hadn't moved, with the exception of taking out Symes. He stared at him for a few moments before stepping forwards. Without another warning, Cox fired his gun. A hole appeared in the black top the youth was wearing, but it didn't slow him.

The youth reached out towards him. Cox fell into his eyes and was lost, unable to move, unable to do anything. Then the boy's cold but fiercely strong hand gripped him. It held his shoulder, and everything went black.

D E McCluskey & C William Giles

When he awoke, he was no longer in the bedroom of the house in Jacksonville. In fact, he was no longer on solid ground. There was a strange smell that accompanied the rocking back and forth. It was boggy and wet. Tentatively, he opened his eyes. It took him a moment to realise where he was, and when he did, he couldn't quite believe it. He was on a fan boat. It was night, and he wasn't alone. There was a man to his left, stood on the side of the boat looking into the water. As he turned, Cox got a look at his face. He looked like the photographs of the victim that they had been working in Georgia. Thad Carr. Behind him, sat at the pilot's chair, was another man. This man had longish hair and a beard. He resembled the photographs they had of Matthew Fitchett.

Within a few moments, after the period of disorientation had passed, he recognised this situation for what it was. He wasn't there, not in real life. This was a vision or an illusion.

Thad, wearing a pair of loud, colourful Bermuda shorts and a plaid shirt, was smiling as he looked back into the water over the side of the boat. The sun was setting behind the trees in the distance, breaking the sky into the most striking oranges and azure blues. A warm wind blew through his hair, and the open shirt he was wearing flapped in the breeze.

Matt was sitting on the elevated seat at the pilot's station. He was holding a can in his hand; the beverage was wrapped in a cooler sleeve. The green logo of a smiling crocodile stood out against the blue plastic.

He was grinning.

The light of the boat illuminated the water below them. There were splashes and bubbles as whatever wildlife lay under the surface and in the bushes on either side of the boat were agitated and excited by their presence.

Cox was surprised to notice that there was a third person on the boat. A woman. A young woman. She was wearing the clothing of someone who had been out partying, on a night out with her friends. The small red skirt was designed to show off her bare legs, and the black, lacy, see-through top was designed to reveal the black bra beneath. She was pretty, or at least she would be if she hadn't been bound and gagged. Tears had dried on her face, ruining her make up. She was shivering, and Cox assumed that it was more with fear than the cold. The poor young woman was on her side, helplessly secured. Her wide eyes were pleading towards the two men who were currently holding her captive.

The Contract

'This'll do, man,' Thad shouted, looking up from the side of the boat.

Matt killed the fan, and the boat began to slow down. He steered it towards the middle of the lake. Thad was smiling at the splashing in the water around them.

What the hell is going on here? Cox thought as he watched both men become animated as the boat slowed.

'How do they always know?' Matt asked as he focused a large spotlight into the water. The rippling and bubbling around them increased as the boat came to a stop. 'It's almost as if they know why we're here,' he shouted.

Cox took an involuntary step backwards as he saw the flashing of dark yellow reptilian eyes emerge from beneath the surface. Large bodies covered in green scales rose from the water, fighting each other for prime location. Instinctively understanding what this boat meant to them.

Food! he thought.

'Okay, let's do this,' Matt shouted as he got up from his seat.

'Don't forget to take all her clothes off this time,' Thad reminded him as he looked away from the mesmerising waves of the competing creatures in the water. He joined his friend and their passenger on the deck.

Both men were laughing, and a wave of understanding washed over Cox as he got a feeling that the reminder to take the girl's clothes off was a kind of ritual. A joke that heralded back from mistakes made the very first time that they had played this game. In his mind's eye, he saw them fishing around in the dangerous, blood filled waters for hours, attempting to retrieve all their first victim's clothing so they weren't found at a later date by inquisitive police officers or nosey tourists.

Matt grabbed the petrified girl underneath her arms and hauled her up into a standing position. She screamed, and thrashed, but ultimately, she was no match for the larger man. Cox could see that he was a big guy and obviously kept himself in shape, much like Thad did.

Thad produced a large knife and showed it to the girl. He was laughing and goading her with it. The poor girl's dark eyes widened as they tried to focus on the blade. Without saying another word, he grabbed at her top. He lifted the knife once more and touched her chin with it. A grin to rival the alligator's in the water, spread across his face.

Cox moved, attempting to accost the man and the knife before he could do what he was obviously going to do with it. He found that he couldn't move. From out of nowhere, a voice spoke to him. It was loud, booming. It seemed to come from everywhere all at once. From the water, the trees, the deck of the boat. He sensed that he was the only person who could hear it.

'YOU CAN'T HELP HER, AGENT COX. THIS SCENE HAS ALREADY COME TO PASS.'

Cox instinctively knew that the voice was telling the truth.

Feeling useless and dirty, like a voyeur peeping through a window, he watched as the blade cut through the fabric of her top like a hot knife through butter. The flimsy shirt fell away. Thad reached out and caught it before it blew in the warm breeze of the night. Next, he cut off her bra, from between her breasts. As the undergarment fell away, he admired the way her small breasts hardly moved. Cox got the feeling that Thad was more than a little aroused by his actions.

'Hurry up, man, you're taking fucking forever with this one,' Matt laughed.

The girl's scared eyes flicked from the knife to Matt, then back to Thad.

'I want to take my time. I like what I'm seeing.'

'Well, you'll be liking what you're seeing a whole lot more in a few moments if you get a move on.' Matt was looking over the side of the boat. The huge prehistoric reptiles were squirming about in the water around them. 'I think there's more tonight. This should be some show.'

Without further preamble, Thad sliced through the girl's red skirt and through the black panties she was wearing underneath it. He collected all the clothes and put them in a small bag to the side. 'Going to burn them later,' he explained to their victim, although Cox had a feeling that the panicked girl didn't hear a word he said. 'We don't want anyone finding anything that they shouldn't now, do we?' There was a pleasant smile on his face, as if he was explaining what he was doing to a small child.

This sent a chill through Cox. He now understood why the white feather killer had selected these two men. Thaddius Carr and Matthew Fitchett were serial killers. They now fitted the white feather killer's modus operandi.

The Contract

The girl was naked and shaking uncontrollably. She had stopped trying to wriggle free, and her eyes passed backwards and forwards between the two men, before resting on Thad. Cox thought that she looked like someone who didn't quite believe what was about to happen to her. He'd seen that look before; it was never a nice thing to see.

'I do believe that this one's yours, dude. I did the last one,' Matt said pointing towards the girl rather theatrically.

Thad smiled as he looked at her. He reached over and pulled off the grey tape that was over her mouth. She pulled in a deep, shaky breath, bending over slightly to allow her body to take in more air.

'Please,' she pleaded, breathlessly. 'Please, I'll do whatever you want. I ... I won't tell anyone anything. I won't go to the police. Just please don't kill me.' The tears flowing down her cheeks were thick and full of dark mascara, giving her more than just a passing resemblance to Alice Cooper's stage makeup.

Thad was laughing now. Cox could see that he was shaking too. He didn't know if this was due to the night air, the adrenaline running though his body, or just for the thrill of what he was about to do. He reached out and stroked her hair. 'Hey, don't worry. Me and Matt here are just having a little fun. We're not going to kill you.'

The two men smiled as the girl's shoulders relaxed and a nervous smile broke out on her pale face.

'You're ... you're not?' she stuttered.

Thad scoffed at the question. 'No, we're not. We're not monsters, we're just two regular guys blowing off a bit of steam.' He reached out and grabbed the girl's arm. Cox saw her skin turn white where his grip cut off her blood circulation.

His face then twisted into an unsettling grin. 'Oh no, *we're* not going to kill you. The gators are going to do that for us.'

Cox cried out impotently as he watched Thad push her, hard. The small railing at the side of the boat only came up to the girl's knees, and the force of the push took away her gravitational balance, making her top-heavy. With a scream, she tumbled off the boat and splashed into the dark water below.

Matt had made his way back up to the pilot's chair, and he switched on the powerful spotlight. He found the struggling girl easily as she thrashed away, attempting to keep her head above the water. Her shackled arms and legs flapped uselessly as she slipped beneath the surface.

Unfortunately, drowning was the least of her worries.

The hungry alligators were her immediate concern.

The two boys whooped and hollered as the large, carnivorous reptiles fought each other to snap and grab at their easy prey. Cox watched as large, vicious yellow teeth tore into the struggling girl's flesh. Ripping, tearing, twisting. Blood saturated the water, turning it darker than it already was. Limbs and innards floated to the surface before being quickly snapped back underneath by powerful jaws.

For the next ten minutes, the friends danced and sang on the deck of the boat, as below them, almost every single scrap of the innocent young woman was consumed. The poor woman now languished in the bellies of several of the monsters below.

~~~~

Reality blinked and Cox found himself back in the bedroom. The bearded youth was still holding onto his shoulder. His bright, piercing, blue eyes were still burning into his head.

The cold, icy fingers released him from their grip. Cox fell onto his knees. He could see Symes's unconscious body lying within the jamb of the door, but he couldn't move, not even to reach out to see if he was OK.

'DO NOT PERSUE THIS, AGENT COX,' the voice, the same voice as he had heard in his vision, spoke into his head again. 'THIS IS BIGGER THAN YOU. BIGGER THAN YOU COULD POSSIBLY IMAGINE.'

With that, the young man was gone. Cox didn't see him leave as he had now fallen to the floor as unconscious as his partner.

The Contract

15.

THE PORTSMOUTH DOCKS were dark, cold, and wet. The constant drizzle had been falling from the grey clouds for the last three days, drenching everything beneath, inch by inch. At this time of night, after ten, the whole area was manned on a skeleton crew; there would be no more than ten workers covering the length of the four miles of warehouses and locks. But tonight was different; tonight, there was a larger presence than normal.

Twenty men stood around the concrete platform of a disused dock. None of them looked as if they were suited for the cold, wet British weather. They were all wearing long, dark coats but were still dancing around in feeble attempts to get warm. Breath was pluming out from their mouths in large, grey clouds.

'Here it is,' one of the larger men who was sporting a closely cropped haircut shouted as he pointed out towards the dark expanse of water before them. The blackness he was pointing to was broken only by a single white light accompanied by a flashing red one. 'Look lively fellas, I don't trust these foreign fuckers, not one bit.' He reached into his jacket and pulled out a small, black handgun. He popped out the magazine and looked at it, satisfied that there was a full complement of bullets inside.

Most of the men around him did the same.

The light got closer, and the faint sound of a horn could be heard over the lapping of the water against the dock wall.

'Is that ship coming in fast?' another man asked as he watched the lights approach.

The big man cocked his head a little and squinted. The light really did seem to be coming in fast. They had done this a few times before. The eastern Europeans had always requested this dock to bring in their product. Police and dock security had been paid off, and the immigration guys had received their—rather handsome—share of that payment, in order to turn a blind eye regarding goings on, on Dock 14F.

Normally the boat was guided in expertly, which meant slowly and purposefully. Tonight, things looked totally different.

The lights were approaching rapidly, and Gerald was not happy about it. 'Get Klaus on the blower, will you?' he ordered in a thick cockney accent. 'Something's not right here.' Gerald shook his head, blowing into the hand that wasn't holding his gun. 'I'm not liking this one bit.'

The man to the left of him took his phone out of his pocket and pressed a couple of buttons. He put the phone to his ear and waited for a few moments. 'There's no answer,' he said.

'What do you mean? There's no answer. There has to be an answer, he's our fucking contact. Try again!'

The man pressed the redial button on the phone, and Gerald watched as the screen illuminated and he held it to his ear. A few moments later, he clicked the button and shook his head.

Gerald looked back out towards the lights that were getting closer. 'What the fuck?' he mumbled. 'Get Ed on the phone. I've got to tell him that we're pulling out. I don't like this at all.'

'Are you sure?' the man asked. 'You want to ring Ed? At this hour? Seriously?'

Gerald breathed out a long, drawn breath. 'I don't want to, but that's not right out there.'

Both men looked out at the rapidly approaching lights.

'Ring him,' he said.

The man began pushing the buttons on his phone again, and Gerald heard the faint tone of the phone ringing. After a few rings, it was answered.

He'd expected to hear the thick, deep tones of Ed's voice, but he was surprised to hear the excited tones of a woman. She sounded agitated, and scared.

'Hey, hey! Calm down! I can't understand you,' the man shouted into the phone.

Gerald turned and grabbed the phone off him. 'Give me that,' he growled. 'Hello, Ed?' His tone was completely different on the phone; there was a noted mark of respect in it. 'Ed, is that you?'

The Contract

'Oh my God, he's dead ... He's dead. The man ... he tore him to pieces.' The voice on the other end was female, high pitched, and in some distress.

Gerald couldn't make out what it was she was saying.

'Mrs Steele ... Mrs Steele, please, calm down, just for a moment! I need to speak to Ed!' He was talking calmly but rapidly down the line, attempting to get the hysterical woman to relax, to take a breath and tell him exactly what she needed to tell him. The hairs on the back of his neck were standing up as he listened to the sobbing of the woman on the other end while watching the rapidly approaching lights in the harbour. He was feeling a deep and dark sense of foreboding, mostly from the ship but also from whatever was happening with Ed.

'Mrs Steele, I need you to calm down for me now. Please, tell me why I can't speak to Ed.'

The woman took in a deep, shaky breath, Gerald thought she was trying to compose herself; and failing. 'Ed...' she sobbed. He's dead. The man, the young man broke in here.' Her voice was shaking again. 'He broke in and he ... he killed my Ed.' The high pitch was back for the last few words of her statement.

'Who broke in, Mrs Steele? Who killed Ed?' Gerald was shouting down the phone now.

The other men in the crew, including the man whose phone it was, were all looking at him. Their expressions akin to being told that there was no such thing as Santa Claus as a child. Complete and utter disbelief.

'The young man. Christ, he was so young. He, he, tore Ed apart, right in front of me. Picked him up as if he were a rag doll. He didn't show him any respect ...' Gerald could hear the tears come back then as a long, high-pitched wail emanated from the phone.

'Where is he now?' Gerald asked; he had no time to listen to the wailing of a hysterical woman.

'Ed? He's right here next to me. The bed is covered in blood. I don't know what to do. Little Brian is asleep in the next room, luckily Mel's out for the night. What do I do? Do I call the police?'

'NO!' Gerald shouted down the phone. 'Do *not,* call the police. I'll get someone around to help you. I need to know who this guy is, the one who's done this to Ed ... and you.' Gerald was shouting now, looking out into the dark harbour, with the rapidly approaching lights of their boat coming into dock.

'He left.'

'Did he say anything? Did he say who he was working for?'

'He didn't say a thing. Not one word. Ed tried to fight him, but the bastard was too strong.'

'Did he leave any message at all? Anything?' Gerald was in a spin now. The boat was almost here, and Ed had been hit by persons unknown.

'No, all he left was a white feather. A big one. Do you know what that means?'

Gerald was shaking his head. 'I've got no fucking clue,' he spoke, more to himself than to Ed's hysterical wife. All his respect for her had washed away with the knowledge that her husband, Ed Steele, the notorious 'Eastend' Ed Steele, was now dead. He hung up the phone. 'Right,' he shouted to everyone on the dock. The other nineteen men turned to look at him. He could see the worry and concern in their faces. They had all heard the conversation, and all of them could see the boat approaching too fast. 'Ed's gone. He's been hit. I'm not getting anything from his missus. We're going to have to assume that we've been compromised. I'm calling this off.'

'Ged, that boat is about to …' The man who had just received the mobile phone back from Gerald didn't finish his shout as he was pushed onto the floor by one of the other men on the dock. This man was in a hurry to get out of the way of the boat that had not slowed down and was just about to crash into the dock wall.

The men were shouting and running as the schooner collided with the wall with a scream. It sounded like an almighty beast that was dying; shot and left to perish.

'What the fuck?' Gerald shouted as he flung himself to the floor, dropping his weapon in the process. An explosion tore through the quiet night as one of the fuel tanks ignited from the sparks created by the ship's metal hull deteriorating against the stone wall.

Gerald looked up, shielding his eyes. The explosion brought about the illusion of daytime as the flames coming from the ship lit up the otherwise dark dock. He witnessed two of his men throw themselves to the floor, both squealing like piglets in a pen. They were covered in the brilliant orange of the flames that had spread from the explosion. He thought about getting up, getting over to them, and trying to help, but he

The Contract

thought better of it as the heat from the inferno prickled his skin, even from this distance.

The initial glare of the explosion was over in a matter of seconds as what little fuel still in the tanks burnt out. It burnt fiercely, catching on the old wood and plastics of the boat and the dock.

Gerald sat up and searched for his gun. It was on the floor, inches from him, and he reached out and grabbed it. His finger caressed the cold metal as if it were a comforting teddy-bear, or a safety blanket. The two burnt men had stopped screaming as the fire that had consumed them was now simmering, mostly on the cooking flesh and fats within their body. The smell of roast flesh mixed with burning gasoline brought a disturbing rumble in his stomach. *That shouldn't smell so fucking nice,* he thought with a grimace. He looked around the dock and saw at least three of his men had fled. *Fucking cowards,* he thought. *They'll get what's coming to them, especially now that I'm running things.*

He looked over at the wreck of the ship that had just fire-balled against the dock. He eyed the windows of the bridge and was surprised to see the captain stood up there, still at the helm.

'What the fuck is going on here? You three,' he pointed at three of the men who were stood around looking as if they didn't know where they were.

All three of them snapped around at the sound of his voice.

'You three, get on board that thing and find out what's just happened. We need to get all the merch off it before it sinks and before the fucking coastguard gets up here to find out what's happened.'

The three men pulled out their guns and made their way over towards the stricken vessel, dodging impromptu fire pits and the two corpses of their fallen colleagues. Gerald watched as they tiptoed through the wreckage and shrapnel from the explosion. He looked up at the bridge again and saw that the man at the helm hadn't moved. He was still looking out of the window, as if trying to navigate his way through the harbour.

A chill ran through Gerald's body, covering him in a cold, greasy sweat, despite the coldness of the evening. He turned his back to the vessel, about to marshal the rest of the men behind him, when an ear-piercing scream emitted from the direction of the boat. He turned back to see what was happening. Nothing looked any different; including the man stood at the helm. 'What the fuck...' he muttered, gripping the handle of his gun tighter still.

Suddenly, he no longer wanted anything to do with this job. He wished that he had listened to his mother, and his uncles, and his teachers. He wished that he had found himself a nice safe job in an office somewhere, working on a computer and a million miles away from this dock and his dead boss, 'Eastend' Ed.

Another scream tore him away from his daydream, back into the reality of the crashed boat that was lined with heroin, cocaine, hash, and at least fifteen teenage girls coming in illegally on the promise of film and modelling work.

There was too much at stake to leave the merch on-board the sinking vessel. Obviously, he wouldn't have to answer to Ed anymore, but even the notorious Edward Steele had people he answered to. The cargo was worth more than the wreck, by at least fifteen times over.

'Fuck ...' he muttered again as he made his way over to the wreckage himself. He could see that the ship was already listing to one side, not dangerously, but enough to compromise the hull and the precious delights inside. 'If you need something fucking doing ...' he mumbled as he dodged through the hot and twisted metal. He wondered how long the authorities, the ones they had paid off so handsomely, would take before they *had* to investigate the explosion on Dock 14F.

He made the short leap from the solid dock to the listing deck of the ship and had to reach out and grab something, anything, as his soles slipped on the wet decking. 'Christ ...' he muttered underneath his breath as he checked back, making sure no one had seen him slip. He couldn't see any of the other men, but guessed that they were still there, standing around and scuffing up the floor, *doing absolutely fuck all.*

Somewhere, he didn't know if it was in the distance or somewhere near, there was a bell; it was tolling a steady rhythm. *That must be on the boat,* he thought. *I couldn't hear it on the dock.* With his trusted gun still in his hand, he made his way further into the ruined craft. He knew that there should be a crew of at least six men on board, but right now, he couldn't see anyone.

He pushed a door that he knew would lead into the main bulkhead of the vessel, but there was something obstructing its momentum. He couldn't get it open all the way. He took his mobile phone out of his pocket, switched on the torch app, and reached his hand

The Contract

inside, illuminating the immediate interior. As he manoeuvred his head to look through the crack of the ajar door, the peeling of the bell suddenly got louder. A shout was coming from back on the deck, but he didn't have time to deal with whatever that was now, he was far too busy with other, more important, matters at hand. Other matters like a one-and-a-half million-pound haul of drugs, not to mention the girls. *Always a delightful part of the job, the girls,* he thought with a wry smile.

An odd smell was coming from inside the bulkhead. It was a smell he recognised but couldn't quite put his finger on. Regardless, he pushed on the door again, and just about managed to squeeze his head through.

He instantly wished he hadn't.

The stark white light from the torch on his phone highlighted the thick, dark crimson that was splattered all over the walls of the anteroom inside. Instinctively, he recoiled from the sight, remembering now what the smell was. It was the gaseous stench of a person's innards after they had been exposed to the air.

He gagged.

He returned his arm and bent over. Knowing that the vomit was coming didn't make it any easier when it did. His number one least favourite thing to do was vomit, always had been ever since he was a sickly child, but smelling that smell, and in such a thick, cloying amount, had induced it.

Chunky, warm fluid streamed from his mouth and his nostrils. Half-way through, he thought he was going to choke with the amount he brought forth, but he managed to catch a lumpy, sour breath that allowed him to calm down.

He knew that he had to go through that room to get downstairs to the cargo hold.

Wiping his nose, squeezing the last bit of lingering chunks from his nostrils, he went back to work on the door. He put his whole body behind the push and managed to get it to give just that little bit more. Resisting the urge to shine his phone through again to see what the blockage was, he tried again. This time it gave way even more.

Something oozed out of the thin opening. Something thick and dark. He knew what it was, and his heart began to beat double. *It's almost in rhythm with those fucking bells,* he thought. He steeled himself, ready for what was about to fall out of the door.

The severed head that rolled out looked like it had been *pulled* off its body. The expression on the face told him everything he needed to know. However, that wasn't the worst part. The head had been stuffed with entrails. It was where the God-awful smell was coming from. Whoever had killed this man had not only pulled his head off but disembowelled him and stuffed his bits inside. The head rolled down the listing desk, leaving behind an unravelling trail of gore. Gerald felt his stomach turn again.

The bell that was ringing on the dock, or on the ship, or in the sky, or wherever it was coming from, had gotten louder. There was something else with it now. Weirdly, it sounded like harp music. Even though he had only heard harp music on some silly films when he was a kid, it was almost unmistakable. It wasn't how he remembered it though. Harp music was supposed to be soothing and calm. This was neither. It was filled with bass! He felt every thrum from his stomach all the way down to his testicles.

He knew that he *had* to get through this room and down into the hold. He was no longer bothered about the girls down there, they could go to Hell for all he cared, but he needed to get to the product. He needed to make sure it was all still intact.

It wasn't until he was about to step into the room that a horrible and dangerous thought occurred to him. Whoever had ripped that man's head off his shoulders was probably still on the ship. Whoever had disembowelled him and stuffed his head with entrails, was possibly, *no, probably,* he thought, still down in the hold.

He gripped his gun tighter, lit the torch app on his phone again, took a deep breath, and stepped into the room.

What he saw inside took his breath away.

There were six bodies. They were all pinned to the wall. Each one had been mixed and matched. Limbs from one body had been forced onto another. One man's head was on another man's body. There were arms and legs dangling from another man's stomach. One man had had his head turned the wrong way around. Gerald found this one just too much to look at. The way the poor devil's skin had stretched, but not broken, brought the saliva back to his mouth as a precursor to vomit. The floor was awash with blood and gristle. It was pooling and rushing towards the door as the ship's deck listed.

The Contract

He could see the stairwell that he needed to access to get down to the hold, to rescue the merchandise, but his way had been blocked. Another man's body had been pinned over the stairs. On closer inspection, an inspection that he didn't really have the stomach to do, he saw that every bone in the man's body had been broken. Each limb hung limply on the rail that he had been pinned against. He had been beaten to death. Only his face hadn't been touched. The look of fear and horror in this man's dead eyes spoke volumes. *Fuck the drugs,* he thought. *I've got to get out of here.*

As he retreated out of the dark room, the bells from the deck were joined, once again, by the harp. The sound had become pronounced. It had become a symphony of unholy sounds that was assaulting his ears. When the trumpets kicked in, it was too much. He leapt out of the room, slipping onto his back and splashing into the wet, sloping deck. The smell of the fresh air hit his nostrils, and he breathed deeply. It was at least a second or two before he noticed that the awful music had stopped.

He closed his eyes, trying to revel in the freshness and the cold spray of the drizzle in the air on his face. But, every time he closed his eyes, he saw them. The men inside, ripped apart like some sick child's wicked fantasy.

He lay on his back, looking up towards the bridge. He could see the captain, still standing at the helm, still in the same position as he had been when the ship crashed.

Now he could see why.

Two large pikes had been pushed through his face. They had come from behind, erupting from his forehead and his cheek. Their sharp barbs, coated and dripping in a dark slickness, had continued through the frame of the window. They were the reason he had remained upright the entire time.

Gerald did something that he hadn't done in a long, long time; he began to pray. He began with the 'Our Father.' He forgot the words not long after starting, so began a 'Hail Mary' instead. He got to the end of that one, and was all set to say another, as an act of contrition or something like it, when the bells, harps, and trumpets began again. This time they were accompanied by a hellish drumbeat. It sounded like a march. *A funeral march,* he thought, wishing he hadn't.

He scrambled to his feet. It wasn't easy, as his grip was lost on the crimson gore underfoot. Somehow, he managed to get up and scramble away from the door, away from the captain, and hopefully away from whoever, or whatever, was down in the hold, killing and butchering everyone.

Somehow, he got back onto the dock, although he didn't know how.

He had been right about his men.

They were all stood around, not doing much of anything at all.

'We need to get the fuck out of here, and right now,' he managed to sputter breathlessly as he ran past them.

That was when he noticed that none of them were moving.

Not one!

He stopped. His hands fell to the side of his body, and he flapped them. His head looked up to the sky, as he breathed in.

Slowly, he brought his head around to gaze at each man. They were all rooted to the spot. Each one impaled on thick wooden beams. Their eyes were wide open, and every one of them was looking, accusingly, at him. Some were still alive. Bloodshot, bugging eyes followed him as their host's bodies twitched and convulsed in the throes of death.

The bell tolled again. This time it was slow and singular. Then the harp joined in. Again, this time it was different. It was harmonious, beautiful, melodious. Gerald hung his head, his chin touching the zip of his gore streaked jacket.

He couldn't move.

Actually, this wasn't entirely true. He could move, he just didn't want to. He had seen enough in this life. He had caused enough misery. What with the drugs, the torture and murder of competition, and what he had forced those poor eastern European girls to do. It was all just too much for him.

'ARE YOU REGRETTING YOUR LIFE DECISIONS?'

The voice was deep. There was a seriousness about it, like it didn't know how to laugh. Like it didn't understand the concept of humour. It came from everywhere, and it came all at once. Gerald understood that it was mostly in his head.

'ARE YOU REGRETTING RAPING AND MURDERING THOSE TEENAGE GIRLS? ARE YOU WISHING THAT YOU HADN'T FORCED THEM INTO DEGRADING, UNNATURAL SEXUAL ACTS?'

The Contract

Gerald knew that this was the end. He dropped the gun and heard it clatter, even over the beautiful music, as it hit the stone floor of the dock.

'WHAT ABOUT THE CHILDREN YOU EMPLOYED TO RUN YOUR DRUGS? THE CHILDREN YOU CORRUPTED! COERCING THEM TO DO YOUR DIRTY WORK ... YOUR WET WORK?'

Gerald closed his eyes. In the darkness, he could see the faces of everyone he had ever killed. The faces of all the children he had ever used, the films of the women being brutally raped and murdered that he sold through his network of taxi drivers throughout London. His life was a sewer. He wanted it to be over.

'YOU ARE NOT WORTHY, GERALD CROSS. YOU WILL PAY.'

He opened his eyes and couldn't believe what he saw before him.

It was a boy. *Just a fucking kid!* he thought. But there was something different about this boy, something ... wrong.

Behind him was a troupe of teenage girls, all of them looking bewildered and lost, all of them following this child as if he were the Pied Piper of Hamelin. Where he walked, they followed.

'I THOUGHT OF ALLOWING THEM TO DO IT, BUT THEY ARE INNOCENTS. I DIDN'T WANT TO DIRTY THEIR... SOULS ON THE LIKES OF YOU.' The voice was coming from the youth's mouth. Gerald was having an issue believing that such a voice could come from someone so young; so small and thin.

He raised his hand and the bewildered women ran off into the night, almost as if it was a rehearsed act. Gerald watched them go. A gladness hit him. He was glad that they didn't have to suffer at his filthy hands. He looked over to the boy and smiled. 'Are you going to make it quick?' he asked, fully understanding what was about to happen.

The boy looked at him. There was no expression on his face, just dark holes where his eyes had been. He simply shook his head. Only the slightest of movements, but Gerald knew then that the end, what he thoroughly deserved, had finally come to greet him.

He nodded, accepting his fate, but glad of his repentance.

The boy advanced.

Gerald did something else that he hadn't done since he was a child.

He screamed.

~~~~

What was left of Gerald was in a heap on the stone cobbles of the old dock. The youth lifted his hood back over his wash of blond hair. He was finished with this one. He had only one job left to do.

He reached into his jacket and pulled out a handful of pristine white feathers. He placed one on the remains of Gerald, he placed one on each of the impaled men in the dockyard, and then one on both of the burnt men still lying on the stone floor.

He reached inside his jacket again, once more removing a handful of the same feathers, and made his way onto the deck of the devastated ship. From somewhere in the distance came the sound of police sirens wailing through the cold, wet night.

The Contract

16.

COX FELT HIMSELF being rocked, gently. He felt like he was on a boat. *Maybe I'm still in the Everglades,* he thought. Somehow, he didn't think he was. He was cold and a little bit damp, but he couldn't feel a warm breeze coming up from the cool water, and the damp, boggy smell was gone. Gradually he began to come around, out of the cotton wool blanket that his drowse had wrapped within.

'Cox! Come on, wake up, man,' a voice, a gentle, lulling voice from somewhere above him, was rousing him. 'Come on, man, snap out of it. We need you awake on this.'

He recognised the voice, but not where from.

The rocking became more forceful and the voice a little more alert. 'Cox, wake the fuck up, man, now.'

It was Symes.

He was trying to wake him up. That meant that there was something wrong. It meant that there was something happening, something important. His senses began to swim back to him. He could no longer smell the salty air. That had been overtaken by the stale smell of a room with an underlying stink of copper and ... shit.

Suddenly, he knew where he was. Suddenly, he didn't want to wake up. He screwed his eyes tighter and wished that he was somewhere else. He wanted to stay on the boat. Staying there was preferable to the images that had started to flow back into his mind. Images of a man strung up on light-fittings, the flesh stripped from his body. Left to die, horribly in pain. Left to be eaten by a dog.

Then the Florida Everglades came rushing back into his head. The horror of the young girl, eaten alive by the alligators while trying to keep her bound body above the water.

The world was a disgusting, horrible place, and Cox wanted, more than anything, to stay away from it. He wanted to live in a dream where he could spend his days floating around in a boat. Wherever he laid his hat, that would be his home.

Against his better judgement, he opened his eyes. He saw a dark, dirty sky above him, and he could feel a cold, wet wind, biting through his clothes, soaking him with a miserable dampness. He knew that he wasn't in Florida anymore. *Shit,* he thought, *this might not even be America anymore.*

He sat up, not really believing what he was seeing. He knew that he'd been in a room, in a house. He was one-hundred percent sure that he hadn't been in a wet, freezing cold dock in the middle of the night. He looked around. The greyness of the night was illuminated only by a shimmering orange. He recognised it as fire. He could smell damp, burning wood and plastic. Everything felt so real. He was wet and cold, and beneath the burning smell, he could smell the coppery smell of ...

Blood!

Oh fuck, please no, no more blood!

All around him were men. None of them were moving. He shook his head, closing his eyes, not wanting to witness the scene, not wanting to give it any reality. Unfortunately, the policeman within him took over and he was forced to look. On closer inspection, he realised that the men were not moving because they couldn't move. Thick, wooden beams had impaled them to the floor. These men were going nowhere ever again. He saw long white feathers flapping in the cold, biting wind. He turned his head and saw the ruined remains of a boat.

That was the source of the fire.

There was someone stepping off the ruin of the boat. It was someone he recognised, but once again he couldn't recall where from. The youth approaching him removed the hood from over his head, revealing the shock of blond hair from underneath. The handsome face with the glowing blue eyes beneath smiled at him.

Cox knew who he was!

~~~

With a deep intake of breath, he jerked upright from the floor of Matthew Fitchett's bedroom.

The Contract

Symes took a step back from the ferocity of his awakening. 'Jesus Christ! You scared me half to death,' he gasped.

Cox looked around him. Police were beginning to filter into the room, and there were two paramedics leaning over him, ready to tend to any wounds he might have.

'I'm fine,' he snapped, dismissing them with a wave of his hand.

'Are you OK, man?' Symes asked as he stood up.

Cox checked himself over, finding that there were no cuts or bruises or broken bones. 'Yeah, really, I'm good. Physically anyway. What about you? I saw you go down.'

Symes began to rub the back of his neck. 'Oh, I'm good. Bastard took me out with some sort of karate chop,' he grinned.

'I take it he got away?'

'Looks like it. Did you get a chance to talk to him before you went out?' Symes asked looking back up at the mutilated body that the forensic team were investigating.

'Nope, but I did get something. I don't know if I was hypnotised or something, but I had a crazy dream. If the dream checks out then our man Fitchett here and his friend Carr, are very much within this killer's MO.'

'Explain it to me in the car, we've got to get to the station. There's been a development.'

'Yeah?'

Symes nodded and helped his partner up from the floor.

Back in the Jacksonville PD station, both men were recovering from their ordeal.

'So, it checks out. Both Carr and Fitchett had hired a fan-boat for a few days. Apparently, they do it every year.' Symes was looking at a computer screen.

'And it seems that if we cross reference these dates with the dates of some of the missing girls from Marathon ...' Cox interrupted.

'We have a hit,' Symes finished for him. 'Carr and Fitchett were serial killers. We can't prove that right now, but we know it's the truth.'

'That's why they were taken out.'

'He only hits bad guys. Do we really need to continue this investigation? I mean, can't we just let him keep killing all these scumbags?'

'I hear you,' Cox nodded. 'I really do. But, just how long is it going to be before he hits an innocent? Or they're caught in his crossfire? Nope, there's no room for vigilantes. This guy needs to be taken off the streets, ASAP. So, what's this development you were talking about?'

'You ever been to England?' Symes asked. There was the ghost of a smile on his lips.

'No, why?'

'Well, that's all about to change.' He threw a file onto the desk where Cox was sitting. It had the seal of Interpol on the front of it.

'Interpol? We're working with the Europeans now?' he asked.

'Apparently, while we were, erm, otherwise occupied, there were multiple murders in an unused dock in Portsmouth, UK. Get this, over thirty people killed. Some of them burnt to death, some just plain torn apart before being purposely put back together ... incorrectly! One guy looked to have been literally beaten to death. Pulverised is what the report states.'

Cox looked up at his partner. 'What?'

Symes nodded. 'You heard me. This guy was bad. Gerald Cross. Drug dealer, pimp, wannabe film producer. He's been suspected of human trafficking and for distributing porn. Nasty stuff: bestiality, snuff, shit like that. A real piece of work. He was an affiliate of an Edward Steele, known locally and nationally as 'Eastend Ed.' An apparent bigwig in the country. He, by the way, is also dead. Killed right in front of his wife. His head was crushed. And guess who the witness said did it? A boy with blond hair, who left a feather when he'd finished.'

'A white feather?' Cox asked.

Symes nodded.

'And the others, at the dock? Did they have feathers too?'

'Yeah, they did.'

Cox shivered. It was his dream. It was less a dream, more a vision. 'Were the men on the dock impaled?'

Symes cocked his head. 'How did you know that?'

Cox dismissed the question. 'Well,' he said, grimacing. 'It looks like we're going to England. Do you remember what this guy looked like?' Cox asked.

The Contract

Symes shook his head. 'All I remember is that dog running off with the fucking strips of meat in its mouth. Then, waking up next to you, and not in the good way, if you get my drift!'

Cox smiled. 'I bet that was a shock for you?'

Symes offered him a sarcastic wobble of his head. 'I've woken up with worse,' he replied.

I bet you have! Cox thought.

17.

THREE THIRTY IN the afternoon, at the same time Cox and Symes were talking in their office in Jacksonville, four thousand miles away in Liverpool, England, a man in his mid-thirties answered a knock on his front door. His name was Simon Cole, and he lived in a run-down estate in the city. Everything about his appearance indicated that Cole had no job, or any source of recordable income.

He was thin, a little too thin, and his hair was long, shabby and greasy. It was in dire need of a wash, much like the rest of his body. He was wearing a vest that had once been white, and as he scratched at the crotch of his stained underwear, he uncovered holes in the garments where they weren't supposed to be.

The small hallway of the house was sparsely decorated, and what little wallpaper there was still clinging to the walls was yellowing and peeling.

The front door had long since seen any repairs, and it rattled as another loud knock shook it from its hinges.

'All right, all right. I'm fucking coming,' he mumbled through his unshaven mouth, spluttering some of the words through his missing teeth. 'Keep your fucking knickers on.' A smile spread across his face as he regarded the old clock that was still hanging on the wall, and miraculously, still ticking. 'Or maybe not,' he concluded.

He put his face towards the small spyhole and looked out. 'Who is it, and what the fuck do you want?' he shouted as the fish-eye lens within the hole offered him a distorted view of his overgrown front garden and the overgrown front gardens of his neighbours. Three-thirty in the afternoon was early morning for a man like Simon Cole. Especially on a Friday, when he'd spent most of the previous night walking the

The Contract

streets of Liverpool's student quarter, dealing whatever he needed to deal to make his sordid living.

He saw what he wanted to see, and his heart leaped in his chest. A young girl in a school uniform was stood in the garden. She was smoking a cigarette. Her hair was pulled back from her head, forming a tight and greasy ponytail. The piercings that she had in her nose made her look older than her years. 'It's me, Nikki. You know what I want.'

'How much?'

'For me? The usual.'

Simon smiled, and his hand involuntarily passed down, back towards the crotch of his underwear. 'How you gonna pay this time?' he asked. He knew how she was going to pay. Her saved up lunch money was not going to cover the price of the drugs she demanded. He had gotten a little bit in trouble last time, *but fuck, it was worth it,* he thought as he remembered what this girl had been willing to do for him to get her fix.

'I've got cash this time,' she replied.

Simon breathed out a sharp breath, and his head dropped a little bit.

'I've got some others with me. Are you going to let me in or what?'

'Hang on,' he shouted and moved back into the living room, grabbing an old, tatty pair of jeans and slipping them on. He took hold of the door handle and breathed in, deeply. *Maybe I can fuck all of them,* he thought, before remembering that the day after a particularly heavy session usually hampered his performances. *Cash would be good too,* he thought, remembering how much he now owed his supplier. He ran his fingers through his hair and then smelt one of his armpits. He was more than a little disgusted at the stink that was coming from him. He shrugged; he knew that she'd done things to him when he was in worse states. *This one is a little addict,* he thought as a dangerous smile spread across his face.

'OK, I'll let you in, but I'll warn you, I'm not decent.'

'Since when have you ever been decent?'

It was a fair question, and as he opened the door, squinting at the sunlight that was now filtering through into his grotty little house, he saw Nikki standing in the alcove. He watched her eyes as they roamed up and down his scrawny body. His brain registered the disgust on her face, but he didn't care. He had the upper hand here.

Nikki's plump body strained her school uniform, and her thick legs were barely contained by the long green socks she was wearing. She looked maybe seventeen at a push, even though he knew for a fact that she had only just celebrated her fifteenth birthday. He knew this because he knew her family. He also knew what they would do to him if they ever found out what he had been doing to her.

'At last. I've been standing out there like a fucking lemon,' she spat as she barged past him, into his hallway. 'Come on,' she commanded the small group of girls, who Simon had missed as they were stood around the corner of the house, out of the scope of the fish-eye lens.

He watched as the group of five young girls marched into his house. The youngest, he guessed, might have been thirteen. He smiled as he closed and locked the door behind the last. 'Right then, what can I do for you girls today?' As he asked the question, he tried his best to hide the stutter that was trying to force itself out of his mouth. He was nervous. He had never been in a situation like this, where it was just him and six girls. He had always been rather wary of the opposite sex.

'You know what we want, Simon. So, stop arsing about and just give it to us ... all of us.' As Nikki spoke, she looked around at her friends. They were all giggling and laughing as Simon squirmed at the intention of the innuendo.

'How much do you want?' he asked as he felt his face change to a deep crimson. He had always had a thing for young girls in school uniforms, and now, having six of them in his living room was making his stomach churn.

'I'll have my usual, plus another half on top,' she shrugged, trying her best to look cool before her friends. 'Because I like it, and because I can,' she laughed. The rest of the girls laughed too. 'I'd say that these lot are going to want a twenty quid bag each. None of them have done it before, and the last thing you want is an unconscious fourteen-year-old on your living room floor, isn't it?'

In the real world, that was exactly what he wanted. One search of the hard drive on his computer, and a quick look at his 'dark web' history would inform anyone that he was a deviant. The thought of a helpless, girl, underaged or not, defenceless to his advances, made him break out in a sweat. But he could see her reasoning. He couldn't bring any heat down

112

The Contract

on himself. If the police got wind of his house, he'd be going down for a long stretch. That's if he didn't grass. But the thought of grassing on Forshaw! That was not an option. He'd be down for years. Years without probation, years without drugs, and years without anyone willing, or able, to prop him up, to watch his back. He wasn't stupid. He knew that he'd be easy pickings in prison. He'd be beaten within the week, someone's bitch within the first six months, and possibly even dead within the year.

No, he knew that an unconscious fourteen-year-old would be bad news for everyone involved.

'Twenty quid bags it is then.' He turned to address the rest of the girls in the room, who were sitting around on his threadbare sofa and chairs. 'You've all got cash on you?' he asked, feeling the blood rise in his cheeks again. He knew, no matter how much he would be willing to give them discount for favours, and by the looks of some of them, they would be willing to take that deal, he knew that including Nikki's score, he would be up nearly one-hundred and fifty. *Not bad for a morning's work,* he thought with a smile.

Each girl produced their money and Nikki went around collecting it from them. 'There you go,' she said with an uplifting tilt in her voice. 'One-hundred quid.'

Simon counted it. Pleased that it was all there. 'Your score's going to cost you fifty.'

Nikki's face contorted into a grimace. 'What? Fifty? I've just got you all these new customers.'

'Yeah, and what you're going to get should be at least seventy-five. So, cough up!' Simon held his hand out towards her.

She dropped her head and cozied up to him, running her hand up and down his skinny, bare arm. She knew that he liked being tickled, she knew that from the last time she had paid off her debt 'in kind.'

'Is there anything I can do to, you know, reduce it?' she purred.

Simon pushed her away. He needed the cash to pay Forshaw, but, once again, he wasn't stupid. He knew that the next time he got to have sex might be weeks, maybe months away. *Unless I get myself a brass,* he thought. But he was in the doghouse with the brothel on Millers Bridge; apparently, they didn't take kindly to him beating up their girls whilst in the middle of a coke-fury. 'Come on then! Get upstairs, but you best be dirty.'

Nikki smiled at him. 'Aren't I always?' As Simon made his way out of the room towards the stairs, she turned around to look at the girls. 'We're just going to sort some shit out upstairs.' She winked at them, getting a few giggles in response. 'Won't be long.'

One of the girls mouthed the words 'dirty bitch' towards her, which she responded to with her middle finger before following Simon towards the bedroom that she had frequented many times before.

'I hope you're going to wash your mouth out afterwards,' she heard one of the other girls shout as she ascended. She shook her head and smiled. As she reached the top, she saw him at the door of another room, other than the small box-room where she normally went to pay her way.

He inserted a key into the top lock and turned to face her with a large smile. *This is going to impress the fuck out of her,* he thought.

He unlocked three other locks and pushed the door. The wider it opened, the wider his smile became. Without saying another word, he flicked a light on and stepped inside.

'Fucking hell,' Nikki gasped as she followed him. 'Simon, there's a fucking tonne of shit in here! Where the hell did it all come from?' Her eyes had grown wide and greedy, like a child entering a toy shop at Christmas.

'Never you mind. All you need to know is that it's not mine. It'll all be shifted in a few weeks. Then, and only then, do I get my payday.'

'Payday?' she asked, not even looking at him. Her eyes were drinking in all the bagged-up delights that were before her. 'How much are you getting?'

'About thirty grand,' he replied, puffing his chest out.

'Jesus! What the fuck is a scruff like you going to do with thirty grand?' she asked, turning around to look at him.

'I'm getting the fuck out of here, that's what. I'm going to take myself off somewhere nice, and never ever come back to this shitty little estate.'

'Will you take me with you?'

With thirty grand? I don't fucking think so, he thought, but said, 'If you want to.'

'Where would we go?'

'Let's talk about that later. I need to get these bags down to your mates, and you still owe me fifty quid.'

The Contract

'What?' she asked, her head snapping back to look at him. 'I thought …'

Simon pushed her away. 'Well, you thought wrong then, didn't you? I need the cash. If you need any more later or tomorrow, then you can suck me off for it then. Right now, is not that time.'

Reluctantly, she took out three notes from her pocket and handed them to him. Two twenties and a ten.

'Happy days,' he said as he folded the notes into the same pocket as the hundred she had given him downstairs. He grabbed a few of the ready-made bags and handed them over to her. 'Here you go, these are pre-measured. Twenty quid bags.'

That was when the crash from downstairs filtered up, past the stairs, into the unlocked room.

Simon stopped talking instantly and looked towards the door. Nikki did the same. In quick succession, there followed another crash, louder this time, followed by a series of screams coming from the girls downstairs. He heard running and shouting as five frightened schoolgirls sped out of the living room, towards the front door.

'What the fuck?' he asked, leaving the room and looking down the stairs. He watched as the girls clawed and scratched at the front door, all of them trying their best to get away from … something that he couldn't see. 'What the fuck's going on down there?' he shouted towards them.

They all ignored him; they were too busy trying their best to escape from something else, something scarier than he was.

He ran back into the room and grabbed a baseball bat that he kept for emergencies. He swallowed hard as he felt the adrenalin surge through his body. For a moment, he thought he was going to be sick. 'You stay here,' he barked at Nikki.

She didn't need telling twice.

He rushed out of the room. He was quite the different person once he had a bat in his hands, no longer the bumbling, snivelling coke-fiend from earlier. He sped down the stairs ready to confront whoever had broken into his house and was currently scaring his customers.

Expecting to see a large man with a mask covering his face and a weapon, he was rather confused when the only person in the living room was a short, young kid wearing a black track suit with a hood covering his blond hair. Simon was momentarily taken aback by the youth's appearance, and he felt a little silly still holding onto the baseball bat. This man, this *boy*, wasn't threatening at all.

'Who the fuck are you? And, what are you doing in here?' he asked, pointing the bat at the youth.

An odd feeling churned within his stomach as the boy's eyes moved to look at him. A sense of relief passed him when they left his face and looked beyond him at the squabbling pack of girls at the front door.

'GET OUT!'

The voice came from the boy, but Simon didn't know how. It sounded like a lot of voices, all shouting together. He very nearly dropped the bat in his haste to cover his ears from how loud it was. That was before he noticed that the front door had opened, and the five girls were all falling over each other to get away.

As they left, Simon, with a ruffled brow, turned his attention back to the boy. He hadn't moved. The only difference was that his full attention was focused back on him. His expressionless, fresh face unnerved him. 'You'd better start talking, kid, or I'm going to wrap this fucking bat around your head and someone's gonna have to carry you out of here. You hear me? I'm fucking talking to you, dickhead.'

The boy said nothing.

Simon readjusted his sweaty palms on the grip of the bat. *Look at this fella,* he thought. *Short and skinny, I can fucking have him.* 'I'm giving you this last chance. What the fuck do you want?'

The boy said nothing still, he just looked at him with his expressionless face.

'Right! You can't say I didn't warn you.' With that, Simon charged. He knew that he had to protect the merchandise, otherwise his life wouldn't be worth living. He needed that thirty-grand payoff, *I need it a lot more than this little prick needs his life.* He swung the bat as if he were attempting a homerun at Yankee Stadium.

The irony of that would have been lost on Simon, with him not knowing much about baseball and nothing about DeGrassie, who had been killed in the stadium by the very same person he was confronting now.

The bat connected with the boy's head.

The Contract

It was a good swing, and on any other day, Simon would have expected the recipient of such a hit to go down in a crumpled heap. Probably never to get up again.

But, the normal laws of reality didn't seem to be working today.

The jolt of metal and wood as the bat bounced off the youth's head ripped through the weapon, tearing it out of his hands. It clanked as it hit the floor. Simon yelled in pain as his hands throbbed from the recoil. He stared at his empty hands for a few moments before remembering that the youth he had just hit was still stood before him.

The boy still had the same expression on his uninjured face.

Simon's brain was not processing this information correctly. *This has got be some crazy drugs shit,* he thought. *There's no way anyone could still be standing after taking a hit like that.* Even though he wasn't feeling particularly cohesive, apparently his thoughts were.

The youth moved his head, ever so slightly, to look at him. Simon saw that his sparklingly blue eyes had changed somehow. They were not like eyes at all, they were like endless black holes. Holes that could swallow him whole. *If I fall into them,* he thought, his body shivering from head to toe, *I don't think I'll be collecting my thirty-grand.*

It was this thought that compelled him. He wasn't bothered that this boy could be some kind of supernatural being, he didn't really care about falling into the madness of his abyss eyes; all he cared about was the thirty thousand pounds that he was due to collect at the end of next week for storing all of these drugs for Forshaw. This thought broke him free of whatever trance he had been caught in. He took one more look at the bat on the floor, squinting to see if there really was a crack through the toughened wood of the shaft or if it was just his eyes playing tricks on him, before bolting back up the stairs, taking them two and three at a time.

Back in the room, he never noticed that Nikki was nowhere to be found. Right at this minute, Nikki didn't even exist to him. All he was interested in was protecting his investment from the hands of the *weird psycho* in his living room.

He reached underneath the table from where he had produced the bat, and his hands fell on something else that he kept under there. Something hard, cold, and metallic. He'd gotten it for situations like this one. Situations where the threat of a baseball bat didn't quite cut it.

He pulled out the handgun and looked at it. There had been many nights, usually high on some of the drugs that he was hoarding, when he would pull this gun out and point it. He would clean it, check the bullets, and then point it. Usually at his own reflection in the mirror, usually muttering some inane quotes from films he had seen as a kid. 'You talking to me? Who the hell else can you be talking to? You talking to me? I'm the only one here, who the fuck do you think you're talking to?' was among his favourites.

Today, there would be no quotes, no joking around. Today was real. Today he was finally going to get to use this thing.

Oh, he had used it on some of the young girls in his house. Things seemed to change, sexually, when he produced a gun. They were suddenly ready to do anything for him. Nikki was different. She liked it when he pointed the gun at her head while she was sucking his cock. Some of the others? *Well,* he smiled to himself, *they got the job done and got themselves a bag of crack for their efforts.*

He weighed the gun in his hand, smiling at the feel of it. Then he looked up, ready to sort out the business waiting for him downstairs. Only the business was no longer in his living room. The business was staring at him from the small landing at the top of the stairs.

The same empty expression was on his face, and the same deep, dark holes were his eyes. Simon fancied that he could see the darkness seeping out of those holes.

He clicked the safety off and pointed the weapon at the boy. 'Get the fuck out of my house. I'm not going to ask you again. This time I'm telling you.'

More blackness seeped from the holes. Like a deep, dark fog, creeping in over a night-time shore. Simon knew that if he didn't do anything about it, that blackness was coming for him.

A banging from somewhere inside the house, *(or was it from inside his eyes?),* filled his head. It was music. He normally preferred music from Manchester's golden age of the Happy Mondays or The Stone Roses, so this *classical shit* was playing with his emotions. Trumpets and harps and *fucking flutes.*

A single tear fell from his own eye. This was the last straw for him. *Fuck this and fuck him. He's not stopping me from getting my money.*

He squeezed the trigger.

The Contract

The gun fired.

His aim was true, and he hit the youth in his chest.

The boy didn't even recoil from the impact. Even though Cole's ears were ringing with the deafening sound of the gunshot and the depressing music, he still had time to notice a small sound. A sound that should never have registered.

It was a small, metallic dink. Simon's eyes searched for its source. His brain was still playing tricks on him. The guy was surely dead. *So why had no one told* him *that?* he thought.

He found the source of the dink. It was a bullet. It was crumpled and distorted, lying on the dirty floor of his house.

Shaking his head to clear it from all stupid thoughts of this guy being some kind of superhero, Simon fired the gun twice more. Both shots hit their target. One in the face, one in the shoulder.

There were two more dinks as both bullets fell harmlessly to the floor.

Kevlar, he thought. *Where the fuck did he get Kevlar?*

He didn't stop to think that there was no Kevlar armour that could protect an uncovered face. His brain, once again, wouldn't register that fact.

Simon shot another three times. Once again, all three bullets hit their unmoving target. Again, all three bullets dinked as they hit the floor.

'What are you? What the fuck are you?' Simon whispered as the useless gun dropped out of his hands.

The stranger didn't talk. He just continued to stare. His expression had not changed from the same blank one he had downstairs.

'What the fuck do you want?' Simon was crying now. It was something about the visitor's face, mixed with the monotony of the music that was filling the room around him, that made him want to cry. It made him feel sorry for all the people he had hurt in his life. For disappointing his mother and father, for abusing all those underage girls, for selling drugs to twelve-year olds and watching them ruin their lives. He wanted to cry for himself. *Look at me,* he sobbed inside his own head. *I'm thirty-three and I'm about to die in dirty underwear in a rented shithole.* He wanted to cry for the little boy he had been, the one who had so wanted to be in the army, and then to be a policeman. The one who had watched the A-Team and so wanted to be The Face. He used to be the little boy who had done so well in school, only to fuck it all up for a hit of coke every now and then. *Now* becoming *then* far too often, before it finally fucked his whole life up.

Simon fell to his knees, flopping his hands uselessly before him. The youth took a step forward. He reached out and grabbed a handful of Simon's disgusting vest. With a strength that he had never felt before, Simon felt himself being forced up. His hands flailed at the hand that was holding him. His fight was pathetic and half-hearted, it wasn't long before he gave up, resigning to his fate.

I deserve this, he thought between stuttered sobs.

He felt himself being thrown. The short flight through the air took longer than he thought it would, probably because everything that was happening to him now was in slow motion. All the air rushed out of him as his back struck the wall. The force of the impact cracked the dirty plaster, making it snow. He then crumpled and folded like a disused rag doll onto the dirty, single mattress below.

In an instant, the youth was on him again. Through blurred, teary eyes, Simon watched as he took hold of a five-hundred-pound, pre-weighed bag of cocaine. As he regarded it, Simon witnessed something that he hadn't seen happen since the youth had come into his life, less than four minutes ago, *or was it a lifetime,* he couldn't tell which. The young man's facial expression changed. He regarded the bag of white powder as if it were a bag filled with filth. Then, without further ado, he tore open the plastic and the room was instantly shrouded in a white mist.

There goes my thirty-grand, he thought. Even though he knew that his life was in some serious danger, it was this that upset him more.

The young man reached out and grabbed Simon's hair. He pulled him forward. Simon had the clarity to notice that a white dusting of powder had settled over his blond beard just before he dragged the big plastic bag of powder over Simon's head.

He was struggling to escape. All his movements were to no avail due to the unnatural strength of the man holding him. His body writhed where it was able, resisting the attack as best as it could. A strong arm restricted the movement of his chest and sternum, causing him to cough and splutter. Each time he did, his lungs expelled his breath rapidly into the bag, causing it to inflate. White dust filled the interior, clouding his vision. Naturally, his lungs needed to replace the air it had just exhaled, and as they did, they also ingested huge quantities of the uncut, almost pure, narcotic around him.

The Contract

The powder raced into his nose and down into his lungs. It filled his mouth, and he gagged as he swallowed. The shock of what was happening to him doubled with the pain in his chest and ribs. He began to choke; he could do little else. His eyes widened and moistened as the drugs filtered into his system. His heart raced, double, treble, quadruple time. He could practically feel it banging against his ribs, dancing, or trying desperately to break free, to escape its earthly prison and make a run for it. Through clouded eyes and the cocaine lined plastic bag, Simon could see his aggressor above him. He could still see those once blue, now blackened, abyss-like eyes.

As if speeding through a tunnel with no brakes, he felt himself doing the one thing he didn't want to do since he'd seen the eyes change. He felt himself being sucked into the black vortex. The darkness was, to him, the only thing visible apart from a blinding white light. A thorough whiteness, like pure, driven snow, with only two deep, dark wells staining the unbroken landscape.

Simon knew that all was now lost.

As if from above, he could see himself bleeding; bleeding and burning at the same time. He watched, fascinated as his own skin darkened to black, flaking like the skin of an over-cooked ham. His flesh glistened, then cracked. Between the cracks, blood oozed and dripped before bubbling and rapidly congealing. Eventually, that too burnt. He could smell the roasting of his own body, even despite his nostrils being clogged with cocaine.

With disgust in his heart, he found the smell alluring.

To his relief, his blurred relief, as the drugs began to take a hold of his conscious thoughts like slippery fingers working their way through to his brain, the bag was removed from his head, and his floating-self crashed from its elevated position back into his physical body. The fresh air hit him like a blessing, and he breathed deeply, attempting to take in as much of the clean, sweet, cold air as he could. His relief was short lived. The bag had been removed because it had emptied, but it was soon replaced by another, fresh, full one and the actions repeated themselves. The bag was split open, and his head was forced inside.

He tried to hold his breath, knowing that it was a futile effort, but he felt like he needed to attempt to exert some control over what was happening to him. This rebellion was quelled by a punch to the stomach. Simon had been hit before, many times in fact, but never like this.

The shock from the assault caused him to breathe in a huge breath. In one breath, he inhaled and ingested almost fifty percent of the air in the bag, and almost the same percent of the narcotic powders with it. Euphoria from the first bag had kicked in, so he didn't feel the pain of his ribs smashing or his sternum cracking, as the drug had begun to numb his senses. Simon's gums and nose were both tingling, he had no sensation within his cheeks whatsoever. As he breathed, he felt the bag push tighter against his face. His lungs filled with the irritant of the grainy powder with every breath he took.

His nose was pouring blood. This, combined with the mucus and the powder it collected, began to roll down his face. His mouth and gums were also bleeding. Thick fluid seeped from between his lips, but mostly it dripped back down his oesophagus, mixing with the residue of the powder inside and causing him to choke.

Simon's mind jumbled and twisted itself inside and out in its frazzled attempts to comprehend what was happening to him. He could feel his body beginning to shut down, and he started to hear phantom sounds. At first, it was a flapping of wings, not those of a bird but of something greater, larger, and much more ominous. The music was back. This time it was louder and faster. It sounded like it was heralding back victors from a battle. His befuddled brain was trying to work out if the sounds he was hearing were real, or if they were the effects of the coke consuming his rational mind. This was a puzzle for another time, right now he was far too busy dying to think about such trivialities.

He began to convulse.

It was the sheer punishment that his body was absorbing that caused it. His heart continued to race ever quicker, and it seemed only a matter of time before it would burst.

The bag over his face had emptied, and a third was put in its place only for the cycle to be repeated.

His convulsions slowed as his body, unable to take any more, gave up. Simon Cole died, laying beneath his attacker. His ribs were smashed, his sternum cracked beyond repair, and his face was bloated and swollen. He was covered in saliva, mucus, blood … and cocaine.

~~~

The Contract

Once Simon's struggles had stopped, the young man holding him reached inside his black, hooded top. He pulled out a long white feather and placed it on the still body before him. Without a word, he got up and left the room.

Nikki was hiding underneath the bed. She was doing her best to stay quiet. She had watched the interaction between her dealer and the strange man, witnessing every small detail of the murder.

She remained in her hiding spot as the man left the room. She waited, anxiously, for the tell-tale sound of the front door banging, heralding his exit.

The sound never came.

For almost an hour she lay under the bed. She had wet herself in her terror, and her legs were now itchy with the dried, cold urine. The worst part of it was knowing that Simon's dead body, the body of the man she let have sex with her, that she had partaken in illegal practices for her age, for any age, with, was lying, dead, mere inches above her.

Eventually, a sound from outside got her attention. It was the wail of police sirens. Someone had called the police.

She knew that she was safe, for now at least.

18.

JAX AIRPORT WAS horrible. It was a mass of sprawling, interconnecting terminals with the same soulless shops selling the same soulless knick-knacks to the same soulless people.

Or so it seemed to Agent Cox.

I'm living my life in airports these days. This thought depressed him, more than it should have. Every airport that he saw just meant another hit by the White Feather Fever killer. A man who he had met, who had knocked him out with just a touch and given him some kind of strange vision. A man who had the ability to kill at will, in front of multiple witnesses, leave little to no evidence in his wake, and then pop up again on the other side of the world, only to kill again?

A man who might as well be a ghost.

They were no further into solving this case, and the bosses back in DC were beginning to crawl up his ass.

They had originally been told to book tickets to fly into Portsmouth, a dock town on the south coast of England. There had been a massacre in an unused dock. A boat carrying drugs and sex workers had crashed into the dock wall. All on board had been mutilated and massacred, along with the men who were on the dock waiting for them. Each kill had their very own white feather. But they had been redeployed to Liverpool, another city in the UK, this one in the north-west. There had been two killings, both with white feathers, and at least one of these had a witness to the whole ordeal. A witness who was able to tell a story, not like the girls from the limousine.

Cox was hoping to be able to interview some of the sex workers from the boat, but as soon as the massacre had finished, they had fled, in the wind. He knew that they would never be seen again.

The Contract

The killings in Liverpool were more significant. Yes, they were smaller, less high profile than the dock killings, but they fitted the MO of the White Feather Fever killer.

One was a Mr Big in the Merseyside area. Grant Forshaw. He ran a security company who worked the doors of the pubs and clubs in the city centre. He also controlled the lion's share of drugs in the city. He was found naked and very dead in a bush in the grounds of his home. More than three hundred syringes had been inserted into his body, in almost every appendage that you could think of. The next one was a low life, scum dealer. He lived in a run-down estate in the north of the city. It was an area well known for drug gangs and prostitutes. Also, by no coincidence, the victim was a known holder for Mr Forshaw. One of many drug holders he employed throughout the area. They were usually residents in small, unassuming houses.

'Tell me again, how did this guy bite it?' Symes asked from the chair opposite him in the bar of the airport. They were both having a well-deserved drink before their flight into Manchester.

'He drowned,' Cox replied. There was a smirk on his face as he picked up his beer and took another long swig.

Symes looked at him, he had a smirk on his lips too. 'Drowned?' he asked, raising his eyebrows.

'Yeah! In a bag of cocaine.'

'*One* bag of cocaine?'

Cox laughed; it was a spluttering laugh filled with beer. 'OK then, he drowned in *three* bags of cocaine.'

'In all my days ...' Symes mused, sitting back in his seat and sipping his drink. 'In all my days, I've seen a lot of strange shit. But it takes going to Liverpool, the land of the Beatles, before I see a man drowned to death in over a grands worth of coke.'

'Let's not forget Mr Forshaw here. I mean, he had over three hundred syringes in him, including some places that syringes are *not* meant to go.'

Symes was laughing again. 'That must have been some painful shit. And, all of these are White Feather murders? I mean, we're sure they're not suicides?'

Cox burst out laughing again, spitting his beer out of his mouth. 'Jesus. I can imagine the coke thing being a suicide, but the syringes? Fucking bad way to go, that.'

'In all seriousness though, how does this MO fit our man?'

'Well,' Cox began. He didn't need his folder for this one as he'd been cramming on this murder, and the murders on the dock in Portsmouth. 'This guy, Simon Cole, had been the holder for Forshaw. He was also allowed to sell a little from time to time, as a reward for good work. Well, he used to cut his shares with some seriously bad shit. The police have stated many times that they think that he was to blame for several deaths from bad drugs in the vicinity over the last few years. They've never had the resources available to investigate it all properly. The worst thing about this guy is that his preferred customers were school children. He used to sell to some as young as twelve. There were rumours that sometimes he'd take his payment in other ways ...' Cox raised his eyebrows to emphasise what he was going to say, '...alternative to cash, if you get my meaning. The police, acting on this information, did some digging into him. They looked at his computer and they canvassed the neighbourhood. It wasn't surprising that there was some disturbing pornography on his hard drive.'

'Kids?' Symes asked, his face telling Cox all he needed to know about his take on that side of things.

'Among other stuff, yeah.'

'Shit man. I know I have my problems with the opposite sex, but fuck! Twelve-year olds. I hope this piece of shit died horribly. If the police knew about this, then why didn't they take him out sooner?'

'Because of this guy.' Cox took the folder out of his bag and pulled out a photograph. It was of a big man, with a bald head. The picture showed him getting out of a large, black, four-by-four car; an expensive one. 'Grant Forshaw. Allegedly, he had a lot of the police in his back pocket.'

'Shit, that goes on in the UK too?' Symes asked, his face showing his disgust again.

'Apparently so. Obviously, this is a picture of him before the syringes.'

'Well, I'm glad this filth has gotten a taste of his own medicine.' Symes sat back again and took another swig of his beer. 'Do you sometimes think that we should just leave this guy to his own devices?'

Cox nodded, it was only a small nod, but it spoke volumes about their work here. 'Anyway ... There was a witness to the Cole murder.'

'That's the drugs one?'

The Contract

'Yeah. There was a fifteen-year-old girl hiding under a bed in the house. She said that she saw the whole thing. She was there to score some drugs, she'd taken a few of her friends along too. I've heard that she's a delight to interview,' Cox rolled his eyes. 'A real credit to her parents. Anyway, she described the man as young, slim, blond, and good looking. Sound like our man?'

'Totally. Anything else.'

'She said she saw Mr Cole, the victim, put six bullets into the guy. Every one of them bounced off, landing crumpled onto the floor, next to her. Then she said that the man took three bags of coke and put them over Mr Cross's head before punching him in the stomach, one punch for each bag. In effect, forcing him to inhale the whole contents.'

'Was he wearing armour?' Symes asked, taking the file from Cox and looking at it himself.

'Maybe, but she's adamant that at least one bullet hit him in the face.'

Symes stared at the printed report. His eyes were narrow as he bit the insides of his cheek. 'Hmm! A reliable witness? Fifteen years of age, in a stressful situation. Possibly strung out on drugs?'

'Scene of the crime officers removed six bullets from the scene. All of them crumpled, and all of them used, just like she reported. They said they looked like they had been fired into a solid metal wall, or some other immovable object,' Cox replied, taking the file back from his partner.

'Flight BA-4403 to Manchester International is now boarding at gate fifteen-F,' the voice over the speakers announced.

'That's us, man,' Symes said swigging the rest of his drink while getting up out of his chair. 'I'm just going over to that shop there to get something to read for the flight. Twelve hours is a long time with nothing better to do.'

'There's always the stewardesses to harass,' Cox replied. He was joking, but just a little bit of him was serious.

Symes winked as he walked off.

~~~

Four hours into the flight and Cox had read and re-read the files on the Portsmouth massacre, the other related killing of Edward Steele, and the two murders in Liverpool back to back and cover to cover. He felt like he had all the information he needed to move this investigation along. He knew what the man looked like, and they knew what his MO was. The only thing niggling him, and it wasn't a small thing, was how would they arrest him if he didn't want to be arrested? Cox had seen him. He wasn't a big guy by any stretch of the imagination, but from all the evidence they had, he was freakishly strong, quiet as a mouse, a gymnast, and now bullet-proof. He was also able to take out twenty or so men all at the same time.

We're going to need a fucking army, he thought with a wry smile.

He was considering the possibility that this was a conspiracy. That it was an inside job, or there was a team of vigilantes all working in tandem to get rid of the criminal, low-life scum. But now that they were travelling across the Atlantic as guests of the British police force, who were now dealing with the same issues, he wondered if such a group could be acting together and collaborating over such large distances. *I suppose that in this age of the internet, it's possible,* he thought. *But they already have a specialist team of computer experts and terrorist cell specialists working on this in the background. They would have come up with* something *by now.*

Cox's head was pounding. He rubbed his eyes, trying to stem the constant throbbing behind them. He looked over to Symes's seat and was not surprised to see it empty, although he didn't remember seeing him leave it. He did remember watching him flirt outrageously with every stewardess who went past. He also watched every one of them respond positively.

He searched in his carry-on bag and produced a small box of paracetamol. He called for the stewardess for a glass of water. He swallowed the pills and settled down into his business-class seat to attempt to get some sleep. *This is going to be a futile effort,* he thought as he closed his eyes.

He must have had them closed for five minutes when he opened them again. As he did, he noticed that Symes was back in his seat. He leaned over and got his attention. 'You OK, man?' he asked.

Symes shot him a knowing smile and a wink. 'You know it, dude,' he replied.

'I can't sleep.'

The Contract

'I never can on these long-haul flights,' Symes replied. 'But I'm going to give it a go.' Cox watched as he snuggled down into his seat and was asleep before he had even folded his arms. He shook his head as he sat back into his own seat.

After a few minutes of squirming around, he knew that sleep was not coming any time soon. He turned on the little television on the back of the chair in front of him and flicked through the channels. There was absolutely nothing that caught his attention. He picked up the in-flight magazine and thumbed through that, but once again, there was nothing that could tear his mind away from the case and allow him some down time.

He looked over at Symes sleeping in his reclining chair and smiled to himself. His head was cocked over to one side, ruffling his usually immaculate hair, and there was a line of drool spilling from the side of his mouth. He laughed to himself. *If that stewardess sees him now, then for once he'll have no chance with her.* Then he saw the magazine that he had been reading. It was the *National Enquirer*. Once again, Cox chuckled to himself.

He caught the attention of the passing stewardess, who came over to him, all smiles and bright white teeth. 'I'm sorry, but could you do me a favour? Could you pass me that magazine that my friend over there was reading?' He pointed to Symes who moaned a little in his sleep before dribbling a little more and scratching at his crotch.

'Are you sure you want to read that? We have plenty more quality publications that are free of charge.' Her English accent was music to Cox's ears.

'No, thanks. I need a little distraction. I want to have a laugh instead of reading about doom and gloom all day.'

'No problem, sir. Is there anything else I can get you to make the flight more comfortable? Another pillow maybe?'

As she bent over to retrieve the magazine from Symes's seat, Cox couldn't help himself but admire the woman's shapely rear. She turned around and caught him looking, and he felt his face flush a bright red. *What would Symes do in this situation?* He knew that he didn't have it in him to laugh, to make a joke, and then probably end up in the first-class lounge toilets, having wild sex at thirty-thousand feet!

'Erm... no. That's all thank you,' he stuttered as the attractive woman handed him the magazine with a knowing smile. 'OK, sir. Have a nice flight,' she said, automatically, as she walked off down the fuselage.

Cox put his hands to his face, attempting to hide his embarrassment.

Well, she won't be coming back anytime soon, he thought as he opened the magazine and began to flick through the pages. The stories were garbage, all of them. Endless drivel about talentless celebrities having affairs with other talentless celebrities. Then stories about people who wouldn't even be famous if they hadn't applied for brainless TV shows where they had to prove just how stupid and uneducated, they were for six weeks while they 'dated.' All of them having major breakdowns and going into rehab. *Who reads this shit?* he thought, looking over at his sleeping partner.

One story did catch his attention, however. It was something that really shouldn't be in a newspaper like the National Enquirer, but there it was. It was a report detailing the polar icecaps, and the cycle they ran in over the course of thousands of years. It was trying to give a balanced argument that the melting wasn't completely due to global warming, but more to do with what it called the 'natural order of the planet.' Its argument centred around the fact that the icecaps expanded and retracted naturally, over the years. Apparently, according to scientists, whoever they may be, we are currently in a contraction phase.

To Cox, the story had meaning, and he was interested in the theory, but it had been dumbed down so much that he lost interest less than half-way through.

He was ready to put the magazine down and attempt some sleep again when another article buried in the back pages caught his attention.

Astronomical Anomalies Happening at Alarming Rate

The headline did its job at pulling him in. He used to love astronomy when he was kid. The thought of looking out at the stars had always fascinated him. He got himself comfortable, drank the last of his water, and began to read.

Leading Astrophysicist Dr Robert Broom from the University of

The Contract

Kent, England, has made a fantastical claim that there has been an abnormal number of strange Astronomical Anomalies in our skies over the last few months, maybe even years. He claims that he can pinpoint actual locations that the anomalies have alluded to and likens them to 'the Star of Bethlehem' event, said to predict the birth of Jesus Christ over two thousand years ago.

'The stars are aligning and then re-aligning at an alarming rate,' he states in his latest report. 'Two thousand years ago, three wise astrologers from the East followed an anomaly similar to these, and it led them to the Lord Jesus Christ. If the same occurrences are alluding to similar events, then it would be like a hundred or so Messiahs being born all within the same year. A lot of these anomalies have gone unnoticed, over the USA, but occur they have, and indicated various locations within in North America...'

The doctor of Astrophysics, who has held the chair at Kent University for several years, went on to pinpoint some of the locations.

'A few of the more recent activities pointed towards Baltimore in Maryland, New York, Wichita in Kansas, Ohio, Georgia, and Jacksonville, Florida ... all of these just within the last month.'

The professor continued to state that these occurrences are rare, and so many within such a short period should be unheard of in the world of astronomy. He also claims that he is able to track these anomalies and even predict when the next ones will occur.

'I have devised a formula, based on the historical evidence, that should predict when and where the next anomaly will occur. I can say, with a certain level of authority, that the next ones will occur, not in the USA where the more recent ones have occurred, but right here in the UK.' He has predicted one over the city of Portsmouth and one over the historic city of Liverpool …'

At this point, Cox stopped reading and put the magazine down. *Did I just read that correctly?* he asked himself, looking over at his sleeping partner. He shook his head and continued to read.

He *had* read it correctly. Baltimore, New York, Wichita, Ohio, Georgia, and Florida. All the places that they had been to recently on this investigation.

He stared at Symes, not really seeing him, but just looking in his direction. His mind was somewhere else. It was reeling with this information. Could it be real? Could it be true that he was reading about these places, the places that he had visited in the past months, in connection with some celestial anomaly? Or, could it all be just a coincidence?

He took the file out of his bag and cross referenced each location against the article. They all matched.

What the Hell does this mean?

The conspiracy theorist in his head asked him if someone had accessed his FBI notes. Gotten them, put two and two together and came up with fifteen, then made a ridiculous story about the stars aligning and aliens. But then, if they did, how would they know that he would end up reading them? Especially if it was printed in a rag like the National Enquirer. The White Feather murders were big news, but surely, if someone was making up wild theories about his investigation, then they would be released to a wider audience.

The Contract

'Tell me again what the perp said to you back in Florida after he'd attacked me.' Symes was leaning over his seat, looking at the investigation folder and the strange news article.

'It's not really what he said, it's more what I saw. He grabbed me. I've never felt a grip like it before in my life. The power he had in his hands was unbelievable. He grabbed me and told me, by name, not to pursue him. He told me that his mission, his contract, was bigger than me, that it was bigger than the FBI. Bigger even than the whole of the USA. I'm not even sure if he spoke those words because I was still reeling from the vision regarding Carr and Fitchett.'

Symes looked at the front of the magazine. It had been published a few days ago. 'This is crazy. This rag was published last week, therefore the information in this article must have been written at least a week prior to that. So, he was reporting events that hadn't even happened at the time. He couldn't have known about Florida, or even Georgia at that point. Let alone the cases in the UK.'

Cox was shaking his head. 'Yet, there it is, in black and white. At first, I thought I was dreaming. Like I'd fallen asleep without realising it. But the fact that you're reading it too ...'

Symes was looking through the article again. 'I don't believe this. I really don't.'

'It looks like we've got our work cut out for us when we hit the ground in the UK. Where did it say he was a professor?'

Symes looked back through the article. 'Um, University of Kent,' he replied.

'Is that anywhere near Liverpool?'

Symes took his phone out of his pocket and connected to the business-class Wi-Fi network. 'It's not that far. About a four-hour drive.'

Cox laughed. 'A four-hour drive in the UK is over halfway across the whole island. It looks like we're going to have to make a trip into Kent and see this Professor Broom. If he's actively predicting these locations, then he just might know something about this case.'

19.

BOTH AGENTS WERE sat in a sparse room in a scruffy police station in Liverpool. The room was bland and beige. They had been given their own desk and a log-in for the computer system. Apparently, this was how they treated their 'cousins' from across the pond.

'You'd think a city like Liverpool would be sick of Americans coming over and poking their noses into everything that they were doing, you know, with the Beatles and all,' Symes whispered as a lovely young lady in uniform came in with a large plate of cookies and two more steaming hot cups of tea.

After gratefully accepting the gifts, Cox turned to his partner. 'This is the fourth cup of tea we've had since we've been here.' He looked at his watch. 'It hasn't even been three hours yet, and I've gone to take a leak twice already!' He was laughing as he took a swig of the hot brew. He nudged his partner and pointed to one of the policemen at a desk just outside the room. He picked up one of the cookies, or biscuits as he'd called them, although everyone knew biscuits were breadcakes you used to mop up your gravy. Both agents watched in horror as the man dunked his cookie into the hot cup he was holding before taking it out and eating it.

'What the hell is he doing in there? Is it some kind of mad cult thing? Are we going to have to bring them in for questioning?'

They watched as the same policeman picked up another cookie and dunked it into his tea. Someone spoke to him, and he looked up towards them, answering the query. When he took his cookie out of his cup, the agents watched in horror as the soggy thing broke and fell back into his cup with a splosh. Both agents looked at each other, shaking their heads with their mouths turned down.

'That's just... wrong,' Symes whispered.

The Contract

A huge man entered the room. He, too, was holding a large steaming mug in his hand, a hand that was dwarfing the cup he was holding. He was wearing a dark blue sweater with a white shirt underneath and a tie that matched the colour of his other garments. The collar of the shirt looked strained, due, mainly to the girth of the man's neck. He wasn't fat, just ... big!

'Gentlemen, I'm DS McNally,' he said in a deep voice, with a thick local accent that the two agents had trouble understanding at first. He put his mug down on the desk and offered them both his hand. His grip was powerful. 'You can call me Steve though, if you don't mind. I've never liked being called DS anything.'

In his other hand he held a brown card file. It didn't look very thick.

After Cox and Symes had introduced themselves, they all sat down around the small desk. Steve McNally had trouble getting his considerable bulk into the plastic, moulded seats that were provided.

'Jesus, these seats are uncomfortable,' he said as he wriggled about. 'Leave it with me and I'll get better ones brought in. Anyway, it's an honour to have you guys here. I'd be right in saying that you're the very first FBI guys we've ever had in our station. All our resources have been opened up to you.'

'Thank you, Steve. What I think we'd like to know first is any intel that you have on the Portsmouth dock massacre.'

'I thought you were here about the Simon Cole and Grant Forshaw case?' he asked. His face looking from one agent to the other.

'We are,' Symes continued. 'But we're going to need to know everything about that case too.'

'Well, I can certainly pull the evidence up on the computers about that one. That won't be an issue at all. But the other two that we have here, well we all just thought that they were another run-of-the-mill drug hit. We've been getting a lot of them lately, ever since our fucking useless government decided that the best way to cut costs were to cut people's safety.' He put the file that he still had in his hands on the table and opened it. 'That was until we found the white feathers at both scenes. Even then, the methods of killing seemed a bit strange, but Christ, we've seen all sorts over here. Anyway, it flagged up on the computer thingy that this could possibly be part of a bigger case. So, we did a bit of digging, and came up with your investigation.'

'Did you keep all the evidence bagged up and separate?' Cox asked.

McNally again looked from agent to agent. A big, soft smile broke on his face. He had the look of a jolly giant rather than a fierce ogre, but Cox thought that that could change in an instant if it needed it to. 'You want to see the feathers, don't you?'

Cox smiled back at him. 'Was it that obvious?' he asked.

~~~~

The evidence room was small and overcrowded. There was 'stuff' everywhere.

How do they keep track of everything in here?' Cox thought as he eyed the bagged items strewn over the racks of shelving.

The big DS took them inside, signing them in as he did. 'Just make sure you don't take anything,' he laughed.

Cox smiled, pretending that he had never heard that particular joke before. 'Did you get the feathers analysed?' he asked.

'Yeah! We sent them off to the labs in the university. They came back with nothing. Just like you guys did over your side. The only acceptable DNA that we could get from it was from the victims themselves. Just blood, mucus, sweat, and flakes of skin. It did flash up as organic. It was a zero for plastics, and they thought that the structure was similar to an eagle but was nowhere near to be any kind of match. The report came back stating that it was not out of the realm of being from a genetically altered creature, or even an engineered one. Although, they said that that's probably just wild speculation.'

Cox was impressed that this force had gone so in-depth in their investigation into where the feather could have come from. 'We speculated the same thing. But concluded why would someone go to the trouble of creating a new species only to use its feathers as a calling card for murder?'

'We've got more evidence down here. There are bags of coke. We have to keep them under lock and key in here,' he laughed. 'There's also Mr Cole's gun, the ruined bullets, the syringes from Mr Forshaw ... and this!' The big man struggled to reach down to the bottom of the shelves. As he came up, he made a loud sighing noise. 'I thought that this might make you guys feel a little more at home.'

The Contract

'What is it?' Symes asked, taking the bag from the big man.
'It's a snapped baseball bat.'
'A baseball bat?'
'Yeah. Apparently Cole attempted to wrap this around his assailant's head. To absolutely no effect whatsoever.'
'Any DNA on it?' Symes asked, looking into the bag.
'Only from Cole. Absolutely nothing else on it at all,' McNally answered, taking the bag back off Symes. 'We took the evidence from the young girl with more than a pinch of salt. She's a known entity around here. She's a loud-mouth, and what we call a hard-knock. She's only fifteen but is already known by us as serial user. She's been arrested for drunk and disorderly charges, assault, and theft. Basically, she's every parent's dream.'
'Or nightmare,' Cox concluded, not quite understanding the sarcasm in McNally's voice.
'Oh no, mate, not round here. If they don't have an ASBO, that's an anti-social behaviour order, by the time they're twelve, then they're seen as a lost cause.'
'Did you speak to her parents? When they came to pick her up?' Cox asked shaking his head.
'The girl's father is on the birth certificate as 'unknown.' Her mother is thirty-one, a druggy herself, on the sick, or what you guys would call the welfare. The grandparents are in their early fifties. This is the world we live in, gentlemen.'
'Can we see her? Can we interview her?' Symes asked, wiping his hands on his long, dark coat after handing the bag back to McNally.
'Sorry, guys. She was too young for us to keep in detention. Also, she'd need a chaperone to be interviewed by you.'
Symes and Cox shared a look.
'Although,' McNally continued. 'We did record her initial interview. It was in-depth too. You want to see it?'

~~~~

The three men and a woman officer were sat in an office upstairs in the police station. They were back in the uncomfortable chairs again. Before them was an eighty-two-inch television. The PC was built into the back of it, and the woman was currently operating it via the front screen.

'These things are excellent,' she was explaining. 'Not only are they high definition, 4K graphics, but they're networked right into the police infrastructure. All we need to do is log on, and we have access to any recorded interviews that are happening or have happened in the whole of the UK.'

'We can get the footy too, if we want,' McNally continued. His face burned a deep red when the two agents turned to look at him. 'Erm, I think you guys call it soccer. Anyway,' he coughed to clear his throat. 'We wanted to get this interview on tape as we knew that it was going to be important evidence.'

The woman officer pressed on the icons of a few folders, and a clear and crisp picture of a drab little interview room appeared.

'I guess those interview rooms don't change much from country to country,' Symes joked.

'I'm afraid not, Agent Symes,' the woman officer replied. Cox noticed her neck turn a deep shade of red as she addressed him. He rolled his eyes as he noticed Symes offer her a small wink in exchange for the look. In a little bit of a fluster, she turned her attention back to the screen and pressed the triangle to begin the recording.

There was a young girl, rather scruffy looking, with tied back hair and a smug look on her face. Sitting next to her was a court ordered official. He could tell by the look in the woman's eye that she wanted to be anywhere else other than there.

'I take it her mother didn't show then?' Cox asked.

The woman officer shook her head. 'We tried for hours and finally got through to her mother, but she was not making much sense. So, we appointed a solicitor for her.'

A deep, male voice boomed out of the speakers, causing the female officer to stand up and adjust the volume. Cox caught Symes staring at her behind in her tight, police issue trousers, and he nudged him. Symes shrugged; his brow ruffled. Cox glared before turning away.

'Can you state your name and address for the record? Also, the name and address of your parents?'

The camera zoomed in on the girl's face. She didn't look scared or intimidated by the questioning at all.

The Contract

'Me name's Nikki Driscoll,' the girl's voice droned. Cox had trouble understanding what she was saying. 'I'm fifteen. Me address is thirty-two Gawford Crescent, Norris Green. Me mar's name's Brenda, and she lives in the same house.'

'We seriously thought of getting subtitles for you guys for this. Her 'scouse' accent is quite thick.'

'Scouse?' Symes asked.

'Yeah, scouse,' McNally replied. 'Can you hear my accent?'

Both men nodded.

'Well, that's scouse. It's unique, but it can get a bit thick at times. If you get stuck, I'll translate.'

'My name is Detective Riley, and this is Detective Broad,' the female voice, off camera, spoke in soothing tones. 'I just want to let you know that you're not in any trouble here. We only want to know your version of events in Mr Simon Coles' house on Monday the twenty-third of September. You know the address Nikki, eighty-six Carnaby Street.'

The girl looked into the camera and surprised the two agents by raising her middle finger up and mouthing the words 'fuck off' in an obvious manner.

Another female voice spoke then, still using the same soothing manner, obviously trying to keep the girl calm and make her feel safe and secure. To Cox, the girl looked more than comfortable, and not in the least bit worried.

'Would you please tell us, for the record, what you were doing at Mr Coles' address on that day? Don't worry, this information will not incriminate you in any way. We're not here to judge, just to get the facts of what happened. Once again, I'll reiterate, you're not in any trouble here, none whatsoever.'

The girl's eyes looked dark as she regarded the two detectives behind the camera with suspicion. The woman sat next to her, her council, leaned in and whispered something into her ear. The girl's distain stretched towards this woman now too, and she shook her head as if the woman was stupid.

'He was me mate. I was there on me own to watch some telly and that,' she replied. Her accent was thick, but Cox was just about able to make sense of what she was saying. 'I was on me own too,' she concluded.

'Now, Nikki, we know that you were not there alone that afternoon. We know that you were there with at least another five girls. We have witnesses that saw you all going into the house, and we have the same witnesses who saw the other girls, without you, rush out of the house in a state of, shall we say, distress?'

Nikki shrugged as she leaned back into her seat. 'What can I tell ya? I'm not a grass.'

'You won't be a grass, Nikki. As I said before, neither you, nor anyone else in your group are in trouble. We just need you to tell us, on the record, how many of you there were inside that house on the afternoon of the twenty-third.'

The other voice from behind the camera spoke then. 'We need you to tell us, so we can substantiate your stories.'

Nikki grimaced, making her double chin a little more pronounced. 'What does that mean?' she asked.

'It means us putting all your versions of events together and linking the bits that are similar. Everyone has a different take on what happens at an incident. As we listen to the stories, bits jump out that are in everyone's versions. We analyse them and come up with as close to the truth as we can.'

'Well then, OK, I *was* with some others. I'm not going to give you their names though. You're fucked if you think I'm getting anyone else into trouble for this. I wouldn't last two minutes out there if they thought I'd grassed.'

'We don't want their names, Nikki. We just want you to tell us that they were there. Now, please go on,' the soothing voice encouraged from behind the camera.

'Well, we went there to hang out, you know?' She gave the two officers behind the camera a glaring look, as if daring them to challenge her on that point. When no one did, she continued. 'I went upstairs with Simon.' Her face changed then as if she'd said something that she shouldn't have. 'Not for anything like that. Fuck that, he's an old man. I'm not a slag. No, I went up to get a coat that I'd left the last time I was there. Anyway, me and Si were upstairs when we heard a crash. A proper bang, and all the others started to scream. I heard them running, trying to get out of the house. Si always keeps the front door locked, you know what it's like around there, robbing bastards. So, none of them could get out. They were all fighting each other at the door. That's when

The Contract

Si must have thought that he was getting robbed, as he took out this big bat from underneath his table.'

'The table with the drugs on it?' One of the voices asked.

The woman next to Nikki leaned in and whispered again. Nikki nodded.

'The table that was in the room. Anyway, I was shitting meself right about now, but he ran downstairs with the bat, ready to defend his house, y'know, like you do. That's when the voice came. This mad voice. It sounded like there were about thirty or forty people all shouting at once.'

'What did the voice say Nikki?'

'It just told the girls to get out. Just like that. GET OUT,' she shouted, making the woman next to her jump a little. 'Then, the door opened, one of them must have gotten to the snip. I watched them all leg it. That was when I heard a bang and a snap. Like Si had hit a metal bar with the bat and snapped it. He came legging it back upstairs and the next thing I knew, he had a gun. I didn't even know he owned one, he'd never shown it to me or anything. So, I thought, 'fuck that' and hid under the bed. I was there for a laugh, not for messing about with guns.'

'The rest is in the report,' McNally interrupted, indicating to the female officer to pause the video. 'She gave us a description of the man. Said he looked like some fella off one of the soaps on the telly. I don't know his name, but this is his picture." McNally rummaged through the thin file on the desk and produced a publicity shot of a handsome young man. Blond hair, blond wispy beard, big blue eyes.

'Can I see that?' Cox asked holding his hand out towards the big DS. As he looked at the picture, he felt his heart drop into his stomach. A flash-back to Jacksonville, to this man holding his arm and ... *What, Cox? What did he do then? Project a memory into your head? No, he assaulted you, and you had a dream. That's all it was!*

'If you removed this guy's blue eyes and replaced them with black holes, then you'd have our man,' Symes said looking over Cox's shoulder.

'What?' McNally asked, cocking his head to one side.

Cox shook his head, dismissing the question.

'Do we have the movements of this guy over the last few months?' Symes asked.

McNally nodded his head. 'Yup. He's been filming in Yorkshire. All accounted for, for every date on record of the White Feather Fever murders.'

The female officer, who had hardly taken her eyes from Symes the whole time, then stood up. 'This is where the tape starts to get interesting gentlemen,' she said pressing the pause button on the big screen.

The girl on the screen was talking again. She was looking like she was enjoying herself now. 'So, he's, like, looking at his gun and stuff when the fella turns up at the door. Si starts to pump him with bullets. At least three, I think. The noise was proper loud, and me ears were ringin'. I snuck a peek out from under the bed, expecting to see the fella lying on the floor, dead or bleeding or something. But he's just stood there. A blob of metal landed next to me. I didn't know what it was, but I could tell that it was hot. It wasn't until another one fell on the floor that I realised that they were bullets. The other shots that Si did ...'

'How many in total do you think you heard?'

'I don't know.' Nikki shrugged. 'Five, maybe six? Anyway, the fella was stood there, dead hard like, so hard that not even bullets could hurt him. Then, the next thing I know, he's on Si. I was going to get out and try to help him, but ...' she put her head down, 'I was too scared. I think I'd pissed me knickers to be honest. I heard a scuffle, and muffled shouts. Maybe a couple of punches, then it went quiet. The next thing, the fella left. I was under there for a bit, like, too scared to move. It wasn't until the busies turned up that I felt it was safe enough to get out.'

McNally pressed the stop button on the screen and the interview went off.

'What are 'busies'?' Symes asked looking at the female officer.

She blushed a little and played with her neck. 'Erm, it's a local slang for the police. You know, busy, as in busy-bodies!'

Symes nodded.

'We've cross-referenced a few of the other girls' accounts of what they saw that afternoon, and they all say the same thing. The assailant was young, good looking, but strange. They all said he had 'dead looking eyes.' To be honest, it's freaked out quite a few of our guys here. Both deaths, both unexplained, and the only witnesses describing something out of a comic book. That's when we ran it through the database and came across your investigation. So, we chased it upstairs, and the call to your bureau was made.'

Cox and Symes both stood up. 'Well, Steve. We must thank you for the information exchange. It's been most invaluable to us.'

'You can have all our files if you want them, and a copy of the interview. Diane, sorry, Officer Gartside, here will assist you with anything else you might need. I'm so sorry, but I've got another matter that I need to attend to.' He indicated the female officer next to him. She smiled at Cox, and he noticed that the smile grew a little wider as her eyes fell all over Symes.

'Anything we need?' Symes asked, his best wolfish grin making an appearance as he looked her up and down.

Officer Gartside blushed a deep crimson as she looked away. 'Not the way you're thinking, Agent Symes,' she laughed as a rebuff.

That's what you think missy, Cox thought to himself. *Once Adam here has you in his sights...* 'Well, thank you Diane,' Cox started.

'We're staying in the Hilton Hotel, downtown,' Symes said, imparting information that the officer already knew, but Cox knew that there was an ulterior motive. 'I'm sure we could find our way there eventually. But I was wondering if you could accompany us, just to make sure we're on the right track?'

'I'm going to read through these documents for a bit longer. Why don't you two go, and I'll catch up with you later?' Cox didn't want anything to do with whatever these two were going to get up to. He was itching to read up on the professor at Kent University.

As Gartside and Symes made their way out of the little office, Cox called his British counterpart back for a moment. 'Erm, Diane,' he shouted. She turned around, the smile on her face told him that they hadn't been talking about the case. 'Do I have a login for the computer system?'

'Oh, yeah. Username is fbiguest, password is fbiguest, the FBI bit is uppercase,' she replied.

'Right, thanks.'

As they left, Cox logged onto the computer. He didn't want to use the big screen. He opened his favourite search engine and typed *Dr Robert Broom, Kent University*. There were quite a number of hits on the name, most of them giving the same photograph of a small looking man, bald on top, with a cheerful face, finished off with thin, gold-rimmed glasses.

He spent a bit of time reading up on him. The man came across as a serious academic and not at all the type to fly off on flights of fancy. He was well thought of by his peers and his students in the University, and also by the scientific society at large.

He made his decision right there to contact him.

Logging off, he made his way over to the front desk and addressed the officer behind the counter. 'How do I get to Kent University from here?' he asked.

~~~~

Later, when he got to the hotel, he knocked on the door of Symes's room, next to his. There was no answer. He knocked again, a little louder.

He heard the sound of giggling coming from inside. He wasn't alone. He tutted. *I'll tell him in the morning,* he thought as he opened his door and entered the darkness beyond.

The Contract

20.

IT TURNED OUT that Kent University was further away than they thought it was.

'I don't understand how a five-hour journey in the UK can seem so much longer than a five-hour journey in the US.' Symes was shaking his head as he gripped the steering wheel of their rented car. His knuckles were white as his grip tightened. 'I mean, do they really need to do maintenance on every road, every fucking twenty miles?'

'It would appear so,' Cox replied, reading his report. 'So, do you want to tell me about Officer Gartside?'

Symes looked at him. Cox thought he saw anger in the stare, anger that soon dissipated into regret and a little shame too.

'There's nothing to tell. We went out and had a few drinks. She instigated everything,' he confessed. 'It's not like I forced her into it.'

'Adam, we need to take a professional approach to this investigation. I feel like we're actually getting somewhere, the last thing we need is for some random woman putting in a complaint against you for sexual misconduct or some other bullshit, and then you're taken off the case.'

Symes shook his head and sighed. 'I know, man. I really do. Sometimes I just don't know what it is. If a girl so much as looks at me, I make it my mission to have her. It's a drive, maybe an obsession.'

'Try addiction,' Cox said looking back into his notes.

Symes shrugged as the traffic began to move again. 'Look, I promise you, when this investigation's finished, I'll take some personal time. I'll get my head straight. I promise.'

'Listen, so far we've gotten lucky. Please refrain from anything of the romantic nature in this university. This is going to be a stuffy, old world kind of deal. The women will be librarian types.'

Symes grinned and turned to look at him again. He raised his eyebrows and a smile at the same time. 'I like to read,' he laughed.

Cox didn't laugh, he just shook his head. 'I thought you might,' he sighed.

The Contract

21.

THE UNIVERSITY OF Kent was in the historic city of Canterbury. The campus was a mixture of old architecture merged with new and contemporary style buildings. It sprawled out underneath the watchful gaze of the gothic Canterbury Cathedral.

'I do love a good British cathedral,' Cox muttered as he stretched his legs getting out of the car.

'Well then, it seems that you've come to the right place, haven't you, gentlemen?' A broad, plummy, Queen's English accent surprised both men as it came from somewhere behind them.

Cox turned and was pleased to see a small man that met the description of Doctor Robert Broom that he had seen from the internet.

'This cathedral is one of the oldest and most valued Christian properties in the world. It was completed in the year five-hundred and ninety-seven, then rebuilt in ten-seventy, before being finished in ten-seventy-seven. Then in eleven-seventy-four, it was rebuilt again, being extended into a gothic style. There had been a fire you see, after the murder of Thomas Becket. Due to ruination, it was largely demolished in the fourteenth century and rebuilt into the structure that you see before you.'

'Wow, you know all that off the top of your head?' Symes asked, smiling towards the small man.

'When one lives in such a historical location, gentleman, one makes it a mission to know all there is about it. I could tell you more, but I'm afraid I would bore you both back to Washington, DC. I am Doctor Robert Broom; you, I believe, are Agent Cox and Agent Symes, of the FBI. Am I correct?'

'You are,' Symes replied gripping the man's hand.

'And to whom do I owe the pleasure?' Broom asked, returning the handshake.

'I'm Symes, and this miserable old windbag over here is Cox.'

Cox smiled at the old man. 'Please excuse my colleague here, he's hurting over a scolding I gave him on the way down here.'

'Ah, I see. Well, spare the rod and spoil the child is what I always say. I trust everything is tickety-boo between you now?'

'Something like that,' Symes replied with a smile.

'Well, welcome to my university. When I say mine, I don't actually own it,' the small man spoke with a laugh. 'It's just that I've been here so long that I feel like one of its relics.' He laughed again.

Both agents looked at each other, not really getting the joke, but they both politely smiled anyway.

'When I found out that two agents from the FBI were coming over to see me, I must admit I got a little worried. I started thinking about that piece of cheese I smuggled into your country a few years back. I can never find decent cheeses in America. It's all processed to within an inch of its life. Anyway, I digress. Would you like to follow me into my study where we can talk over a nice cup of tea and some jammy-dodgers?'

'What's a jammy-dodger?' Cox mouthed to Symes, who shrugged his response.

'That would be lovely, thank you, doctor.' Cox hoped he was doing the right thing accepting the invitation to a jammy dodger.

∼∼∼

Broom's office was as overcrowded and as stuffy as Cox had imagined it to be. It was every bit the cliché of a fuddy old professor's office from every old British film he'd ever seen. They were sat around a huge, old oak desk that was crowded with papers and trinkets. There was a steaming mug of tea before them, and a plate with the strangest cookies either of them had ever seen. They were beige, with a filling of jelly and some kind of cream. There was a smiling face on either side of the cookie, where you could see the reddish-pink filling beneath it. The professor was happily dunking them into his tea, a ritual that Cox felt he would never be able to understand.

The Contract

'Well, gentlemen, I understand that you are fans of my work?' he asked, poking his gold rimmed glasses so they sat on the bump of his nose.

Symes was a little relieved that they were finally getting down to why they were here after the guided tour that he had given them of the facilities, the preamble of the tea and biscuits, and the general faff of the man.

Jesus, I've been in Britain for three days, and I'm using the word faff. Cox smiled as he put his cup of tea down on the desk.

Dr Broom immediately lifted it up and slid a strange, cotton design underneath it.

'We always put the doily beneath the tea, it keeps the hot cup from staining the veneer,' he said, sitting back. 'Carry on, Agent Cox.'

Cox slipped another look over to his partner, who was trying his best to stifle a smile behind his own cup. 'Well, we're here because of your article in the *National Enquirer* magazine. The one regarding astronomical anomalies.'

'Ah yes, the one that all the major news outlets I contacted chose to ignore. I think I was actually lucky to get it into your *Enquirer*. Although, I understand that that publication is not held in such high regard in your country.'

Cox grimaced as he nodded.

'You could say that,' Symes interrupted. 'Although, I did find it rather … illuminating.'

Dr Broom laughed. 'Ah, yes, I get that, Agent Symes. That's very funny.'

'Please, call me Adam.'

Broom nodded, still smiling. 'Indeed, I will, Adam. Indeed, I will. So, what was it about my article that caught the attention of the FBI, and got you to fly all the way over here from Washington, DC to meet little old me?'

'Well, we were intrigued as to how you knew all the locations of the murders that we are investigating,' Cox replied.

'Not to mention the locations of a couple that hadn't occurred at the time of the publication. Including the two here in the UK. In Portsmouth and in Liverpool,' Symes continued.

Dr Broom's face dropped as he put his cup down on his own doily. Cox noticed that his hands were shaking somewhat.

'Murders?'

'Yes, murders. In the plural sense. In your article, you mention the strange astronomical anomalies that have been occurring in the skies over the last few months.'

'Years, agent,' Broom added. 'It seems as though these have been happening, unnoticed, for years.'

'Really?' Cox asked, taking his notepad out of the inside pocket of his jacket. 'Well, each one you mentioned in your article, every location you pinpointed, was the location of a killing. A series of murders that we've been tasked to investigate.'

'They all correspond to the dates and times you mention in the article,' Symes interjected.

'These murders, they're not your run of the mill, ordinary killings, Dr Broom. These are rather grizzly and violent. All of them targeting a particular kind of victim. Bad people. Violent, corrupt people. Even so, we have a moral obligation to investigate every murder,' Cox continued. 'We need to know how you were able to get the locations correct, including the ones that hadn't yet occurred at the time of publication.'

Broom raised his eyebrows and blew a breath out from between his pursed lips. He shook his head as he regarded the two men before him. 'Gentlemen, you have me at a disadvantage. I know nothing of any murders. All I did was watch the skies and report my findings.'

'Can you show us the calculations that you used for these events?'

'Or a model or something?' Symes added.

Broom stood up and moved to the computer that was on a desk in the corner of the room. He wiggled the mouse and the screen came alive. 'I love these things. Most people my age hate them, but I'm fascinated. It was through a computer programme that I developed a way for mapping the *celestial dances*, as I call them. I wrote a paper about them that'll be published next month, but I was just too excited about it to wait. So, I reached out to the main-stream media. I can assure you that I knew nothing of any murders. All I knew was that I had discovered something everyone else had overlooked. All the evidence and the workings are in my programme here.'

The Contract

Over the next two hours, he proceeded to map out his research into the anomalies for the two agents. 'Here's the longitude and the latitude workings,' Broom pointed at the screen; it was just a jumble of numbers and computer code. Neither Cox nor Symes understood what was being explained to them. Broom smiled. 'I can see that I might have lost you two gentlemen. Well, watch this ...'

He clicked a button on the screen and a graphical representation of the sky opened up. The stars were moving, aligning, and as they did, a shaft of light was produced. The shaft pinpointed locations on the graphic of the Earth below.

Both agents noticed that the locations were indeed the sites that they had been visiting for the last month or so.

'And you can use this model to predict future alignments?' Symes asked.

'Yes,' Broom answered, not looking at either agent. His eyes were wide, and there was a glazed smile on his lips as he watched what was unfolding on the screen. 'All I need to do is ...' he typed in a few commands and clicked a few buttons.

Cox guessed that the good doctor had almost forgotten that they were still here.

'There you go,' he announced, stepping back and cocking his head at the screen.

Symes smiled as he saw the love that this man had for his programme.

'Using the analysis of the past movements, and basing the prediction on the historical evidence, it was possible to accurately predict the two events in the UK.'

All three men watched the shafts of light hit the UK in two different locations.

'So, this is the first prediction. I linked the programme up with an internet map site so I could accurately pinpoint the positions the alignments were alluding to. It produced this one, Portsmouth. And this one in Liverpool ...'

'There were four events in the UK,' Symes added, looking at his partner. 'Portsmouth, on the dock. Then 'Eastend Ed' was killed a few miles away from this scene. Then there were two in Liverpool. The first one was this Forshaw character, and then Cole, in ...'

'Norris Green,' all three men said in unison.

Broom looked at the other two with his head half cocked. 'How could you be so specific?' he asked.

'Because that's where we were before we came here,' Symes said, impressed with the whole set up and preciseness of the calculations.

'Are you sure?' the old man asked.

'I don't think we're going to forget a place name like Norris Green, do you? It sounds like the old groundskeeper in one of those crappy soap operas,' Symes laughed.

'Yes, it does rather. I think it sounds rather quaint. I'm imagining fields, a lovely old English pub, and a picturesque village green,' Broom dreamed.

'Yeah, well, you keep on imagining that, doctor,' Symes laughed in reply.

'You said that this thing is accurate. But it only read two events,' Cox mentioned.

'Two large events. Some of the larger events seem to have ...' he pushed his glasses back up his nose again as it looked like he thought about the word. 'Offshoots,' he concluded, eventually.

Can it tell us roughly what time these events occurred?' Cox asked, breaking through the joviality.

Broom looked at him and smiled. The smile was smug, but there was no malice to it. It was the smile of a proud parent telling his friends about the progress of one of his offspring. 'No, Agent Cox, it can't tell you *roughly* what time the event happened ...'

Cox sighed.

'It can tell us *exactly* what time the event happened.' With newfound enthusiasm, the old man fussed about on the screen for a while, then turned around to face the others. 'It happened at three-thirty-eight and twenty-seven seconds, pm, that is ... Oh, and Greenwich Mean Time, of course.'

Cox's eyes were wide with excitement. 'Of course,' he replied, not really knowing what he was replying to. 'Doctor Broom, can we hijack you from your work here and extend to you an invitation to Washington, DC? I'd love our guys to cast their eyes over this model. You'll be paid, obviously, and anything we come up with, it will all be credited to you and your work.'

The Contract

The doctor's eyes lit up. 'I'll be credited?'
'Of course. If your model proves vital in the capture of our perp, then of course you'll get all the accolades you deserve for assisting the capture.'
'Do I get to carry a gun?' the doctor asked, eyeing the shoulder holster that was visible beneath the agent's coat.
'No, not unless you have a permit,' Symes slapped him on the back. 'Believe me though, you probably don't want to.'
'Well, let me clear my schedule. Let me speak to Mrs Broom, oh, and the Dean of my faculty, don't want him taking any credits that he hasn't worked for, eh?'
'Excellent. You get things moving at your end, it's got to be as soon as possible. Shall we say tomorrow morning? You do have a valid passport, don't you?'
'Yes, I do. How long do you think we will be away for?'
'A while,' Cox answered.

22.

'IN YOUR ARTICLE, you mention that Our Lord, Jesus Christ would have been born at least a hundred times by now. Can you elaborate on that?' The director of the FBI was sat at the head of the grand table. The room was large, and there were eight people sat around the table, all of them wearing suits, with the exception of Dr Broom. He was dressed in an eccentric ensemble, including cravat and cummerbund.

'Oh yes, sir, I don't just speculate when I write an article. I can back them up with scientific proof. The first time I noticed it, it was about six months ago. I can tell you that it shocked me to my core to see the stars dance as they do. I always thought of them as static celestial bodies, as still as the sun. When I noticed, I simply had to research it. It was just too fascinating for me to pass up. The part that hooked me, like a big old trout on a line, was when I read about the Star of Bethlehem event. It was very real, you know.' The old doctor was nodding now, trying to keep the attention of everyone in the room. 'I read that the very same thing that I was witnessing happened around the time that Jesus was said to be born, over two thousand years ago. I was drawn in. So, I continued my research. What I had witnessed was not the first time it had happened, recently I mean. It seemed that it had occurred a number of times before. The first one I noticed had been about four weeks prior. Including the events you saw on my simulation in Liverpool and Portsmouth, there've been at least ten.'

Symes leaned forwards onto the table. He was looking directly at Broom. 'Where were all the others? The others that were prior to Baltimore?'

'Well, for this part of the presentation, I'd like to bring my model into play.' He looked up at the people present in the room and his

The Contract

face began to flush. As he opened his laptop and looked at the large screen behind him, the poor soul looked like a lost lamb. 'Erm, could anyone be so kind as to help me hook my laptop up to this telly?'

One of the women on the table got up with a smile on her face. She took the laptop out of his hands and attached a small dongle to it. She opened up a folder and ran an application. After pressing the big button on the dongle, Broom's desktop was projected onto the big screen. He jumped back a little.

'Oh, would you look at that!' he laughed. 'It's a good job there wasn't any pictures of Mrs Broom in her all-together on there, isn't it?'

A small laugh rippled through the room.

'Right then,' he mumbled as he connected to the wi-fi and clicked away at his files. Eventually the programme that Cox and Symes had witnessed in Kent came up on the screen.

'So,' Broom began, 'the first one that I could fathom, retrospectively, pointed to a location in Albuquerque, in New Mexico. That one was on March the twenty-sixth of this year. The second one was New Orleans, Louisiana, on April the ninth. I thought there might have been a third and fourth one, both of them over locations in the middle east, but I couldn't quite get the locations. The next one I could track was in Springfield, Missouri, on April sixteenth.'

'Have you got that longitude and latitude info that you showed us in Britain?' Cox asked.

'I do, sir. It's all held in the files within the programme and backed up onto the cloud.' He smiled at the room. 'I'm betting that none of you thought I'd know what the cloud was, am I right?' There was a small mumble of amused agreement.

'OK then. Let's fire this thing up and get that information. We can test our theories. If we're right, then there will have been a murder, or some kind of event at each of the locations the system throws at us.' Cox felt more enthusiastic than he had in months. 'Hopefully, at each location, something bad will have happened to a bad person, and we can see if there had been any white feathers left in the aftermath.'

Broom was busy clicking away on the keyboard as the group in the room, made up mostly of the high-level directors and the stakeholders of this ongoing investigation, sat by and watched.

'Can somebody link this computer to a printer?' Symes asked.

The same woman who had stepped up to the screen volunteered. Within a short while, there was a printout of potential White Feather Fever murders in a pile on the desk.

'This is fantastic,' Cox enthused as he began to hand out the printouts to the group. 'Can each of you take a copy and do a little bit of research on the locations and the dates. I'm betting that this will raise more than a few questions.'

Each person present took a printout and left the room. Once they were gone, leaving only Cox, Symes, and Broom, Cox leaned into the professor.

'Now that we're in the process of getting the older cases out of the way, can we make any headway on the future ones?'

'Well, in all this excitement, I mean finding out that my work is wanted on a murder case, by the FBI, that's a little something to digest. I have let my research go a little bit awry. But, if you give me a few hours with unhindered access to a fast internet connection, then I'm sure I can give it my best shot,' the doctor replied as he tapped away on his keyboard. 'I should be able to provide you with an exact time of the next anomaly, and the exact information, give or take a few feet either way, of the location it corresponds to.'

Symes stood with his arms folded across his chest, watching the little man type. 'I'm sure we can deal with a few feet. This is fucking epic,' he spoke more to himself than to the doctor. 'We might actually have a chance of cracking this case wide open. Imagine having a computer programme that told you the exact locations of all future crimes!' He tapped the doctor on the shoulder. 'You're going to make a name for yourself on this one, Dr Broom. You could be a national hero.'

'I think, technically, it would be an international hero, but either way would be nice.' The doctor smiled at the agents just before they left the room.

~~~~

Within forty-five minutes of handing everyone their assignments, Cox and Symes were back in the meeting room. The table before them was filled with printouts, files, and old photographs.

'Well, it looks like we've had ourselves some hits,' Cox laughed as he looked at the faces of the people around him. 'I've got a feeling

The Contract

that this case might just be opening before us here.' He looked around the room and noticed that the doctor was missing. 'Where's Broom? He should be here for this.'

'I think he's off predicting the next murder,' the director spoke up as he sat back at the table. 'So, what are we doing with all of this?'

Cox picked up the printout that the director had before him. He broke out into a big smile as he read the contents. 'March twenty-sixth, Albuquerque,' he read out aloud so the room could hear him. 'Nob Hill to be exact. Just a few blocks away from the university campus. The local police were called to Monte Vista Catholic Church, just off Campus Boulevard. There had been reports of a foul smell coming from within the nave of the church, and no one had seen Father McCrea for days. After a thorough search of the exterior of the premises, they found no signs of a break in or any vandalism. They attempted to gain access, but there was no communication with anyone inside. They made the decision and gained permission to force access. What they found in there was horrifying. The aging priest was hanging upside down over his own decorated alter. There were multiple bread hosts lying around, a lot of them had been covered in blood and what looked like vomit. The priest's stomach had either been cut open, or had burst open, and the poor wretch had been left to die of his own wounds.'

There was a general intake of breath as the more gruesome details were read out.

'It seems that our very own Father McCrea was under investigation for murder. Apparently, he was running a book on what they call 'bum fights.' He was enticing the homeless into his parish, giving them food and shelter in exchange for fighting one another. He ran the club from a remote location, and there had been reports of multiple deaths. His bank account was looking rather healthy too, for a parish priest. This guy fits our killer's MO.'

'Were there any white feathers found at the scene?' Symes asked.

Cox looked into the other papers for a moment or two. 'Not that I can see, but it does state that someone had gone into the church and cleaned up the mess. Apparently, the Church has a tendency to cover their own tracks. Who'd have thought?'

'So that one fits the MO, but it's a maybe on the investigation,' Symes added. 'What's next?'

Cox picked up another slip of paper. 'New Orleans, April ninth this year. Well, look at that. This fell slap bang in the middle of Mardi Gras season, due to the lateness of Easter. There were numerous assaults reported and a few murders. Nothing new there, eh?' Cox asked and was greeted with more than a few murmurs of agreement. 'There was one murder that stuck out from the others apparently. That was the disappearance of a Ms Angela Bryson. She was found in a garage on the morning of April tenth. She was semi-naked, and had various electric clamps attached to her body. It looked like a mob hit. Apparently, she had been working Mardi Gras and had been dressed in carnival clothing.'

'Including white feathers?' the director asked.

Symes nodded. 'Including white feathers! Lots of them. None of them bagged and tagged as evidence, presumably because they were incidental to the crime scene.'

'But why would this woman be a target for our killer?' the woman who had fixed the laptop earlier, asked. 'Do we know who she was?'

'Good question,' Cox replied. 'We do know who she was. Or at least it's in the file.' He scattered some B&W photographs on the table. 'They are for mature audiences only,' he stated as he watched everyone move forward to reach for them. 'Her professional name was Andi Laid.'

The pictures were glamour photographs of an attractive young lady clad in glamour wear and exposing the flesh.

'Not every glamour model is a bad person, you know?' the woman said as she looked at the photographs.

Symes smiled at her, and Cox watched as her face flushed.

'That's true, Agent Webb, but glamour was only how she began her career.' Cox held up some more photographs. 'Now these are the worst ones. They are not for the faint hearted. You have been warned.'

As he threw the new photographs onto the table, he watched the hesitancy in the people present to pick them up. Eventually, Agent Webb reached forwards and picked up a handful. This prompted the rest of the room to do the same. There was a chorus of disapproval as the images on the photographs began to sink in. A number of the agents present threw the offending images back onto the table.

'Yeah, not pretty is it?' Cox began, reading from the file he was holding. 'Andi Laid was an infamous porn star. Infamous due to who, or

The Contract

sometimes even what, she was willing to have sex with. Please, don't get me wrong, I'm quite a broadminded person, not quite as broadminded as Agent Symes here ...'

Symes laughed and nodded. Cox noticed that Agent Webb began to blush again.

'... but, what does it take for an attractive young lady to begin having sex with farm animals?' Cox shuddered, then continued. 'That just blows my mind. But, even though that's illegal in itself, it's probably not bad enough to warrant the attention from our friend. That comes from what I'm about to tell you next.' He looked around at the faces in the room, every one of them were looking back at him. He could see intense fire burning in their eyes. A lust for knowledge. 'She was on the wanted list because she was a sex trafficker. She was involved in bringing young girls and boys into the country and selling them off to the highest bidders. Some of these children would go on to feature in her videos. I used these photographs here to shock you, but I wouldn't even entertain printing some of the other sick stuff that we have on file regarding this evil bitch.'

The room was silent.

'Paedophilia, torture, enforced drug taking, group sex, and even snuff. This woman was a sick individual. The ring was eventually busted. But, due to the involvement of some high-level individuals, nothing about it was ever publicised. And, Andi Laid, AKA Angela Bryson, walked.'

A small gasp from the room made Cox smile a little. *It's like story time in school,* he thought.

'Yeah. She was out on a technicality. Apparently, the officer who arrested her, blinded by the horror of the case, forgot to read her rights. He was a rookie, and never passed probation. So, do you think she fits the MO of our killer?'

'Definitely,' Webb spat.

'Do we have any more hits, Cox?' The director asked as he screwed up the photographs that he had in front of him. He was about to throw them in the bin, before Symes stopped him. 'I'll take them, sir. I'm going to shred them. We don't want the cleaners coming in and having a heart attack now do we?'

The director nodded and handed the offensive material back to Symes.

'We do. Third one is a charmer. Meet Travis Hawkins.' Cox pulled more photographs from another file. 'Travis was an income tax investigator. He worked for the government for twenty-four years. He stopped working for them when he was found dead, wrapped to a table in cellophane with a sheet of fabric over his face. The coroner said that cause of death was drowning. Basically, he was water-boarded to death. Our killer is such a humanitarian.'

There was a nervous laugh from the room. Cox thought that it was more from relief after the last case.

'Anyway, at the time of his death, April the sixteenth, he was being investigated by the IRS. He had at least sixteen offshore bank accounts and had amassed a personal wealth in excess of fifteen million dollars. He was defrauding lower income families, loaning them the money to pay their debts, then using bullying and terror tactics to get his money back. There were a number of suicides related to his cases, including at least one high profile suicide pact case, where the parents killed their three children before killing themselves. At the time, it was seen that they were in debt to Mr Hawkins for over three-hundred thousand dollars.'

A number of the agents, including the director, threw the photographs they were looking at back onto the table. 'It's a fucking sick world that we live in,' he mumbled.

'He was found in a boat that he owned that was moored on the Mississippi, by Chickasaw wildlife resort. He wasn't killed there; his body had been moved.'

'Any feathers?' the director asked.

'There's a bird sanctuary over that way. When they found his body, it was covered in feathers and bird shit. So, there may well have been a white feather, and it was overlooked.'

'Our findings have led us to believe that there is a bona-fide, psycho, serial killer running around out there. One that has, if you'll pardon the expression, a hard-on for bad guys. One with at least ten kills to his name,' Symes added. 'Not to mention the assault on two of the FBI's finest agents.'

Another ripple of laughter passed through the room.

'So, to that end, we have scoured the globe and found the finest. Dr Broom has thrown down a gauntlet. He says that he can predict not

The Contract

only where the next murder will be, but when! So, if you guys want to take a small comfort break, I'll go find him and bring him back in.'

With that, everyone stood up from their chairs and left the room. There was quite a bit of excited chatter between them.

'I hope the little guy can deliver on his promise,' Cox whispered to his partner. 'There's a lot riding on this.'

'I'm sure he will. The guy's a genius. You can tell just by looking at him,' Symes pointed out of the office to where Broom was stood at the coffee machine, attempting to take a swig out of the glass jar. 'Besides, he's British. Everyone always believes the Limey.'

Cox shook his head and sighed. 'I hope so!'

~~~

As Broom entered the meeting room, there was a sheepish look on his face. He was obviously enjoying his time here at the J Edgar Hoover Building in Washington, DC. It was also obvious from his strut into the room carrying his laptop that he was rather enjoying the attention he was getting too. 'Good afternoon, ladies and gentlemen,' he addressed his rapt audience as he went about setting up his laptop again so it could project onto the big screen behind him. 'I'm afraid I have a little bit of a mixed offering.'

Symes looked over at Cox whose head was half cocked, listening to the man. 'Can you elaborate, doctor?' he asked.

'Well, I'm afraid that in order to purvey to you the bad news, I must have relayed the good news prior. So, I'll relate the positives first and then move directly to the negatives. That way, you should be able to make your own minds up as to what is what!'

Cox was confused. 'Can you just give us the update please? I think we're all big enough to be able to decipher the good from the bad,' Cox smiled. The smile was devoid of humour and was hurting his jaw to maintain.

'OK then, here goes. The positive is, my programme works. I fed all of the information into my algorithm relating to the current location and last known configuration of the stars I have been monitoring.' He stood as tall as he could, straightening his back with his hands at his sides. His smile and the wild look in his eyes gave away his pride. 'I'm proud to announce that I have been able to predict the next location *and* the time of the event itself!'

Symes was up off his seat. Dr Broom had the attention of everyone in the room. There was silence as each face stared expectantly at him.

Dr Broom stood, wallowing in the moment.

'Dr Broom, can you tell us where and when please?' Cox asked, looking rather red in the face, due to the fact that he had hardly breathed in the last minute, awaiting the information.

'What?' Broom asked, snapping out of his reverie. 'Oh, yes. Well, that is where the negatives come into play, Agent Cox.'

Symes was breathing from his nostrils and clenching his fists. 'Doctor Broom?' he urged.

The doctor's gaze shifted over to Agent Symes, and he raised both hands, he looked like he was surrendering. 'Oh, yes. Well, the bad news is that, the most recent event will be in …' he looked at the watch on his arm and shook his head. His face looked dark. 'In just under ninety minutes. Eighty-eight actually.'

Cox was up, next to him. Inside he could have kissed the man, but there was also a part of him that wanted to fling him to the floor and beat the living hell out of him for not rushing in and giving them the information five minutes earlier. The more time that they had, the better. 'OK, so eighty-eight minutes. That doesn't give us much time to get mobilised. Where's the location, doctor?'

The smile was back on Broom's face. 'I have worked out the exact location, down to the street. Maybe even the house number.' The doctor turned to face the big screen behind him and pressed a few keys on his laptop. A large map of Oregon appeared. 'Eleven-hundred Southwest Alger Avenue, Beaverton, Oregon. Zip code nine-seven-double zero … erm,' he leaned back into the screen of his laptop, ignoring the large screen before him, 'Five … yes, definitely five.'

'Broom, if you weren't a man and so hideously ugly, I'd kiss you right now.'

Broom smiled and blushed before fixing his glasses on his face.

Within less than a minute, the doctor was in the room on his own, scratching his head at what had just occurred.

The Contract

23.

BEAVERTON, OREGON, ROUGHLY seventy-five minutes later, was awash with FBI agents. A number of non-descript black cars had pulled up and were now encamped on SW Allen Boulevard, just around the corner from the Avenue that was the focus of their attention.

After some heavy reassurances from the Director of the Bureau, a SWAT team was mobilised and were less than five minutes away. The FBI were backed up by the city police, there were state police on the way too.

Helicopters had been organised, and Agent Coombs, a large African-American gentleman with thinning hair and a greying beard, was standing outside his blacked-out SUV, talking into a mouthpiece that was connected to the interior of the car. '...the area is cordoned off and surrounded. The house that we're looking at, eleven-hundred, is on the corner of Southwest Sixth Street. We've got eyes on the building now. The last of the local residents are being moved as we speak. Can you give me any more detail on what we're doing out here, Agent Cox?'

'Right now, all I can tell you over this channel is that it's a major operation and part of an ongoing, international investigation. In house number eleven-hundred there may or may not be a high-profile fugitive.'

Agent Coombs was silent for a short while. 'A fugitive?' he asked eventually. 'A ... as in one? Please tell me, Agent Cox, that I haven't just scrambled a SWAT team, a fleet of helicopters, local and state police, within ten minutes, just for one man?' Coombs hoped the annoyance in his voice was coming across on the other end of the line.

'If this intel is correct, and we've got reason to believe it is, then this is no ordinary fugitive. I'm going to tell you that you may still be undermanned to take this felon down. You need to continue with extreme caution. Do you have the files on the location that we sent you?'

Coombs, shaking his head, leaned into his car and pulled out the faxed document he'd received. 'The property is owned by a ... Mrs Nancy Pritchard. She's sixty-seven years old.' Coombs cocked his head. 'She doesn't sound like much of a threat to me.'

'She's not living at the address, Agent Coombs. Please continue,' Cox requested.

Taking a deep breath, Coombs continued. 'The property is currently rented to a Mr Devon Lattis and a Miss Enola Greaves.'

'Correct. We never had the time on this end to pull either of their records. Did you manage to get anything, Agent Coombs?'

'Lattis has a few outstanding warrants on him, mainly for misdemeanours. Spousal abuse and drunk and disorderly, nothing that warrants a SWAT team!' Coombs replied testily.

'Is he the focus of any current investigations, locally? Anything that would make him the target of a vigilante? I understand your frustration here, Agent Coombs, and I know that this sounds vague, maybe too vague, but it *is* of vital importance to the on-going investigation.'

The agent leaned back into the car and pulled out another sheet of paper. He looked through one of the windows and noticed the SWAT armoured vehicle as it pulled up behind the other FBI cars. 'Let's see now. There's been some aggravated burglaries in the area lately. Two of which have resulted in deaths. They're being treated as murders.'

'Was Lattis involved in these burglaries? Do you have any information regarding any of his prior addresses? See if there were any other aggravated burglaries around his other addresses. Please, Agent Coombs, this is of vital importance. I'll almost guarantee that this Lattis guy or the Greaves woman are into some bad shit. That's why they're being targeted by our fugitive in there.'

'This is all sounding hoky, Agent Cox. I'm thirty seconds away from pulling this operation. It'll give me a red face, and won't bode well for the bureau, but I need more to go on than a fucking burglar.'

The sound of Cox exhaling from the other end of the radio brought a satisfied grin to Coombs face. 'Look, the guy you're facing in there is unnaturally strong, and he has the ability to wriggle out of situations and locations undetected. I can't be sure, and I don't want to

The Contract

go all Mulder and Scully, but there may be some elements of the supernatural on this. Either that or he is a damned good astronomer.'

'What? Super-fucking-natural? That's it, Cox, I'm wrapping this up. You've wasted too much of my time already. I'll be putting in a complaint to the Director ...'

'The Director is with me, he's right here in the room. Look, I didn't want to say it over a radio, but this is part of the White Feather Fever murders investigation. We have reason to believe that our man is in there right now.'

'The White Feather murders? You have my attention now, Cox,' Coombs said as he began to calm down.

'You need to be *very* careful, Agent Coombs. We've been monitoring all the murders and incidents related to this case. Everything comes down to this location. This could be your moment. You could be the one to take down this vigilante.'

'Now you're sharing intel, Agent Cox,' Coombs gushed. He liked the idea of his name being attached to the capture of this White Feather bastard. 'OK, you have my attention and my full co-operation. Can you tell me how to move forth on this bastard?'

'With caution, Agent Coombs. Extreme caution.'

'OK, were going to move in, but it's on your authority.' An agent wearing a bulletproof vest handed him another piece of paper. 'We have conformation of at least two people inside. One of them could be your fugitive,' *or it could just be a man and woman having breakfast,* he thought.

'God speed, Agent Coombs. Please keep radio contact, and remember, extreme caution,' Cox spoke over the radio.

Coombs put the handset back into its cradle. *Prick,* he thought. *How the fuck do I explain to the SWAT team that were going in for one fucking fugitive?'*

He motioned for his team of FBI agents and local police officers to gather around him. They all did, dutifully. There were twelve pairs of eyes watching him. He could feel them all burning into his skin, waiting for him to instruct them, to tell them what they were here to do.

'OK, people. This is not a drill. We're going into that house and we're going in hot. We'll need everyone at their most vigilant. Not everything inside will be what it appears to be. We have conformation of two people inside ...'

A murmur rippled through the assembled team.

'I know, I know. It all seems a little overkill for two people, but there may be more. The description of the perp is as follows. He's white with blond hair and a beard. He is roughly five foot six inches and about one hundred and thirty pounds.'

More murmurs through the team.

'Sir,' one of his agents addressed him.

'Yes, Platt, what is it?'

'Sir, one-hundred and thirty pounds? Five foot six? We have twelve men on the ground, there are snipers in helicopters, shit, we've got SWAT. Who the fuck is this guy?' Platt asked, a number of the others nodded and spoke their approval of the question.

Coombs shook his head. 'I hear you, Platt. I had the same reservations myself when I heard that it was only two people in the house. But these orders have come down from the Director himself.'

Platt nodded and stepped back into the crowd.

'Great, I'm glad for the question. We all need to be on the same page here. Platt, I want you and White to come in with me. I want you others to find positions and cover all the other exits, including windows, doors, look for a basement. I want the other houses on the street to be covered too. I was on an operation once where the perps had tunnelled through to the next house. The brief that I've had on our man tells me that he's bad news. We're to operate with extreme caution. We want him alive if possible, but if that goes off, then so be it. I want to be in and out of this shithole in ten minutes. I want everyone who goes in to come out. Everyone got that?'

The excitement of the team was evident in the enthusiastic response he got from them.

'Ladies and gentlemen, it's time to earn your wages!'

Coombs walked over to address the SWAT team, as he did, the other agents and officers geared themselves up, tightening their bullet-proof jackets and checking their weapons.

'All right, guys,' Coombs directed. 'Let's do this.'

Coombs and the two other agents made their way slowly towards the front porch of the house. The street was silent as the other agents and police officers, who had gotten themselves into position to cover the exits, as instructed, watched them go. As the trio got to the

The Contract

porch, Coombs, with his gun in one hand, reached out and pulled open the screen door. It opened with a scream of rusted metal.

So much for surprise, he thought.

Without further ado, or even thinking about what he was about to do, he turned the handle of the front door. To his surprise, it opened. Swallowing hard, he instructed his partners to enter as he covered them with his gun. He took the rear, closing the front door behind him carefully so as not to let it slam.

Once inside, the first thing that hit him was the smell. It smelt like the raw meat that he fed his dog. Only this was thick, cloying. He'd never been in one before, but he imagined that this would be what an abattoir smelt like. It didn't bode well for the residents of the house.

'We're inside,' he whispered into the small headset he was wearing. 'The place stinks to high heaven. It stinks of raw meat, like dog food.'

Coombs watched as his men covered all the shadows and the exits within the lower rooms. Something moved. He thought he saw something dark flick across the room.

'Platt, did you see that?' he whispered.

The small shake of the head told him all he needed to know. He signalled for the two agents to complete their search. He wanted to see what the flicker had been.

In a pincer movement, the three agents began to converge on the large living room that was through the partially open door. The smell was stronger over this way. He saw White begin to gag. He caught his attention and signalled for him to calm himself.

White recovered almost immediately, nodding and signalling that he was all right.

Coombs gestured for them all to continue through into the room.

He was a seasoned professional. Similar to quite a few senior agents, he had a military background. He had seen action in Desert Storm, Afghanistan, and in Libya. He had seen things that would turn the stomachs of the strongest mortician. But, none of the training or memories could have prepared him for what was in this room.

The only word he could think of to describe what he saw was carnage. But he felt even that word fell short.

There were pools of blood everywhere. The old and decrepit carpet was ruined with the dark pools soaking into it. Blood spatters splashed across the walls, the furniture, and the ceiling.

Something on the couch caught his eye. It was dark, but it was wriggling, of its own accord. Through the rush of blood running through his ears, he could hear something, something akin to mumbling.

Gripping his gun tighter, he took a step closer to the furniture. He instantly wished that he hadn't. What he saw there made him want to vomit. It made him want to quit the FBI, quit civilisation, Hell, maybe even quit this planet.

The thing on the couch was black. On closer inspection, the object became a torso. The torso became a person, and that person was still alive.

It was lying on the couch. Its skin was covered in dark blood. It took a small while for Coombs to be able to identify it as human. All four limbs had been removed. They looked like they had been hacked, or maybe sawn off, and recently too. Blood was still oozing from the wounds, and the limbs had been scattered on the floor. Coombs felt a panic rising in his chest. His heart was hammering, and he felt like he could be having a heart attack. He looked around the room, neither of the other two agents had noticed the horrific scene on the couch. He saw the bloodied wood-saw lying discarded on the floor. There were clumps of flesh and raw meat between its teeth. A gorge rose in his stomach and he crossed himself. It wasn't because he was religious, it just felt, to him, like the right thing to do.

'THAT FUTILE GESTURE WON'T HELP YOU HERE, AGENT COOMBS.'

The voice was loud. It sounded like it came from upstairs, and outside, and from behind him, and next to him, all at the same time. It was like he was listening to a well-engineered album through headphones, with the sound crossing from one speaker to another.

Coombs jumped at the voice. He hadn't wanted to, he didn't want to give away the idea that he was scared, but he hadn't been able to help himself. 'Who's there?' he shouted. He impressed himself with the fact that he didn't sound anywhere near as scared as he felt. 'Give yourself up, we've got the house surrounded. There's no way out of this.'

The Contract

The other two agents had just seen the thing on the couch. Agent White lost it on the first glance, and Coombs watched as he turned away and vomited over the floor. Platt, with his gun in his hand, was looking over towards the kitchen. His eyes were wide. The hand that was holding his gun was shaking, badly. Coombs followed his stare and was surprised to see a young man stood in the doorway of the kitchen. He was exactly as the description had stated. He was small, athletic, thin. His bleached blond hair hung out of the woollen hat he was wearing, and his beard looked wispy.

'YOUR GESTURE OF CROSSING YOURSELF, AGENT COOMBS. IT HAS NO SIGNIFICANCE.'

Coombs found it difficult associating the voice with the diminutive figure stood before him. A noise from behind distracted him from the strange, expressionless boy who stood before him.

'Uhhh ... pheeeeeuuug pluuuuuuuugh fiiiig muuuuh'

The words were unintelligible, nonsensical, but they meant the world to Coombs. They meant that whoever this was on the couch, if it was Lattis, was still alive. *The poor bastard,* he thought. *He'd be better off dead.*

'Pheeeeeuuug pluuuuuuuugh fiiiig muuuuh.'

Coombs looked at the wretch and realised why he was mumbling. His mouth, or what was left of it, was filling with blood, and it was pouring out, down his chin and onto the cushions of the couch he was lying on. His eyes had been gouged out and were now nothing but deep, black and bloody holes in his head. Coombs had never seen such torture inflicted onto one man who was still alive.

'Platt, White, take this son-of-a-bitch out, will you? He's fucking crazy,' Coombs half whispered as he made his way over to the couch to comfort the stricken man.

The two other agents raised their guns, pointing them at the young man.

There was a moment where he thought about how ridiculous this situation was. The remnants of a man on a couch and three agents standing off against what amounted to a featherweight boxer.

'Lattis,' Coombs whispered, hoping that the man, or what was left of him, could hear him. 'Lattis, stay with me here. You're going to be fine. Stay with me now!'

'LEAVE HIM BE,' the booming voice from everywhere that should not be coming from the man/boy spoke. 'HE WILL DIE VERY SOON. IT IS THE REWARD FOR HIS WICKED WAYS. THERE IS NOTHING THAT YOU CAN DO TO STOP THAT NOW.'

Coombs turned away from the horrific site on the couch and looked at the two agents. 'Will one of you pricks arrest or shoot this bitch. Anything just to shut him the fuck up.'

Both Platt and White were dumbstruck by what they witnessed on the couch.

White dragged his face away from the freak show and looked back at the small man with the big voice. 'Get on your knees,' he ordered. 'You're under arrest. You have the right to ...'

White didn't finish his well-rehearsed speech as the young man moved forward with almost lightning speed.

Platt watched as the boy merely touched his partner on the head. He saw White, a big man, drop his gun, close his eyes, and sink to the floor, unconscious.

~~~~

Agent Platt didn't hesitate for one moment before opening fire on the youth. He fired and fired, then he fired again. The three bullets hit their mark with ultimate precision. He had been a fine student in Quantico, and shooting had been a passion of his from an early age. He had been taught by the best to do something he was already good at. So, when each of the bullets made absolutely no impact on the man, the most they mustered was to make him flinch slightly, he couldn't believe what he was seeing. He had seen men in bullet-proof jackets taking bullets, he himself had taken bullets from this range, it hurt ... a lot. Enough to incapacitate a man. Platt's eyes grew wider as his target, unhindered by the shots, continued to approach him. He had two options now. Either he could run, get the hell out of there and figure out some kind of excuse later, or he could continue to fire at the man, put him down and deal with the consequences later. As Agent Platt had never run away from anything in his life, the only option he had left was to continue shooting. This he did. Platt continued to squeeze the trigger on his handgun. He fired until his magazine was empty, and the hollow clicking echoed through the room.

The Contract

The man stood in front of him. There were no visible effects from the bullets that he knew had hit him. Platt had gone for head-shots. He should be dead; but he wasn't. The small man stared into his eyes. For the first time in a long time, Platt was scared, more than he had ever been in his life. He felt the stare burrowing deep into his mind, *and my soul,* he thought. In a desperate bid, and out of the sheer frustration of feeling like he had no other recourse, Platt swung his fist at his assailant. The strike caught the boy squarely on the jaw.

The only result of the hit was the shattering of Platt's hand. The pain felt like someone had stuck him with a million pins up and down his arm at the same time. Every bone, every piece of cartilage in his hand shattered.

His gun dropped to the floor as he grasped at his destroyed and useless hand.

The stranger's face was stoic, but even in the throes of agony, Platt fancied he could see something almost akin to faint amusement flick across his lips. He raised both his hands and placed them on either side of the agent's face.

Platt had no idea what was happening, but he knew that he was powerless to stop whatever it was. 'Coombs, help me,' he shouted through a squashed mouth. He tried to turn his head to see where his colleagues were, but the hold this man had on him was vice-like. He couldn't move a muscle.

That was until the vice began to turn.

He felt the pressure on his cranium. The steel grip got tighter and the pressure on his skull replied in tandem.

'YOU HAVE SAVED ME A JOURNEY, JACK PLATT. I WOULD'VE BEEN COMING TO SEE YOU SOON, ANYWAY.' The voice was whispered, but it still had the same effect of a multitude of voices coming from everywhere. With very little effort, the youth increased the compression upon the sides of the agent's head.

If it had been possible, Agent Platt's eyes would have grown wider with incomprehension. *How the fuck does this guy know my name?* he thought. The fact that this man *did* know him raised a fear deep in the recesses of his mind. *It's not possible. Is it?* The forced eye contact intensified as the pressure on the sides of his head did likewise. He watched as the deep blue of the boy's irises faded. Slowly but surely, they changed, the colour fading as a creeping blackness overtook them, devouring them, swallowing them. The agent was forced to stare into the deep, black pools. *Is that infinity?* he thought, not really understanding the question. He wanted to close his own eyes to rid himself of the awful sight, to put it out of his mind. But it was too late! He could already feel himself falling, tumbling, deeper and deeper into the never-ending night within those hellish holes. If the absence of light were a substance, like water, then Agent Platt felt as if he were about to drown within it.

Suddenly, he was no longer in the living room of the house on the corner of the street. He was swooping and swirling in the blackness. His body was gliding and tossing as if he were in free-fall, in space. There was nothing above him, nothing below him, there was only him, and the deep, petrifying darkness.

Then, as suddenly as it had started, it stopped. Gingerly, he opened his eyes. He was hoping not to see the hideous nothingness that the young man offered and was taken completely by surprise to find himself somewhere else entirely. He woke to a sparsely furnished room. It was, however, a room he recognized.

The peripheral edges of his vision began to tilt. The effect was akin to a fairground ride that he remembered as a child, one where the walls would distort and flip. The room began to turn hazy and blurred. Platt's eyes teared up, causing the blurring to double as his focus swayed. The sense of nausea was overwhelming.

His vision began to focus, and an image opened to him.

It was him.

He was in the room, but it was a different him, a younger him. He didn't like where this was going. Not one bit. He wondered what Coombs was doing right now, why he wasn't trying to get the freak who was squashing his head off him, the same freak who was orchestrating this stupid vision.

He watched as the image of himself began to buckle up his trousers. He could hear sobs in the background. The cries were deep, sorrowful, and filled with fear. They were also in close proximity.

He knew where this room was. He knew whose sobs he could hear, and he knew why he was buckling up his trousers. Absently, he wondered why he was seeing this vision now.

He looked away from the sweat-lined face of himself slipping his shoes back on, and over towards a filthy, bloody mattress on the other side of the room. Ahead of him were two uncovered windows. Outside it

The Contract

was dark, almost pitch black, the windows should have been acting like mirrors right about now, and he expected to see himself, staring into the blackness. But all he could see was the back of this 'other' self as he slipped on a thin, light brown, leather jacket. His gaze moved again. Each time his vision shifted; it caused his stomach to churn. Nausea swept through him as his eyesight blurred. The fact that he *knew* what he was going to see helped build on the nausea and he felt the familiar rush of saliva in his mouth, he was going to vomit.

He realised that the point of this vision was to see what he had been trying his best to ignore.

Upon the mattress, huddled together, were two children; neither of them could have been older than ten years of age. One was a girl and the other a boy, brother and sister. He knew they were brother and sister as the memory was fresh in his mind. They were comforting each other, the younger of the two had his head buried into a dirty, tear stained pillow as his sister, herself crying, was trying her best to comfort him.

They were the children of one of his informants.

The informant was a woman with a dubious life style. She had a severe drug addiction and a penchant for selling whatever she had to get her next fix. It didn't matter to her what it was she sold. Her car, her clothes, her TV, her body ... even her children. Platt had her in his pocket. She was someone who he could take out whenever he wanted, someone to amuse himself with because of everything he had on her. Like a cat with a terrified mouse, he played with her, toyed with her life. She was only thirty, but she looked sixty. Because of this, Platt was not interested in her sexually. Her children, however, they were another matter.

It had been her, a drug addicted prostitute, whom he had abused and used so often that the novelty had worn off as she let herself go, who had offered him the services of her children. It was a pay-off, just so she could go and get another score. He had taken a shine to the two children. There had always been an innocence about children that he loved. An innocence that he loved taking away from them. He could have told them that there really was no such thing as Santa Claus, or that their mother was really just a drug hag and not the woman who could bring them up properly and protect them. But there was something in his twisted nature that wanted to inflict more onto them. There was nothing that she could've done to prevent him having them. He had told her as much, and she believed it. Once, when she was half sober enough and had plucked up the courage to defend them, he had beaten her to within an inch of her life, right in front of them. He had left her in no doubt about what would happen should she go against him again.

This vision was terrifying. It was so real. It left him stumbling, thinking about why he could see it now. He knew it was a low point in a life of many, many lows, but he was a good federal agent, and a few misdemeanours shouldn't bring him down. He had done more good than bad in this world. *Haven't I?* he thought.

Something distracted him from the thought and the sobbing. It moved within his eyeline. As he tried to follow it, the windows began to shift. He could hear a sound coming from somewhere outside. It was distant, but distinctive. It was the sound of trumpets. This change confused him. He remembered this scenario as if it were only yesterday, but he didn't remember the sound of any music. He turned to see his old self leaving the room, slamming the door behind him. He then looked back to the naked children as the sister put her bruised arm around her brother. They weren't reacting to the music. He shook his head and put his fingers in his ears, attempting to block the annoying, sinister sound. A vision of an advancing army riding into view from across hills burst through his head. He could see banners and horses as searing pain flashed through him. Rapidly, the volume increased to ear-splitting levels. The floor began to vibrate, and he could feel the strange sensation of his teeth rattling. A pressure was building. It might have been inside his head, or it might have been the whole room, either way he felt his eyes become moist and tear up.

Suddenly, whether from the volume of the noise outside or the building pressure within the room, the windows shattered. Large, dangerous shards of glass flew across the room towards him, and the edges of his peripheral vision blurred some more. The room felt like it was tilting. The window frames contorted and rounded. With some considerable effort, he blinked as he saw that they had become, unquestionably, eyes. Huge black-filled eyes staring directly at him.

The darkness of them swirled with anger and rage. He watched as they narrowed. Something was triggered then, something that had remained unspoken. That something was fire. It licked, hungrily out from the skirting boards of the wall and rolled upwards like boiling liquid until

The Contract

it hit the ceiling on all sides. The flames spread above him, and black smoke drifted from the raging inferno like a thick crust of tarry film.

Without thinking or even knowing why, Platt screamed. Something wet crawled across the flesh on his arms and hands. He expected to see a large slug, or something similarly hideous, but what he saw instead shocked him to his core. There wasn't anything crawling across his hands. The crawling, slithering feeling was caused by his flesh literally melting and dripping from his bones. It oozed and pooled onto the floor below him.

The sobbing from the children had stopped. He initially thought the maddening music in his ears had drowned them out, but it wasn't the case. The cries had been replaced by laughter. The two naked children were laughing at him. Both of them were sitting up on the mattress, a mattress that was now on fire. They were pointing at him. The girl had her arm around her brother, supporting him, as he was laughing the hardest.

What the fuck do you have to laugh about? The thought had too much venom in it; it shocked even him.

A fresh breeze blew in from the endless window/eyes before him. It caught on the exposed, raw flesh of his limbs. Sudden, severe pain swerved his attention from the insolent children before him, causing him to scream. Half way through he stopped, as hot, sour vomit spewed from his mouth, splashing onto the floor, mixing with the mound of his own semi-liquid flesh.

The continuing triumphal tune was halted by a roar. Again, in his addled mind, it sounded like a roar of victory and triumph.

His vision blurred again as the room tilted and the vision was torn from him. He was back inside the living room, back in the investigation, back with Agents Coombs and White. The youth was stood before him, and the black eyes that he could see now were no longer windows, but gaping holes into the man's face.

He felt the hands on either side of his head again and felt the mounting pressure as they squeezed with uncanny strength.

'Get ... the ... fuck ... off ... me ...' was all he could croak. These happened to be the very last words of Agent Platt, decorated FBI agent, torturer of women, and paedophile.

The youth forced his hands together, and Platt heard an almighty clap of thunder resonate around him a second before his head caved in.

Bone, blood, and grey matter exploded. Steaming gore splattered forth from his body as his lifeless corpse collapsed, unceremoniously, onto the floor before a disbelieving Agent Coombs.

The youth reached inside his black top and produced not one but two long, white feathers. He placed one upon the crumpled mess that had recently been Agent Platt before moving across the room towards Lattis, who was lying on the couch.

~~~~

Coombs couldn't believe what he had just seen.

Within the last few moments, he had seen their suspect knock Agent White out cold with a mere touch of his hand, the same small man being shot multiple times to no effect whatsoever, and then, without any effort, crush the skull of one of his finest men.

He stepped away from the couch as the man approached Lattis, holding one of the infamous white feathers in his hand. Coombs dropped his gun to the floor and raised his hands in the air.

'What the fuck are you?' he whispered and stuttered at the same time.

The youth ignored him as if he wasn't even in the room. He knelt on the floor, leaning over the twitching torso, that used to be a complete human. What was left of this man became agitated, as if acknowledging someone was there. Lattis began to mumble incoherently. It sounded to Coombs as if he was praying, or maybe he was confessing.

It could have been both.

'Uhhh... pheeeeeuuug cuh ooo pluuuuuuuugh fiiiig muuuuh'

The young man whispered something back in response. Once again, the booming voice came from everywhere, all at once, only this time it sounded softer. 'YES, HE MIGHT BE ABLE TO,' he said, 'BUT, I CAN'T.'

Coombs was helpless. He watched the young man insert his fingers into the eye sockets of the man, and press, firmly. He thought that, if he survived this encounter, if he lived another day, the sound of that poor man's brains popping in his head would haunt him until the day he died.

The man placed the white feather he had in his other hand onto the blood covered chest of the decapitated man. He wiped his hands on

The Contract

his black sweat top as he stood. He looked at Agent Coombs and tilted his head to one side. Coombs felt the gaze bore deep into his head, *maybe deeper,* he thought.

Then, without another word, he turned away from him and walked out of the room.

Coombs felt his legs buckle underneath him, and he fell to the floor. From his prone position he looked over at Agent White, who was twitching and rousing from his assault. He then shifted his gaze towards the body of Platt, who would never rouse again.

He pondered the white feather on the body of his colleague.

24.

THE FRONT DOOR of the house opened, and a young man wearing a pair of black sweatpants and a dark hooded top stepped out into the small front garden of the property. His shoulder length, blond hair was blowing in the breeze. His head was down, and his hands were in the front pockets of his hooded top. He appeared to be covered in blood.

The team of FBI and local police had been joined, as promised, by a contingency of state police. The SWAT team had taken positions on the roofs of the other houses on the street and the surrounding streets, covering all accesses to and from the property.

Agent Blackwell had been left in charge of the operation when Coombs and the others had gone inside. He had been attempting to communicate with his superior via the radio but hadn't had much luck. They had heard everything that had been said inside the house, although not a lot of it had been legible. All he knew was that it had been going wrong in there and something seriously bad had happened. He considered sending the SWAT team in but thought twice about it as neither he nor anyone else seemed to understand the full extent of the shitstorm they would have been walking into.

Right now, as he watched a man, who perfectly fitted the description they had of the perpetrator, walk out of the door, covered in blood, his blood rose, and he was ready for action. *OK you motherfucker, we've got you now,* he thought. He picked up the megaphone that he had been given by Coombs and pressed the button.

'You,' he shouted into the device. There was a loud scream of feedback, but it didn't last long. 'Don't you take another step. Right now, there are at least seventy high-powered weapons trained on you. We have you covered from every possible angle. Drop any weapons you may be holding and lie down on the ground with your hands behind your head.'

The Contract

The man looked up.

Blackwell saw his face from his vantage point in the front garden of the house opposite. *Fuck me, this guy must be twenty years old,* he thought as he looked at his bearded, bloodied face through his binoculars. He also noted that the blood that was all over him didn't appear to be his. In his opinion, it didn't bode well for Coombs, White, and Platt, who were still inside.

The man continued walking, with his impassive face, towards the garden gate.

'I said HALT,' Blackwell shouted through the megaphone again. 'I will not warn you again. If you do not comply, I will have no other recourse but to use extreme force. Stop your progress right now, lie down on the ground, and put your hands behind your head.'

The young man still didn't respond to his demand. He continued walking as if he were out for a Sunday afternoon stroll.

Blackwell shook his head. 'Fuck!' was all he said before picking up his radio and pressing the talk button. 'SWAT One, do you have a visual on the suspect?'

'Copy that,' came the swift reply.

'Don't let that man reach the gate.'

'Am I going for a kill-shot?'

'Negative. Hit him in the leg. Drop him. We want this bastard alive.'

'Confirmed.'

'Take him down now,' Blackwell commanded.

The shot rang out into the quiet street. Blackwell heard the single report ricochet off all the other buildings in the street. He wasn't watching through the binoculars; he had no desire to see a man being shot in the leg close up. But he was watching. He saw the shot from the high-powered rifle hit the man's leg, saw the trouser leg tear up as the projectile hit him, but still he continued to walk. His face ruffled, and he picked up the radio again. 'SWAT One, did you hit him?' he asked.

'It's a confirmed hit, direct into the thigh of the target. It looks like the bullet bounced off him. He must be wearing body armour.'

'Shit fuck!' Blackwell cursed as he watched the man walk, unimpeded, through the gate and into the street. He picked up the radio again. 'SWAT One, can you give me a shoulder shot? I want that man on the ground.'

'Ten-four,' came the reply, and within moments, another shot rang through the street. This time Blackwell did watch through the binoculars. He witnessed the shot hit the man in the shoulder. He saw a slight wobble in his walk, but that was all. There was no entry wound, there was no splash of blood as the projectile entered his body, there was no look of pain or shock on his face. But, most off all, the man did *not* fall down wounded. He didn't stop at all.

He couldn't believe what he was seeing.

Looking through the binoculars again, specifically at the blood that the man was covered in, he knew that he needed to make a decision, and it needed to be made quickly. He had to assume that this man had killed the two residents of the house and the three FBI agents that had gone in there to confront him, and he needed to take control of the situation.

'Agent Coombs, do you copy me?' he spoke into the radio again, hoping beyond hope that his boss would reply.

There was nothing but static. All the other officers looked at each other; young and old, experienced and rookies. A wave of unease flowed through them as the suspect continued his walk despite two confirmed hits from the sniper and his high calibre weapon.

The youth had left the garden and was now heading down the street. Blackwell knew that his procrastination was over, no matter his personal feelings, the time to act was nigh. *Oh, Lord Jesus please forgive me for what I'm about to do,* he prayed. As he did, he saw the suspect turn his head and look directly at him. Blackwell felt the man's glare burn his skin. Then, after a few moments, he looked away and carried on with his slow journey.

'Let him have it … fire at will,' Blackwell shouted down the radio. He needed this suspect taken down, and if the snipers couldn't do it, then maybe a full-on assault would. He had wanted to bring the suspect in alive, but he knew that was now no longer an option.

A cacophony of gunfire ensued as all the nervous trigger fingers of the local and state police began to fire at once. The SWAT snipers were firing their high-calibre weapons, but the FBI guys abstained. To Blackwell, this was appropriate action.

The smoke of the gunfire began to cloud up the street, and he soon lost sight of the target. It began to feel like all of this was extreme overkill for one man, but cops did tend to get itchy fingers when one of

The Contract

their own, or perhaps three in this case, didn't return from a situation, when the perp did.

He must be down by now, Blackwell thought through the deafening noise of the gunfire. He looked around, hoping that the media blackout that they had ordered had been maintained. This situation would not look good on the TV.

'CEASE FIRE,' he shouted through the megaphone. He had to shout it three times before the order got through to all the cops and the SWAT snipers. Eventually, silence pervaded.

The smoke took its time to clear from the street. When it did, the car that been parked on the street outside the neighbouring house was destroyed, riddled with bullet holes and smashed glass.

Blackwell looked around at the police and the FBI on the ground. They were all either checking their weapons or shuffling their feet, looking more than a little embarrassed at the over-the-top reaction.

'Hold your fire,' a shout rang out from the silence. Blackwell looked up to see where it had come from. The voice sounded familiar.

'Don't shoot, we're coming out!'

Coombs and a wounded Agent White appeared in the doorway of the house. With one hand in the air and the other one wrapped around his colleague, Coombs stepped out of the grim darkness, into the smoky street.

'Well I'll be darned,' Blackwell muttered with a smile on his face. He was thankful that his old friend and boss had made it out alive, but mostly he was thankful that he could now hand this whole cluster fuck back to the man who had been tasked with it in the first place.

~~~

'Where's the body? The body! Where the fuck is it? DC wanted this perp alive.' Coombs was shouting at anyone and everyone the moment White was taken from him by the paramedics.

Blackwell stepped forward. 'When he came out of the door, I gave him the order to place himself on the ground with his hands behind his head. I gave him two chances, but he chose to ignore both. He continued walking both times.'

Coombs was looking at him. He didn't know whether to be angry at his friend or feel sorry for him. This whole thing was a shit storm. Both he and Blackwell would feel heat for this. Mostly, he was angry with that prick, Cox. He had set them up for this fall without any kind of genuine warning of what they were up against. Although deep down in the pit of his stomach, he'd known something was off. There would have been no way that another FBI agent would have deployed so many resources on a whim. He cursed himself for not entirely taking Cox at face value.

'I heard the warnings. I also heard the shots. Explain to me what happened.'

Blackwell was shaking his head. 'We fired a shot to the leg, and then another one to the shoulder. Either one of them should have incapacitated him. Neither of them did. The kid just kept on moving.' Blackwell hung his head a little then. 'I thought you guys in there were dead. There was no word from you on the radio, and I knew how much DC wanted this guy stopped.' He paused for a breath, before looking up and staring into Coombs' dark brown eyes. 'I gave the order to fire at will.'

Coombs turned away to survey the devastated battle zone with gritted teeth. Then, he heard the words that he least wanted to hear right at that moment.

'Sir, I've got DC on the Sat-phone for you.' A police officer was next to him holding a large phone towards him. He was holding it as if it was something distasteful, something he wanted to get rid of as soon as he could.

Coombs looked at it, and his stomach churned. *How the fuck do I explain this?* He snatched the phone out of the officer's hand and put it to his ear. The officer retreated to a safe distance.

'Is this Agent Coombs?' the voice on the other end asked. It sounded different from the one earlier, which annoyed Coombs even more, as he was wired to give Agent Cox a piece of his mind. 'I'm Agent Adam Symes, Cox's partner. He's otherwise engaged at this moment, but he's asked me to get a status update from you.'

A fucking status update? Coombs was furious now. He'd lost one of his best men, and a whole fucking battalion of police and SWAT couldn't take out one featherweight suspect, or at least supply him with a corpse.

'Well, Agent Symes …' he hoped the inflection on Adam's name would tell him exactly how he was feeling, '…your update is that the mission was a failure. An *abject* failure.'

The Contract

'A failure? Can you elaborate?'
I'll elaborate your fucking face in a minute you prick, Coombs thought. He took a couple of deep breaths and felt the rush of the oxygen swilling through him. He then began to relay the full operation down the telephone for the Agent who he was beginning to despise. 'Then the fucker had the audacity to leave one of those damned white feathers on him.'
'He left a feather on Agent Platt?' Symes asked.
'Yeah, he pulled it out of a pocket within his top or something, before casually leaving it on top of his body. Next, he made his way over to me to finish the job on Lattis. Christ, he stuck his fingers right into the poor bastard's eyes. That was a mercy.'
'Did he leave a feather on Lattis?'
Is this guy even listening to me? I'm pouring my heart out here and all he's bothered about is the fucking feathers, Coombs thought. He shook his head, clearing the bad thoughts and continued his report. 'Yeah! He took two feathers out of his top, one for Platt and one for Lattis.'
'Did he say anything to Platt before killing him?'
Coombs thought for a moment. 'Yeah, he mentioned something about him saving him a trip. God only knows what that meant. Anyway, I watched Platt put two bullets in him, and believe me Platt was one of the best shots in Quantico. I don't mind telling you that I feared for my life right there and then. He looked at me, no, I'd say he looked through me, then he turned and left. I made an informed decision that if he left the house the cops outside would take him out. Which they did, or at least tried.'
'They tried? Agent Coombs, can you confirm that the target is either in custody or dead?'
'Well, this is where the mission seems to be a failure,' Coombs confessed on the phone. 'When the smoke cleared, there was no-one there. There's no way on God's Green Earth that a man, any man could have gotten out of there alive. I'm telling you, there's no fucking body.'
Coombs paused then, waiting a reply from Symes on the other end. All he was rewarded with was silence.
Eventually the silence was broken. 'Right...' was all Agent Symes said.

Coombs felt the accusation of it. He felt the condescending sarcasm drip right out of the handset he was holding. *Right?* he thought. *Right? I just told him that after the shitstorm of bullets and the direct hits from the SWAT snipers that there's no corpse, and all this prick can say is 'right'?* 'Agent Symes, I'm a little bit confused here. I've just informed you that there's no body to be found. That the perp has either disappeared into thin air or escaped a hailstorm of bullets. Your response is a non-committal 'Right.' Am I out of the loop here? I've just watched one of my men, the man who he killed, pump bullets into him from close range, to absolutely no effect whatsoever. Then I watched him crush that same man's skull with his own skinny ass hands before fleeing a scene where over fifty cops shot at him. This isn't your average perp, is it?'

Once again, he was greeted with silence on the other end of the phone. 'Agent Coombs. We still don't know what kind of entity we're dealing with here.'

'Entity?' Coombs interrupted.

'We did tell you that there was the possibility of a supernatural element to this case. The agent who was killed, was it a targeted attack? It didn't sound like an accident to me. Can you elaborate?'

It was time for Coombs to be silent. Anger was building up inside him. Platt had been a trusted agent and he'd had his back on a number of occasions. 'Agent Platt challenged the perp. With very little effort, the freak picked him up and stared into his eyes. I wanted to help, but for some inexplicable reason, I couldn't move. The next thing I saw was him squeezing Platt's head. He said what he said to him and then killed him.'

'Was your body recorder working?' Symes asked him.

'Yeah, it's always on when we go into situations. Why?'

'Can you send us the audio file?'

'Yeah, I can. There was something odd about his voice though, it was too deep and too ... I don't know, something, to be coming out of such a small man.'

'I hate to ask this, Agent Coombs, and believe me, I'm not speaking ill of the dead. But, Agent Platt, just how well did you know him?'

'Platt had been under my supervision for over five years; he came to my office right out of Quantico. He finished his class with honours, Agent Symes. You can look that up yourself.'

The Contract

'We already have. I'm going to have to know more about him, more about his personal life. What did he do after work? Who did he hang out with?'

'What are you getting at, Agent Symes?'

There was a sigh on the other end of the line. When Agent Symes resumed, he sounded as if he was trying to whisper. 'Well, if the man, our perp, made a targeted attack on Agent Platt, and especially with the exchange of words that they had between them, then there just might be something in his past, something in his methods, that was not quite right. The two men he killed recently, both of them seemed like fine, upstanding citizens. It wasn't until we dug deeper that we found out that they were, in fact, serial killers. If you don't want to investigate it, Agent Coombs, I'll get someone else to do it. But, believe me, he will be investigated.'

This information hung in his head. *Platt, crooked? No way,* he thought. 'Fine. I'll commence with a hushed investigation. But put this on the record, Agent Symes, I have severe reservations about snooping around about one of my men, especially one who has just died in the line of duty.'

'Duly noted,' Symes replied. 'Thank you so much for your co-operation, Agent Coombs,' Symes said before signing off.

Think nothing of it, you arrogant dick, Coombs thought before pressing the red button on the phone. He rested his hands on the roof of the car as he looked around at the mess of this operation. He sighed, deeply.

25.

IN AN OFFICE in the J Edgar Hoover Building, Washington, DC, a few days after the events in Oregon, Agents Cox and Symes and Dr Broom were sitting in a meeting room. An atmosphere of gloom hung over them, as if they had lost something valuable, which, in essence, was exactly what had happened. Cox did not take the loss of an agent's life lightly, even if the method of his killing cast a spotlight upon his personal or professional life.

Before them on the table was another open file. *My whole life seems to be consumed with open files,* Cox thought as he flicked through the report within. 'Multiple hits, confirmed. Not including the shots from Platt himself inside the house.' He shook his head as he flung the file back onto the desk. 'This guy is unstoppable. What the hell are we dealing with?'

'The supernatural,' Broom spoke up.

Both agents looked at him as if they had forgotten that he was there.

'Do you really think that?' Symes asked.

Broom shrugged. 'It makes sense. I've proved that my model works. I pointed to the exact location and the exact time. All of this came from the stars.'

Symes leaned back in his chair, crossing his arms as he shook his head. 'I've seen a lot of shit in my life. I'm really struggling with this supernatural beings shit. Where the fuck was God when I was in Afghanistan? When I watched the twin towers fall back in '01?'

'Maybe that was all the work of the other side?' Broom asked. 'There are plenty of beautiful things happening every single day that go unnoticed and unrecorded. Then, as soon as aeroplanes go into a building,

The Contract

people scream 'where was God then?' If you believe in the devil, then you have to believe in God. It's yin and yang.'

The corners of Symes's mouth pulled down as he pouted towards the doctor. 'That's a good speech, Doc, but right now, what does it do to help us with this ...' bending two fingers of each hand to air-quote the next words, he continued, 'supernatural perp?'

'Well, for one, we'll have the location of the next attack,' the doctor continued with a smug smile.

Symes leaned in to continue the argument when Cox's mobile phone rang. 'Hang on, you two,' he said, stopping the two men from arguing while he answered the phone. 'Agent Cox,' he announced to the unknown number.

'Agent Cox, this is Agent Coombs, from Oregon. Have you got a moment to talk?'

'Of course, I do. Give me a second.' He held his hand over the phone and pointed at Broom. 'Doc, can I get you onto that model right now? I need you to be working non-stop on it for however long it takes to predict the next celestial movements of our man.' He then pointed to Symes. 'It's Coombs from Oregon. I'll take this outside. Make sure the doctor here has everything he needs. I'll update you on this conversation right after.'

Symes winked as Cox stood up and left the room with his phone in his ear.

'Coombs, I'm sorry about that, we were just addressing what happened out there.'

'Not a problem, sir. I wanted to give you a heads up. We've been working on the audio file from my set. I'm sending you the files now.'

'Thanks, Coombs. But I've got a feeling that you didn't just call me to tell me that.'

'You'd be guessing right. We've analysed the recording, and it's only one way.'

'Meaning?' Cox asked, he thought he sounded a little harder than he meant to.

'Meaning ... the guy's, our target's, voice hasn't recorded. Everything else is fine. My voice is as clear as day, as is Platt's. But our man's? Just dead space.'

'You said I have the files now?'

'You should have. There's something else, Agent. Something about Platt. I started an unofficial, silent investigation into his activities. Let's just say there are a few *things* about him that we didn't know. Some things that must have flown under the radar during his federal evaluation. I don't want to say too much right now, but I promise that I'll keep you informed. Also, can you keep me in the loop on this one, as a professional courtesy? Even if there was the possibility of him being dirty, I still lost one of my men!'

'Yeah, of course, Agent Coombs. Listen, don't beat yourself up too much over what happened. You did a great job. Everything that was required, you did,' Cox whispered down the handset he was holding. 'I'd like to offer you my thanks for that.'

'It's appreciated. Let's hope we get this son-of-a-bitch.' With that, the line went dead.

'Play that file,' Cox ordered as he re-entered the room, pointing to the audio file that had appeared onto the shared drive on the computer screen.

Symes double clicked it and an audio application popped up.

It was pretty standard stuff, except that Coombs was right. Every time they would have expected their perpetrator to say something, the file went blank. Then, there was a muffled cry. It made the hairs on Cox's arms stand up.

'Rewind that bit, would you?' he asked, standing up.

'Rewind?' Symes asked. 'What century are you from?' he laughed.

'You know what I meant, dickhead,' he shot back, playfully, even though he felt far from playful. 'Turn the volume up too.'

'Uhhh... pheeeeeuuug pluuuuuuuugh fiiiig muuuuh'

'Is there any way we can speed this up?' Cox asked. 'Broom, you're a computer expert. Can you speed this up please?'

Broom stepped up to the computer and pressed the button to speed the playback up.

'Uhhh... pheeeeeuuug pluuuuuuuugh fiiiig muuuuh'

'Can you do it a little bit faster?' Cox asked listening to the high-pitched sounds now.

'Uhhh... pheeeeeuuug pluuuuuuuugh fiiiig muuuuh'

'Is it just me, or does that sound like the man is praying?'

The Contract

'Praying?' Symes asked. 'Can you play it one more time please, Broom?'

Broom rolled his eyes. 'I'm a doctor, not a bloody disc jockey,' he tutted as he pressed the button again.

'That sounds, to me anyway, if I'm not putting in words where there are none, like he's saying Father, please forgive me,' Cox said after the final listen of the soundbite.

Symes stood up straight and looked at him. 'It does sound like that! If you're right, then it would fit right in with what Coombs wrote in his report. Look ...'

Symes shoved Broom out of the way, and the doctor moved where he was shoved with a disdainful look.

'Where is it?' Symes clicked around until he found what he was looking for in one of the shared drives associated with the case. 'Here we go,' he said as the email filled the computer screen. *It's not on the recording, but I was close enough to hear what he replied to Lattis right before killing him. Lattis moaned something unintelligible, he had done it twice, then our man leaned into him and said 'Yes, he might be able to, but I can't'.*

'Could this be some sort of religious connotation?'

'Maybe so!' Cox said shaking his head. 'It's another piece of this blank jigsaw. Doc, how is it coming with our prediction?'

Broom took the seat back at the computer, fixed his glasses, and stared intently at the screen. 'I hate to say I told you so, Agents,' he mumbled as he began to type.

Both Symes and Cox stared at him, both men were smiling.

26.

THE DIRECTOR OF Operations office was vast. Pictures of every agent that the director had mentored through the years and had passed through training adorned this wall next to copies of their certificates. It was something that he was very proud of. When he was in a thoughtful mood, trying to work some things out, he could be found staring at this wall. He claimed that it helped him organise his brain.

Right now, he was staring at a photograph of a young George Cox smiling into a camera. He was dressed in a suit and was holding the original of the certificate that was next to the picture.

The real Cox was sat at the meeting table that was in the corner of the large room. He was joined by Symes and Broom. The professor had a laptop in front of him and was clicking away at the keys on it.

The Director turned around to look at the motley looking crew sat before him. He said something, and Cox appeared to agree. Cox then pointed towards Symes, who shrugged and continued to talk for a small while. All the time, Broom continued to type on the laptop. Eventually, he turned the small computer around to show the other three men the screen. Cox and Symes leaned in to look at what he was showing them, and the director made his way over to look too.

The director shook his head. It wasn't a negative shake, he looked impressed by what he was seeing. When he stopped shaking his head, he began to nod. Then he pressed a button on the telephone and spoke into it for a short while. Cox, Symes, and Broom all stood, shook hands with the director, and left the room. Broom left last, carrying his laptop as he went.

The Contract

27.

FOURTH STREET NORTHWEST, Alameda Valley, New Mexico, three days after the meeting in the Director of Operations office in Washington, DC. Cox and Symes sat in an unmarked rental car staring at a house with quite a bit of land around it. The plot was surrounded by other deserted plots, making it an ideal location for the nefarious activities that had been going on inside.

It was not long past noon, and the heat was almost unbearable.

'Can we put the AC back on?' Symes asked, 'I think I'm sweating alcohol here.'

Cox reached over and turned the dial to cold. In fairness, he was sweating like the pig who knew he was for dinner too. He looked at his colleague in the passenger seat and smiled. 'You weren't drinking last night,' he observed.

Symes smiled and winked at him. 'I wasn't, man, but the young ladies at the hotel, they were.'

Cox shook his head for what he felt was the millionth time at his younger counterpart. 'You never?' There was no humour in this question, and there was no hint at being impressed. His face looked as if a dark thundercloud was brewing just behind his eyes.

Symes nodded.

'How many?' Again, this was not a light-hearted question.

'Three,' he replied as he rubbed his hands through his hair.

'Did we not talk about this?' Cox was angry now. Not only had Symes gone back on his word and succumbed to his addiction, but he was in danger of putting the mission in an ill-light, not to mention the bureau.

'We did, and you agreed that I would keep my ... activities, limited to non-bureau related situations. But, come on, man. You saw how hot those girls were.'

'I saw how hot two of those girls were. The third went to bed well before we left the restaurant. Who was the third?'

Symes's head fell even lower. 'The manager,' he half whispered.

Cox stared intently at his partner. 'The manager? Adam, she was double your size and double your age. Not to mention she had a wedding ring on. What the fuck is wrong with you?'

Symes shrugged. 'I can't help it. If a girl looks at me, then I have to have her.'

'I'm serious here. When we get back to DC, I'm recommending you, officially, for counselling. I think this case is affecting you.'

'George, I can't lose this job, it's everything to me,' Symes pleaded.

'I'm going to recommend you for a commendation, but only on the condition that you get yourself some help. One day you're seriously going to fuck up an investigation with that dick of yours.'

'Never, man, I never talk about anything that we're doing. Actually, after the initial flirting, there's never much talking happening at all.' He turned away from the reproachful stare of Cox and looked over towards the building they were monitoring. 'It always seems just so ... mechanical!'

'OK, let's shelve it for now. We've got a job to do. Broom said this building here.' Cox reached over into the back of the car and grabbed the laptop that was on the seat and opened it. 'The doc said that the event will be happening at ten past twelve, which gives us roughly three minutes before the shit hits the fan. Are you ready?'

Symes took his gun out of his shoulder holster and checked the magazine. 'Always, man, always.'

~~~~

They had decided to go on this little adventure alone. Cox thought that there was little point in bringing in any backup. The amount of times that their suspect had taken a bullet, or even a hundred, without it slowing him down, had convinced them that their best weapon against this being was probably words. Cox wanted to talk to him, to ask him what his motivations were, and if they were honourable, which they seemed. Then he would ask him politely to accompany them for

The Contract

questioning. He really didn't think that they would be able to bring this one in if he didn't want to be brought in.

Looking over at the address, they saw a few expensive looking cars parked in the driveway, and there had been quite a bit of activity, coming and going to and from the building.

'Do you think it's some kind of party?' Symes asked. There was a knowing grin on his face, and Cox, for one split second, regretted bringing him along with him today. Given the nature of his addiction, busting a porn shoot, no matter how sick and depraved it was, was not playing to his best interests.

'You know it, man,' Cox replied.

'So, how do you want to play this? Do we go in and warn these people about what's going to happen to them, or do we wait until he's in mid flow and bust his ass?' Symes asked.

Cox could see the sweat on his partner's brow. *He's just as nervous as me,* he thought. *What do we do if this guy won't come in? We can't chase him forever!*

'Forget that question,' Symes continued. 'It looks like our quandary has been answered for us.' He pointed over towards the lot.

'Quandary?' Cox asked.

Symes laughed a little. 'Sorry, I think I've been hanging around with Broom a little too much!'

Cox looked back towards their target building. A young-looking man wearing black sweatpants and a black hooded top was striding purposefully towards the house. The hood on his top was down, and his blond hair was blowing in the dry, hot New Mexico breeze.

'He's early. What the Hell is he doing?'

'Do we go?' Symes asked.

Cox ignored him and picked up the binoculars from by his feet and looked through them. He was shocked by what he saw. 'I think there's something wrong over there. Take a look at our guy through these.' Cox handed the binoculars over to Symes, who took looked through them.

'Is that even him?' he asked.

'It would appear so,' Cox answered.

'What's up with him? He looks, I don't know, old somehow.'

Cox took the glasses back and looked again. Symes was right, he appeared stooped and was walking slower than he had been reported in the past. Also, there appeared to be quite a bit of grey in his hair, more than blond. Cox watched as he leaned against the wall of the house. He appeared to be resting. *He looks sick,* Cox thought. *Maybe this is our chance to bring him in.*

'OK, we take nothing for granted with this guy. What do you have on you?'

Symes reached around his body. 'Standard Glock, Sig backup, knife in the ankle sheath and another in my inside pocket.'

'Did you see what the 308s did to him?' Cox asked. 'Our handguns will be like toys to him.'

'Are you seeing the state of the guy today? He's ripe for the taking.'

'Do you want to test that theory? Make him mad?' Cox asked. 'I don't. We wait until he makes his move. I don't think we have what it takes to take him out, but I do want to talk to him. Find out what his agenda is, maybe even find out who he's working for. You up for that?'

Symes smiled. His cheery demeanour was back. 'You're the boss, boss,' he laughed.

It was Cox's turn to become a little maudlin. He stared at Symes and smiled. It was a resigned smile, a smile that said Cox was ready for whatever would happen to them today. It was a smile that said that he'd made his peace with the world, and if the ultimate sacrifice was to be made, then so be it. What did cheer him up though, was Symes's smile back at him.

'Cox,' Symes whispered.

'What, man?'

'Bring it in, big fella,' he laughed, before opening his arms out to his partner for a hug.

Cox laughed and took the opening.

'Whoa,' Symes said pushing him away, playfully. 'You gotta watch that shit. I've got a reputation, remember? Besides, they'll think we're doing a rival porno in the car here and might just want to take out the competition themselves.'

Cox laughed as he opened the car door. 'Come on, we've got work to do,' he finished.

The man entered the property, opening the door and letting himself in, almost as if he had been invited. Cox knew that there was no

The Contract

way that the front door wouldn't have been locked and guarded. *Then again, this guy doesn't need an invitation to gate-crash a party.*

A loud bang, the unmistakable sound of rapid gunfire, a lot of female screaming, and male shouting ensued. Both Cox and Symes took cover behind the car, guns drawn in automatic response to the situation.

'Who the fuck are you? How did you get in here?' came a shout from inside the building.

Cox tipped the nod to his partner, who ran from behind the car, towards the yard of the address, and stopped behind a sleek looking Audi. Cox watched as Symes peeped and looked towards the open door, then crouched back down and turned to signal Cox.

The meaning was understood.

The coast was clear.

Cox ran in the other direction, across the yard from his partner, to crouch behind a sleek BMW. He also looked over the car door. This location gave him a different view inside the house through the open door. From this vantage point, he could see a body lying on the floor, but no other movement. He made a signal to Symes, informing him of the body, and that there was no other activity. Symes then made his next move, based on that information.

He ran to the house, flinging himself next to the door with his back to the wall. Symes followed him. Both men stayed where they were for a few moments, just listening. Male and female voices were still shouting and screaming from somewhere inside. Cox heard a voice that made his skin crawl.

'YOU, OUT. ALL THE REST STAY!'

He could feel goose-bumps rise on his arm. The last time he had heard that voice was back in Jacksonville. The vision of Fitchett hanging from his own light fitting with most of his flesh peeled away from him was not something that would easily pass, if it ever did. He took a moment to compose himself before nodding to Symes, informing him that he was going inside.

Once inside, he checked the body lying on the floor. It was of a young man. He was dressed in a nice shirt and an expensive pair of trousers. His head had been turned all the way around. His lightly bearded face, stuck in a rictus of fear and pain, was looking upwards. His sightless, dead eyes stared at whoever, or whatever, had done this to him. Cox knelt down. Even though it seemed like a useless gesture, he placed his hand to the man's throat to see if he had a pulse; he didn't. That was when he noticed the white feather, placed on the man's back. He pointed at it, indicating its presence to Symes, who was now inside the door.

Symes nodded. He saw it but was more interested in what they would be finding around the corner.

There was a babble of excitement from somewhere ahead of them. Suddenly, a group of people burst into the room, running towards them. They were mixed male and female, and they were all naked.

'Cox,' Symes whispered to his partner.

Cox turned around, just as the group rushed past them, towards the open door. Every one of them ignored the two agents in their hurry to exit the building.

'What?' he answered.

Symes was laughing. 'Nothing! I was just warning you about the naked men.'

Cox rolled his eyes. 'Concentrate, will you?' he snapped, although he did think the quip was funny.

'Get away from me, you freak! Get a ...' came the shout from inside the room. This was followed by a number of gun shots. Then silence.

'We go on three,' Cox whispered as the two agents made their way towards the location of the shots. He then began to countdown, slowly, using his fingers.

One... Two ... Three...

Both agents burst into the spacious room.

~~~~

The scene that opened up to them was nothing like what they were expecting. Two rooms in the building had been knocked through and made into one, large film set. There were cameras and lighting rigs set up all around. Most of them were pointing towards a large, long couch that was next to a lavish looking bed. Symes was also disgusted to notice a number of cages racked up around the room. Inside the cages were a number of dogs, and in another there was a child.

The child was naked and curled up into a ball. The animals, as well as the child, were all sleeping. The sleep looked too deep to be natural.

The Contract

Drugged, was Cox's first thought. He couldn't tell what gender the child was, but he took a guess at their age. He thought that whoever it was, they couldn't have been older than three or four.

On another couch in a corner were two people huddled together. One man and one woman, both dressed in expensive clothes. They turned towards the agents as they entered the room. Their faces lit up, as if they were here to save them from ...

Cox turned to see what it was the couple were staring at. Cox could only see him from behind as he was turned away from them. He was holding a large man up in the air. At first, Cox thought he was holding him by the throat, but on closer inspection, he saw that his hand had entered into the chest of the man, whose arms and legs were dangling and twitching as thick, almost purple blood spewed from the hole in his chest.

Another noise from the other corner of the room, and Cox saw two more people huddled together. They were both naked and shaking.

By the young man's foot was a gun, which obviously had belonged to the man who was currently adorning the wall.

'This is the FBI. I'm ordering you to cease and desist assaulting that man,' Cox ordered. His voice was calm, and this amazed him, as everything else about him felt like it was going crazy inside.

He didn't turn around to look to see who had just come in. All he did was shift his arm to throw the large man across the room. He hit the wall next to the naked couple with a wet crunch and crumpled to the floor in a heap, leaving a greasy red stain, like a mural, behind. Without saying a word, he walked towards the dead body, pulling a white feather from his top as he went. When he got there, he lay it on top of the body.

Cox watched as the naked couple began to squirm, attempting to crawl out of his way.

They didn't get far.

With what looked like minimal effort, he reached out his hands and pulled both of them back towards him. He then smashed both of their heads together. The crack was dull, and Cox winced at the sight of the collision. It made him weak at the knees.

The couple fell to the floor when he let go of them. Cox saw that both their heads were ruined, caved in and bloated. Like someone had turned on a tap, thick blood was pouring from the devastation in their craniums, the mouths, noses, and ears. The old looking youth drew another two feathers from inside his top and placed them onto the bodies at his feet.

'Don't take one more step, or believe me, we will fire,' Cox ordered. He looked towards Symes who also had his gun levelled at the youth's head.

The man turned to look at Cox. For the first time in this encounter, Cox saw his face. It had changed since the last time he had seen him. The blond was losing the fight with the grey, in both the hair and the beard. Lines were etched into his face, and his skin looked sallow. Without any recognition, he turned away and walked towards the other, fully dressed couple on the couch.

'I said not to move,' Cox spoke.

'I DO NOT RECOGNISE YOUR AUTHORITY, AGENT COX.' Even though the voice still boomed and sounded like it was coming from multiple directions, there was something about it that Cox didn't like.

It sounded tired.

He walked over to the couple and grasped one of the lighting rigs that was still illuminating the couch and bed. As he grasped one of the metal flaps, Cox heard Symes take in a deep breath as the sizzle from his skin on the hot metal must have burnt him. If it did, he didn't show it. He took the metal flap and bent it, then thrust the shiv into the woman's neck. Her screaming and crying ended in a sick gurgle. Her blood, under pressure from the carotid artery, spewed forth and splattered over the man sitting next to her. As it began to pour from her mouth, she reached out towards her colleague, grasping at him, non-verbally pleading for help.

The man screamed. It was a high-pitched scream that looked and sounded strange coming from someone so big. 'Keep away from me, you motherfucker, keep the fuck away,' he squealed.

The four reports from Symes's gun were loud to Cox's ears. He hadn't been ready for them, and they took him by surprise. Another four reports rang out as their target, unthwarted by the shots that had hit him, turned his attentions on the whimpering man currently attempting to simultaneously wipe the woman's blood off his face and push her dead, lifeless body away from him.

The four shots hadn't even slowed him down.

The Contract

He grabbed the crying man's head by his hair while his other hand wrapped around his face in a vice-like grip. With an almighty pull, he ripped the head right off the torso.
Cox marvelled at his strength. It was then that he realised how he had pulled Carr's body up from his office seat with just that wire.
Symes was fitting another magazine into his gun as Cox looked at him. He shook his head and held his hand out towards his friend. 'Don't,' Cox half-whispered. 'There's no point.'
Symes's eyebrows came together in a question.
'Trust me. What use are they against him?'
The youth moved so fast that he took both of the agents by surprise. He reached out and grabbed Symes by the shirt. He yanked him towards him so hard that his gun flew out of his hands and his feet left the ground. He pulled the surprised agent close, and both men stared at each other, eye to eye.
No one moved.
Cox didn't know what to do. He had an idea that Symes would be OK, as they knew that this man only ever killed anyone who was a bad person. Other than a few dalliances with the ladies, *OK, more than a few,* he contradicted himself, he was a good man. He had nothing to worry about.
The youth looked Symes in the eye. It was a long and laboured look. Cox felt his heartbeat raise. *What if Symes has something to hide?* he thought. The old boy looked a little confused as he stared at the petrified agent. He took in a deep breath, closed his eyes and exhaled slowly. To Cox's relief, he let go of Symes, allowing his body to fall, ungracefully, to the floor. He reached into his top and pulled out a white feather. Cox's heart fell to this stomach again. *He's going to kill him after all,* he thought. Then, to his relief, the young man placed the feather onto the headless torso lying bleeding on the couch.
By force of habit again, Cox pointed his gun with a shaking hand towards the now not-so-young-looking man.
'YOU WILL NOT NEED THAT GUN, AGENT COX,' he said in his strange voice.
'Maybe not, but I feel a whole lot safer with it in my hand. How do you know my name, by the way?'
The man took a moment before he answered. The expression on his face never changed. 'I KNOW EVERYBODY'S NAME. I KNOW

YOUR PARTNER, ADAM SYMES. I KNOW THE FORNICATORS WHO WERE IN THE BEDS. THEY WERE JAMES JULES AND KATARINA SHINKLO. I KNOW THIS MAN …' he pointed to the man he had killed first after they had entered the room, 'HE WAS WILLIAM HOLT.'

'What do you want? Who do you work for? Why are you killing all of these people?' Questions were flooding out of his mouth. Months and months of frustration on this headless chicken of a case poured out of him, seemingly at once.

'THESE PEOPLE,' he swiped his arm out before him, taking in the whole room, 'AND THE PEOPLE BEFORE THEM, THEY ALL DESERVED TO DIE. THESE TWO HAVE CHEATED PEOPLE OUT OF ALL OF THEIR LIFE'S SAVINGS ON MORE THAN ONE OCCASION.' He was pointing towards the two bodies on the couch. 'THEIR GREED HAS CAUSED FOUR SUICIDES. THIS WOMAN HERE …' He indicated towards the body of the woman by the window, 'SHE RECRUITS THE INNOCENT AND CORRUPTS THEM INTO WHAT YOU SEE HERE. THE CHILD IN THE CAGE? SHE HAD NO PROBLEM SUPPLYING THESE PEOPLE WITH WHATEVER THEY REQUIRED OR LUSTED AFTER. SHE CAUSED MISERY AND DEATH WHEREVER SHE WENT. DO I NEED TO GO ON, AGENT COX?'

'You still haven't told me, who, or what, are you? Where are you from? Where do you go? Who the fuck do you work for?'

'AGENT COX, PLEASE DO NOT GET EMOTIONALLY INVOLVED. YOU WILL BE CONSUMED. I IMPLORE YOU NOT TO PURSUE THIS.'

'I have to, it's my job. It's what I do. *You* are now my job. I know that my gun here is useless against you, and I know that I'm physically powerless to stop you, but I have to know! I just have to.'

'AGENT COX.' The youth's voice had become audibly weaker now. Even though there was still a boom, it was nowhere near as powerful as when he had first encountered him. The rapidly aging man leaned in to look Cox in the face. It was an unnerving feeling for him. Even though he was physically bigger than this man, there was an enormous sensation of power emanating from him. Cox couldn't find the words to express the feeling he was encountering. His brain searched and searched, but the best that he could summon was—vast.

The Contract

There was a vastness about this man before him. It was almost as if he was the personification of eternity. *What the hell does that even mean?* Cox asked himself.

'AGENT COX, DO YOU REALLY WANT ANSWERS TO YOUR QUESTIONS? DO YOU THINK THAT YOU CAN HANDLE THE ANSWERS YOU DESIRE?'

'Yes, I think I can, and if I can't, then I need to know that too.' Cox felt like a young boy being taught a lesson by the oldest and wisest master in a university. He did need to know these answers. But now, it was not only to quell his professional curiosity, he felt like this man had become something of an obsession to him.

'You're old, aren't you?' As the question left Cox's lips it felt like a stupid thing to ask. It felt small and useless.

The man looked at him and smiled. It was the first time he had witnessed an expression change on his face. Cox noticed that even in the short time of them being here, the lines on his face had deepened, along with the yellow sallowness of his skin.

'WITNESS!' The boom in his voice was back.

He stood to his full height. Cox thought that he was somehow taller now than he had been less than a few moments ago. He lifted up his blood-soaked, black hooded top and pulled it over his slight frame. He then removed the jogging trousers that he had been wearing. Cox was more than shocked at the boy's nakedness beneath. Not because it was unexpected, but because of his physical differences to other men he had seen. The boy had a great physique, he was well muscled, but there was something odd about his torso. It wasn't just the distinct lack of hair on his body, even though that disturbed him somewhat. There was something else. It took a few moments to realise what his eyes were missing.

The man had no bellybutton, or nipples. There was just smooth skin stretching over his muscular fame. There were also no reproductive organs either.

'YOU CALL ME 'THE PERP' OR 'OUR GUY,' BUT YOU HAVE NEVER CALLED ME BY MY NAME.'

'We don't know your name, we don't know anything about you,' Cox replied.

'YOU DO KNOW MY NAME, AGENT COX. CLOSE YOUR EYES AND THINK OF ME. MY NAME WILL COME TO YOU.'

Cox felt that he had no choice *but* to close his eyes. He was compelled to obey. As the darkness enfolded him, he thought he could hear music. A loud, terrible music, but from far away. There were trumpets and bugles and drums. There was chanting and screaming, and laughter all mixed together. Then a white light appeared. It drained the darkness out of his eyes, giving him a perfect vision of a shining being.

It was him.

Cox couldn't see him clearly, but he was sure that it was him.

'You're god-like,' he muttered. As he did, he opened his eyes. 'Michael!' was the simple word that rushed to his lips.

'THAT IS CORRECT,' Michael replied.

As Cox looked at him, he smiled again. A magnificent expanse of white wings unfurled out from behind his back. When they reached their full potential, their span filled the room.

Cox didn't know what to do. He didn't know if he should fall down to his knees before this being, or if he should run. All he did was rock a little on his heels as the enormity of the situation engulfed him. His senses began to focus again, and he narrowed his eyes, staring at the wings. He noticed that there were a lot of the white feathers missing.

'I AM MICHAEL, THE ARCHANGEL. I WILL REVEAL TO YOU, AGENT COX, MY MISSION.'

The wings, as if with a mind of their own, reached out to the agent and began to wrap him into their soft embrace. Although he felt no force on his body, he was lifted up, off the ground, and bathed in a golden light. Cox could not fathom where the light was originating.

~~~~

The golden glow intensified, and Cox found himself revelling in it. It was warm, it was comforting, and it was all-encompassing. It was the safest he had ever felt since he was a babe in arms, held by a proud and protective father, while a tired but jubilant mother looked on. He opened his eyes, expecting the glare from the light to blind him, but it didn't. The golden glow around him had gone, only to be replaced by a light blue. Instead of standing in the dingy, horrible porno studio, Cox was now floating in the clouds. Michael was next to him, guiding him. He had returned to his former glory. His long, lustrous hair was back, as was his golden beard. His face was beautiful. Cox had never been aware

The Contract

of human faces ever being beautiful before, but Michael's, probably due to his lack of humanity, was. His wings were spread to their full capacity. All the missing feathers had been replaced with golden ones.

Cox felt lost in the euphoria of being with this Angel.

'In order for you to know my mission, my contract, so to speak, you must first understand the beginnings.'

Cox didn't associate the words with Michael. He had heard his voice before, twice. Both times it sounded harsh, otherworldly. Now he knew why. But now, his voice sounded like the sweetest music that he had ever heard in his life. He likened it to honey, dripping from the hive.

'You must witness the beginning of all things.'

Cox looked down and around him. There were structures below. Golden towers and sprawling lands. He saw other flying beings swooping through the air around them. *There is peace here,* he thought. 'Where are we?' he asked. The wonder in his voice was practically childlike.

'You might call this place Heaven, or Paradise. Maybe Zion, Utopia ... it has many names. I call this place HOME.'

'Home?' Cox asked. 'You live here?'

'It is HOME, but not in the same sense as you understand the word. We know it as the original word. It has multiple meanings in multiple languages. Domov. Thius. Kodu. Bagay. Koti. Maison. Heim. I could go on. Multiple words with just one meaning. It is the place you return to.'

Cox couldn't help but fly around and around. He was awed. The tranquillity, the feeling of fulfilment, it soared through him, through his very being. *My soul?* he thought.

'You are in another time and space. You think of it as a different dimension, another planet if you will. All of those descriptions have the same meaning here. This is the land of *The Originator*. He thought of you all, and you all must return to him in the end.' Michael paused for a moment before continuing 'Or, most do!'

Cox stopped flying and looked at his host. 'Most? What do you mean by most?'

Michael breathed a sigh. As he did, Cox noted that it was mostly for effect. Very little, if any breath expelled from him. He was using human traits. *Probably for my benefit.*

'You are familiar with the concept of Hell, Perdition, Limbo?' Michael continued.

'Yes. Of course, I am. It's instilled upon us from an early age. Most religions on Earth have their own version. That is, if you believe the stories we're told.'

'Well, that place is an unwelcome side-effect of *The Originator's* biggest mistake. It was the one idea He thought would be His biggest and greatest triumph.'

'What would that mistake be?' Cox asked hoping that he wasn't overstepping his mark.

'His biggest mistake, one that was made by His own self-righteousness. He decided, in His wisdom, to give humans free-will.' Michael said this as if it left a terrible taste in his mouth. He looked like he was about to spit.

Do Angel's spit? Cox thought that this was a funny idea. *I'd like to see an Angel spit.*

'There will be no spitting tonight, Agent Cox,'

Cox felt guilty at having such a ridiculous thought, but also felt violated because Michael was so easily able to enter into his thoughts.

'Come, let me show you my mission. Please be aware that some of the images I will show you may distort your view of humanity for the rest of your natural life.'

'That's OK. Some of the things I've witnessed in my time have already given me a dim view,' Cox replied.

Michael flexed his wings, and once again they wrapped themselves around Cox. The beautiful, golden glow returned and began to pulse around him once more. He bathed in the glorification of that light.

He opened his eyes as the glow began to subside. Disappointment overcame him as he realised where he was. It was a dim and depressing police interview room, just like many he had frequented on numerous occasions, *too many occasions,* over the years. 'Where am I?'

'We are still in HOME. I made the surroundings a little more comfortable, familiar for you. More in keeping with what you're used to. We are going on a journey, Agent Cox, a very illuminating journey. It will hurt, not physically, but it will hurt nonetheless.'

Michael offered out his hand, and Cox took it without even thinking.

~~~~

The Contract

A jolt ripped through Cox's body, forcing him to open his eyes. It wasn't an entirely unpleasant feeling; it was more of a strange sensation. Once his eyes were open, it took him a few moments to realise where he was.

He was in a forest. It wasn't dark, but he was having trouble seeing. Then he realised why; it was snowing. It was snowing, and there was a fierce wind blowing, yet he didn't feel any of the ill effects. He wasn't cold, nor was he being blown.

'You are within my will, Agent Cox. I willed you here to show you my mission and *The Originator's* biggest mistake. Think of yourself as my passenger,' Michael assured him as he pointed through the trees. 'Observe,' he said.

Cox looked towards where Michael indicated. Through the mist, he saw a group of men striding through the forest. They were walking towards them. Two men at the front were carrying a long. Tied to the stick was a dead animal, one that Cox didn't recognise. He did recognise the men though. Not personally, but by the way they looked. They were small, wide, and hairy. Their long, black, dirty hair and beards were covering jutted jaws and overbearing foreheads.

'Are they our ancestors?' Cox whispered.

'Yes, they are. You do not need to whisper, Agent Cox. They cannot hear or see us. We are shadows in this world. I wanted you to witness what is known as original sin.'

Cox saw that there were four of them, each heavily muscled and carrying bloodied weapons. They were grunting at each other as they made their way through the trees. To Cox, it looked like a primitive form of communication.

Suddenly, from out of the bushes, sprang another group of men. The original group, in their shock at the attack, but with surprisingly fast reflexes, dropped their cargo and stood to defend themselves. The newcomers although similarly dressed and armed, were greater in numbers. With absolutely no preamble, the fight ensued. It was swift, and it was violent. Cox, although detached from the scene, thought he could feel every punch, every kick, every scratch and bite. The four men were quickly overpowered by the larger group, and three of them managed break free and run away. They ran back in the direction from whence they came. Cox saw their wounds. They were deep, and they were bloody. He thought of the primitive way that these men lived and imagined the pain and agony they would endure over the next few days as their wounds festered.

This left just one man, alone to protect the carcass. The new group ignored the dropped meat, as they concentrated on him. He put up a brave fight, but it was futile. He was soon overpowered, lying cowering on the ground as punches and kicks rained down on him from above. The frenzy of the attack was not over until the man was no longer moving. He was dead, killed in the melee. It was not until they had realised that he was no longer moving that they then turned their attentions to the meat he had been attempting to protect. The group picked up the carcass, stripped the man's body of all his clothing and any weapons or tools, and then they fled the scene, whooping and hollering as they went.

Cox reeled from the violence that he had just witnessed. He leaned on a tree, his mind a dichotomy of wanting to help the man and wanting to get as far away from this scene as possible. 'What did I just see?' he asked.

'You have just witnessed free-will at work Agent Cox. That was original sin. Man's baser instinct. They were not content until the man was dead and they had taken everything he owned away from him. They could have just taken the meat, there was no way he could have defeated them. But they didn't. They wanted to kill him.'

Without any warning, Cox blinked and found himself inside an old and dirty amphitheatre. Sand and blood covered the floor. He looked up and saw a huge crowd. They were sitting in their seats in a circle around the staging area. Loud cheers and shouts were roaring as the mob leered and leaned from above. Items were being launched into the arena. *Some things don't change,* he thought as he remembered the last football game he had attended.

There were two men in the centre of the theatre. One man was on top of the other, pinning his rival to the ground. Both were covered in blood, but the man on top was holding a large sword to the chest of his grounded victim.

This fight was over.

'Witness this, Agent Cox. The man is defeated. He has yielded. The other man does not want to kill his colleague, but he looks to his leader.'

The Contract

Cox watched as the gladiator looked up towards a sheltered region of the crowd. There were few people in that area, and they were seated in splendour and affluence. Several armed guards surrounded them, sealing them off from the rest of the baying hordes. One man was standing up, wearing brightly coloured robes that looked expensive. He was listening to the crowd as they jeered, booed, and cheered in equal measure. Cox could see that he was attempting to make a decision, a decision that he was rather enjoying.

He raised his hands, and the whole crowd fell silent.

It was obvious to Cox that this man enjoyed the feeling of control and power as the crowd eagerly awaited his whim. Eventually, he clenched his fist and thrust his thumb into a downward signal. That was all that the triumphant gladiator needed.

Cox flinched as the thrust of the man's sword sunk deep into the chest of his defeated colleague. He died, screaming for mercy, a mercy that would never be forthcoming. The triumphant gladiator then proceeded to hack at the man's neck until his head fell away from his body. He picked it up by its hair and held it aloft for all to see.

The roar from the crowd was deafening.

Cox turned away from the bloody spectacle to look at Michael. 'Everyone knows that this was a bar—'

Michael shushed him, mid-sentence. 'Watch, Agent Cox. The games are not yet over.'

Even though he didn't want to, Cox turned his attentions back towards the spectacle.

A smile broke onto the face of the man in the expensive robes. It was not a pleasant smile. It was filled with wickedness and malice. He offered a gesture to someone who Cox couldn't see, and the crowd went silent again. They were certainly getting their money's worth today.

With an almighty squeal of metal on metal, four large doors began to rise around the arena. The gladiator dropped the severed head he was holding and turned to see what was happening. His triumphant glow was replaced with fear as four thin leopards were let loose inside the circular stage. All of them eyed the tired gladiator with hungry eyes.

Wielding his sword, he took a defensive position, ready for their attack.

The crowd was loving the sport as they cheered for more blood.

The attack was swift, and in the end, bloody. The fickle mob were in a fervour now, ecstatic at how these games were panning out. The man they were yelling in favour of mere seconds ago was now devoured by the hungry cats, and they screamed and yelled in support of the violence.

'You were about to say barbaric, were you not, Agent Cox?' Michael asked. Cox noted that he had not been watching these events as they unfolded.

'I was,' Cox replied.

'And you would be right. It is barbaric. The Governor had every chance available to him to spare both men's lives. But, instead, he chose to end them, on a whim. Once again, this was free-will in action. Examples of this are rife through your history.'

In the wink of an eye both Michael and Cox were back inside the drab police interrogation room.

Before him, there was now a large television screen, much the same as the one they used to display the model Broom had been working on. At that moment, the screen was black, but Cox was sure that it wouldn't stay that way for long.

He was right.

An image in the centre of the screen flickered into life. It was a disgusting image of a man holding a large knife as he cut deep into the throat of a young woman lying before him. There was something about the image that disturbed Cox more than it should. It was the realism in the act. It didn't look staged. It looked like he was watching something unfold that he was never supposed to see.

This image was joined by another one. Three women were kicking another woman on the ground. Their faces showing the enjoyment of what they were doing.

Another image joined the other two. This was of an old couple cowering in terror as a group of masked youths ran riot around them. More and more images began to flash up. Men in white sheets raping a young black girl, women beating up young children, masked men shooting live guns into crowds. Men, stick-thin in concentration camps, being beaten by larger men in uniforms. Humans eating other humans, people beating and killing defenceless animals, aeroplanes flying into buildings, cars and trucks driving into crowds, people wearing bombs and

The Contract

detonating them in busy crowded areas. War, hunger, greed, pestilence, but most of all, death and suffering.

'STOP IT ... STOP IT ... STOP IT!!!' Cox shouted at the top of his voice as the images multiplied and spread across the seemingly never-ending screen. But the images kept on coming. Sexual perversions, paedophilia, necrophilia, bestiality, group rape, beatings, mass suicides, genocide, snuff ...

Cox turned his head away. He couldn't watch any more of it. A strong pair of hands took hold of his head and forced it back towards the screen. He was forced to watch as progressively sickening act after progressively sickening act filled the screen, multiplying, relentless.

'You wanted to see my mission, Agent Cox. Gaze upon my life for the last two thousand years.'

Finally, after what seemed like a lifetime to him, the images stopped, and the screen returned, thankfully, blank.

~~~

Cox's head hit the table with an almost comical thunk. It wasn't for another minute, until he moved, that he realised the screen was still dark, and his ordeal was over.

When he lifted his head, his eyes were pink, and his cheeks were wet. A pool of tears lay on the table before him. He looked around, realising that he was still in the police interrogation room. Michael stood by the door, looking at him, the impassive, emotionless face was back.

'Now you see my mission! My Contract! I have been on earth for two thousand years. I see all that every minute of every day. What you saw was but a snip of my life.'

'I understand what you've been tasked to do; but I don't understand why. If God, or whatever he calls himself, wants a reckoning, then why not just smite us all out of existence? Undo all his mistakes. Start again?'

'The Originator loves His creations. He loves the human race far too much. He can't bring himself to destroy what He has come to love. It is the only point of contention within HOME. There are some of us here who do not share His vision. These Angels are set in their ways to destroy it.'

'Are you one of them?' Cox asked, hoping that he didn't already know the answer.

'I am not,' Michael replied. 'I have been tasked to seek out and destroy one that has been walking among you.'

'Is that why you're killing the bad people?'

'No. That is another part of His plan. He dislikes the more extreme versions of humanity and tasked me to remove them from what you call 'society.' I have been working this mission for a long time. But, only now, after two-thousand years, have I the scent of my real prey. The Interloper, The Berserker, The Corruptor, The Fornicator. He is among you and must be destroyed before his seed is laid.'

'Why not just seek him out and kill him?' Cox asked, confused.

'He is hidden from me. He doesn't walk the earth like I do. He hides within the essence of man. He is from AWAY and seeks to change the order of things. He has grown tired of The Originator's ways and wishes to change things from within. His mission is to corrupt humans and bring about a new race of hybrid Angels.'

'The essence of man?' Cox was getting confused now.

'Yes,' Michael continued. 'The Berserker's spirit lodges in that of man. His seed corrupts the essence of the individual he resides within, without the vessel being aware of his presence. This is how he hides from me. He also has the power to jump from vessel to vessel until he finds the one. I fear that he has found his prime vessel and his work has begun. I have recently found traces of his activities and feel that I am close to finding out his identity, but alas, my time here is done. I have depleted my feathers and must return to HOME.'

'Is he like you?'

'No and yes. Our laws, although different from your own, are very similar. There must be a yin to our yang. The Berserker, he is the yin. He revels in rape and violence; he is a fornicator. He endorses sickness to the Kurrn.'

'The Kurrn?' Cox asked. A seed of a revelation was growing inside him. He didn't want to give it a voice. If it had no voice, it couldn't grow.

'The Kurrn is what you call your soul. It is your individual marker. This is what The Originator uses to keep a record of your deeds, so when He calls you back, He knows who you are and if you are worthy of entering. It is how I was able to target the subjects of my contract.'

The Contract

'Well, can't you see The Berserker's Kurrn?'
'He does not possess one. That is why I search.'
'Will you kill him when you find him? If he's like you, then ...' Cox asked.

Michael grabbed him by his jacket and pulled him close. 'He is not *like* me. He used to be *like* me but is not anymore. He has spewed himself from the vagina of one of your females. He is born again as flesh and blood, bone and sinew. He knows who he is and what he does and has lived for many of your lifetimes. His role here is to corrupt and turn as many of you humans towards their darker impulses as he can. He also needs to spread his seed in this world. To be killed, the vessel he uses to spill his seed, although an innocent tool, will need to be destroyed too. If he resides too long in that form, the tool will become the very essence of corruption. When that happens, the human's Kurrn is forever lost. Alas, you have seen me in my earthly form. You have seen me deplete and diminish. I tire on this mission. I must return to HOME to cleanse myself of the two thousand years of filth and depravity that have tainted my crux. This is how you would see me now.'

He spread his wings within the darkened room. Cox's eyes were drawn to how haggard and decayed they looked. The previously white feathers were now an unhealthy grey. Many were missing or wilting, ready to drop from the former magnificence. Then Cox's eyes left the wings and concentrated on his body. His youthful, muscular torso was gone, replaced with the pudgy, sallow body of an old man. His thick arms were now stick thin, and his skin hung limply in an unhealthy shade of yellow.

'My time here is complete. Today, I say that my work is done.'
'Does that mean that The Berserker has won? You have lost the chase?'
'No! The Interloper hides himself well, but I have a trail of him now. He resides within your North American region, hence how I have come to your attention.'

Cox had a terrible feeling, the seed that he was trying not to grow within him was budding right now. He hoped that he was wrong but felt that the next question needed to be asked. 'You want me to continue your work, don't you?'

'No, Agent Cox. You would not understand the complexities of the contract I have. Your human brain would not be able to contain the information I hold. You would go mad; you would succumb to the lesser urges of the men and women you would be chasing. You would become a dog, chasing its own tail until it became wrathful, frustrated with the futility of what it was doing. I am to be replaced. I cannot emphasise this more, but I would urge you and your partner not to pursue my replacement. He will not be as ... accommodating towards you as I have been.'

Cox had to laugh, and the confused look on Michael's face made him laugh even more. 'Accommodating? You've been far from accommodating.'

'You have not met my replacement, Agent Cox. Pray that you never do.'

'I have one further question for you. I see holes in your wings where you're missing feathers. Why have you been leaving feathers at the scene of your crimes?'

'You call my life's work crimes? They are not crimes; they are punishments and rewards. Free will has corrupted their Kurrn. The white feathers are a sign of purity. The world is one more step closer to purity with the feather in situ. If ever one of my projects was The Berserker, The Interloper, The Fornicator, then the feather would have burnt in a crimson light. That will be a sign to The Originator that my contract has been fulfilled. When the Kurrn of these people reach HOME, if it has been marked, then they will not be allowed within. They will reside in the AWAY, for the rest of eternity.'

The golden light from earlier enveloped Michael, and Cox watched with widening eyes as he began to transform before him. He observed a wave ripple through the old man, leaving the young, revitalised Michael in its wake. The youth spread his wings and his arms and lifted up from the floor. His beautiful face was bathed in a golden glory.

'I must return. Look to see me no more!' he warned. The luminescence intensified and became a blinding white light, before blinking out of existence.

~~~

Cox was back in the film studio within the house. He was back on Earth. There were numerous dead bodies scattered around the room.

The Contract

As he scrambled to his feet, he looked for Symes. To his relief, he found him struggling to his feet, using the door jamb to lever himself back into an upright position.

'Cox, are you OK?' The voice sounded like Symes's, but he couldn't be too sure due to the muffling and ringing in his ears.

'Symes, is that you?' he replied. That was when he realised that he was on the floor of the studio. He held his hand out to his partner, who looked like he was trying to reach him. 'It's over,' he called out. 'The contract is done. Michael has gone.'

'Who's Michael?' Symes asked as he grabbed the offered hand, allowing it to pull him up to his feet. 'What are you talking about?'

'Michael, the Angel …' He realised that he wasn't making any sense. Symes would never believe anything about what had just happened to him.

'You fell. That bastard attacked us. I was over here, and when I got to you, you were unconscious. Are you OK?'

A blinding light burst through his head. Searing pain shot forth from the centre of his brain, sending pins out in every direction. A voice spoke to him. The voice scared him. It reminded him of …

'Michael?'

'AGENT COX,' the voice boomed. It sounded young and brimming with energy. Something about this voice filled Cox with dread. 'MICHAEL INFORMED ME ABOUT YOU. YOU ARE THE ONLY HUMAN TO GET CLOSE TO HIM. I URGE YOU, NAY, I COMMAND YOU TO NOT PURSUE ME. DO NOT ATTEMPT TO GET IN MY WAY.'

'Are you Michael's replacement?' Cox croaked.

'I AM!'

'What is your name?'

'MY NAME IS IRRELEVANT TO YOU.'

'You might need me. Michael told me about The Berserker.'

'WHAT DID HE TELL YOU?'

'He told me that he is your contract, that he was *his* contract.'

There was a pause for a moment. Cox thought that he had gone. He hadn't.

'MY NAME IS LUCIFER, AND I AM THE LIGHT.'

With that, the light and the pain in Cox's head left him as quickly as it had arrived. All it left for him was a lingering vision of a feather. A long feather, of the kind that he had seen before. Only this time, the feather was black.

When he opened his eyes again, he was back on the floor.

'Come on, partner, we need to get you checked out,' Symes said as he held out his hand towards him. 'What's this contract you're talking about?'

Cox looked around the room. He had to make sure that they were alone. 'I think it's something that we have to steer well clear of. I don't think there's going to be anymore white feather killings. Not for a while anyway.'

Symes smiled at him as he pulled him up. 'How do you know that?'

'It's just a feeling. I think the killer has bigger fish to fry.'

'Well, let's go and get you cleaned up and get the situation reported. Maybe afterwards we can get ourselves a drink. What do you say?'

Cox nodded. Despite what he had just gone through, he felt better than he had in years.

'Good.' Symes nodded and tipped him a wink.

Sirens were beginning to blare from outside the building. Symes had called the massacre in to the local police department.

Cox shook his head, trying to clear the visions he had received. He groaned as he accepted his partner's help to get up off the floor. Symes was smiling as he pulled him up. Cox nodded as he accepted the help. Once he was stood, he dusted himself off and looked at his partner. Something about him caught his eye. *How have I never seen that before?* he asked himself.

His heart sank into the pit of his stomach. Something squirmed inside him, something that he knew he didn't want, but had been given anyway. It was the seed of revelation, the budding revelation that he had during his time in HOME. The more he thought about it, the more he allowed it to bloom!

For the first time in his life, in all the years that he and Symes had been partners, he noticed something.

There was something in Syme's eye.

It was a small fleck of crimson!

The Contract

D E McCluskey & C William Giles

Author's Notes

I'm writing these notes on the night that I found out that my collaborator on this project, my partner in *The Contract* passed away.

I didn't know Craig for too long, but what I did know about him was that he was a top bloke, a quiet, unassuming man who was passionate about what he did. He was a fellow author who wrote under the name C William Giles, and I was introduced to him by good friends Max Da Silva Willis and Chell Da Silva Willis (Chell is his girlfriend).

When we met, we talked books, we swapped books, and there was an instant, mutual respect. I read his first works, *...Of Tortured Faustian Slumbers,* and was instantly hooked. His writing style and the grasp he had on the mythical Heaven/Hell tales spoke to me, and it brought to mind a story I had written a long time ago that had been left to hang on the 'to do later' list. I knew that his style would be the perfect finishing touch to bring this story back to life. We talked, he read it, and to my pleasure, he enjoyed it! We decided that it would be a collaboration. 50/50.

So, we began working on it, bouncing it back and forth until we ended up with a tale that we were both not only happy with, but proud of. So proud that we instantly talked about making it into a trilogy ... We fleshed the story out, and ended up with the bones of a fantastical extended tale ... A story that I fully intend to continue, and proudly display his name as a collaborator and partner.

Very recently, I was honoured to host the launch party for his latest anthology novel, simply called, *BLACK.* A great night was had by all, and I only wish I had had a little more time to talk to him on that night. He was so busy trying to thank everyone, and we had plenty of time to talk shop later...

Or so I thought.

Craig was taken, cruelly, at a very young age. He will be sorely missed by me and by the people he has left behind. But ... he has left a legacy. His books and stories.

It's my intent to launch *The Contract* as a tribute to this man in the hope that it becomes a legacy to him and to his work. The two other books we had planned will be written, and both will proudly bear his name on the front covers.

The Contract

Craig/Carl/Foetus ... may whatever Angels you believe in carry you to wherever you need to be. Rest easy when you get there ... you deserve it!

Goodnight mate!

D E McCluskey & C William Giles

I originally wrote *The Contract* as a rhyming story a long time ago (it wasn't very good, but I've added it at the end just for shits and giggles). A tale of a supernatural serial killer on the loose. I extended it, with the full intent of making a graphic novel, but like my other novels that were meant to be graphic novels, the scope of the project proved to be VAST. I ran it by a few people and was rejected due to the sheer amount of work that would be required to complete it. One artist called it 'A lifetime's worth of work!'

So, the story was shelved ... never to see the light of day again.

In truth, although I really loved the story and the characters within, I never thought it strong enough to hold up on its own. I always thought that it was more than a little weak, not enough gumption to it. So, the years past and I allowed the dust to settle on it.

A few times I gave it a little peek, just so it wouldn't get lonely, but every time I did, I ended up walking away again. There was just too much work to do on it, and I always had something else on the boil.

Then, by chance at *The Liverpool Horror Club's* Alternative Christmas Market, my trading table was placed next to a delightful young lady artist who was very chatty, and I ended up having a great laugh with. Max Da Silva Willis. She then introduced me to her sister, Chell Da Silva Willis. These girls made me laugh all day. They are like opposite book ends, one blond and one dark.

Chell then told me that her boyfriend is an author. He lives in Liverpool but is from Bolton. So, I asked her for his name, and I got a copy of his book.

...Of Tortured Faustian Slumbers is a great read filled with brilliant, flawed protagonists and beautiful imagery. The book instantly made me think of *The Contract*, and maybe that C William Giles was the missing link that the story needed to blossom into the novel that it could be!!!

We met, we got on, and the book was made!

I'm rather glad it was, because it's a story I was already rather invested in, and I would have hated it to be left on the shelf.

As we got the end, we both realised that there's more to this story ... a lot more. So, we fleshed out our ideas to extend the series into a dark trilogy.

The Contract

Unfortunately, very unfortunately, Craig passed away in March 2019, weeks before the book was back from the editor. He never got to see the final print. He did, however, express his love for the cover art.

So, we are proud to offer you: *The Contract*. A stand-alone novel that will thrust the reader into a dark world, albeit an engaging one.

I sincerely hope it does C William Giles proud (His name was Craig, Foetus to others, but for some reason, I always called him Carl).

C William Giles bibliography is as follows:

...Of Tortured Faustian Slumbers
The Darkness of Strangers
Black
The Contract

All of these titles can be found on Amazon.

There are a number of people I need to mention and to thank for the completion of this book.

Deep breath here goes:

Obviously, I need to thank Craig's family. This must be a tough book for them to read, knowing that he was hugely excited about it. Special mentions go to Chell Da Silva Willis, the love of Craig's life, and her sister Max Da Silva Willis for introducing us.

Once again, Mr Tony Higginson has pulled it out of the bag. I honestly believe that my writing would be a bag of spanners without his help and guidance.

My BETA readers and 'lookers of the mistakes.' Natalie Webb, who has been a long-time collaborator for Beta reading, as has Stella Read... both love my books and style of writing, and both not afraid of saying something doesn't work!!! Good work, girls.

My final BETA reader is also my girlfriend Lauren Davies. She has an eye for all the small, tiny mistakes that even the best beta reader can overlook. Keep it up, girl, and you never know what will happen!

A big mention goes out to DEADFLICKS... it's a youtube channel of reviews and other beautiful macabre going on. Pippa and Myk, thanks for the edits, and also a BIG thank you for the quote for the back. Pippa, you were right... I loved it!

A MASSIVE thank you to Stephen Harper of Folklore Illustrations for the hard work and the fantastic vision for the cover of this book. I know that C William Giles was blown away with the look for this, as was I. I will be working with Stephen on more covers and illustrations in the future.

A huge thanks goes out to Lisa Lee. Her editing skills and eye for detail is what makes a jumble of words, thrown together to attempt to make some kind of coherent sense, into a novel. Thank you so much for your help in this and also for writing the blurb (a task that is so completely beyond me)!

I need to thank my family and my friends for living with me during the difficult times of writing books, especially this one. Craig's loss hit me hard, and if it hadn't been for both of our hard work and perseverance in getting it finished, I don't think I would have been able to do it after that, not on my own.

Lastly, WE need to thank you, the readers. After all, it's you that we do this for.

Stay strong and look after each other.

Dave McCluskey
Liverpool
May 2019

The Contract

Michael looks through a window
It's a familiar family scene
A wife, a husband, and their three kids
A gunshot, then a scream

Out jogging early morning
Michael's hiding in a bush
A serrated blade on one soft neck
Blood, it starts to gush

An air-conditioned office
With comfort and good size
A ceiling tile slips aside
Another person dies

Michael has a contract
He really is the best
Guaranteed, those on his list
Will be laid to rest

D E McCluskey & C William Giles

He always leaves a calling card
It's found at every crime
A long, white single feather
Each and every time

A man is in a limousine
He's a long time at the lights
Michael's in the driving seat
The man is in his sights

A teacher has been bound and gagged
A priest hung from a beam
A homeless man with his throat cut
No pattern it would seem

With the police completely baffled
These crimes will go unsolved
Mobsters, dealers, paedophiles
A vigilante has evolved

The Contract

Michael is no vigilante
Of this he would purvey
The criminal element of this Earth
Will make his list someday

His feathers now are running low
He stands and spreads his wings
There is too much filth in this world
For all these Heavenly things

His contract's nearly over
Another will take his role
Although his list is still quite full
He needs to rest his soul

Michael is an Archangel
On a contract that he landed
His mission here to rid the Earth
Of scum as God commanded

Printed in Great Britain
by Amazon